A DAY IN JUNE

GUERNICA WORLD EDITIONS 13

A DAY IN JUNE

Marisa Labozzetta

GUERNICA
World
EDITIONS

TORONTO—BUFFALO—LANCASTER (U.K.)
2019

Michael Mirolla, editor
Cover design: Allen Jomoc, Jr.
Interior layout: Jill Ronsley, suneditwrite.com
Guernica Editions Inc.
1569 Heritage Way, Oakville, (ON), Canada L6M 2Z7
2250 Military Road, Tonawanda, N.Y. 14150-6000 U.S.A.
www.guernicaeditions.com

Distributors:
University of Toronto Press Distribution,
5201 Dufferin Street, Toronto (ON), Canada M3H 5T8
Gazelle Book Services, White Cross Mills
High Town, Lancaster LA1 4XS U.K.

First edition.
Printed in Canada.

Legal Deposit—First Quarter
Library of Congress Catalog Card Number: 2018956497
Library and Archives Canada Cataloguing in Publication
Labozzetta, Marisa, author
A day in June / Marisa Labozzetta.

(Guernica world editions ; 13)
Issued in print and electronic formats.
ISBN 978-1-77183-382-0 (softcover).--ISBN 978-1-77183-383-7 (EPUB).--
ISBN 978-1-77183-384-4 (Kindle)

I. Title. II. Series: Guernica world editions ; 13

PS3562.A2356D39 2019   813'.54   C2018-905156-6
                                               C2018-905157-4

To my grandmothers:
Francesca Maglio Medori
and
Grazia Cotroneo Labozzetta

2013

Chapter 1

When I was four years old, I was a flower girl in a lavish wedding. In a floor-length lilac organdy dress with a satin bow that also went to the ground, I reluctantly walked down the aisle dropping rose petals from a white wicker basket. My mother asked: "Why the pout?" I told her I wanted to be the bride. Getting married meant nothing more to me than being the star surrounded by all my playmates in the ultimate game of dress-up; it meant eating lots of chocolate cake with fluffy white icing and pink heart-shaped candies. My sour expression ruined what would otherwise have been perfect photos of a perfect wedding, and I have always regretted that. So I would like a do-over.

What was impossible for me to imagine at such an early age was the most important component of a wedding—love. As an adult, however, I'm fortunate to have come to understand that this is the easiest part of a wedding to fulfill, for I have found my soul mate in life. But I still want my wedding to be beautiful and have my guests love being there as much as I'll love getting married, and that's where the natural beauty of Vermont comes into play. What could be more fun than gathering not just in a hall for a few hours, but in a town where all the residents have opened their hearts to us for an entire weekend and labored to create our dream wedding? In a way, I hold Brackton up as a model and inspiration for my marriage. (I have researched your history.) I want it to last and triumph through adversity, to maintain a sense of grace and charm through the years it weathers, and to be a source of happiness for all those who come in contact with it.

I don't have a funny story for which you asked that would make you laugh, or one with a twist of fate to make you cry, but I can tell you that Jason and I have more love, more heart, and more strength than many couples today. And we will appreciate the gift of this wedding more than I can express in 500 words. The engagement ring I wear on my finger is the same one that my fiancé's grandfather gave his wife 60 years ago. It symbolizes love everlasting and I am proud to be a part of this cycle of life and love. A dream wedding is not necessary, but it would be an amazing way to honor not only our love, but the love of everyone who has helped us get where we are today.

Brackton certainly fulfills the requirement for something old; being the recipients of your first wedding contest will be something new; loaning us your town will be something borrowed; and leaving after a magical time will make us very blue.

Thank you for considering us.

THAT'S 493 WORDS. Perfect. Ryan Toscano takes a bite of her hummus-and-avocado sandwich. She is sitting on a bench in the Boston Public Garden during her lunch hour on an autumn day hot enough to rival one at summer's peak. She clicks on Submit and forgets about Brackton and the prize of a free dream wedding for one hundred and twenty-five guests as easily as she forgets about what literary journals she submits her short stories to. What are her chances of winning? How many millions of people read the shrinking *Boston Globe*? In how many other newspapers has the contest been advertised? Besides, she has no sob story about a boyfriend who returned from a tour of military duty minus a leg, and all of her

Pap smears come back negative. She has no comedy of errors about having fallen in love with a Rockefeller seeking independence from his burdening wealth by disguising himself as a shoe salesman at Macy's. Or of a lost engagement ring having fallen into a wastebasket and been retrieved by a fiancé who spent hours sifting through a smelly landfill.

She does have a job as a paralegal for New England Environmental Law Center that pays her rent and more. She has a roommate in Jamaica Plain (or JP, as it's referred to) with whom she shares her funky but trendy apartment. What she no longer has is the fiancé who had a change of heart—not only about her but about the entire direction of his life—and entered a Jesuit seminary. At least she didn't lose him to another woman but to God, who her Catholic grandmother always said takes the best for himself. She no longer has a diamond either, since she gave it back, leaving her ring finger as naked and unclaimed as her thumb.

Chapter 2

"OH MY GOD! They want to *meet* us!" Ryan puts down her mug of coffee and looks up from her phone.

"Who wants to meet us?" Tiffany asks, scooping tofu-and-turkey-bacon scrambled eggs onto a dish. The plate is gray, with a large white crane pattern. It's also chipped. She bought the set from the new Goodwill Store on Centre Street, where the Foot Locker used to be. Her parents offered her their old set of Limoges china—the one with the gold rim and delicate pink flowers—but Tiffany turned it down. Not to prove her independence: Her parents cover the rent for her two-bedroom semi-run-down triple-decker apartment and send her a monthly stipend while she searches for the perfect job. It was simply a matter of taste, something Tiffany's parents embrace about her just as they do her lesbianism. Although it baffles them how such a beautiful and delicate-looking female with a heart-shaped face, whose hair color changes more frequently than the seasons and who loves makeup and expensive stiletto heels, doesn't desire other lesbians as equally feminine—and rich.

Ryan's parents, on the other hand, can't wrap their heads around someone turning down anything of value. That is the difference between those who have always had and those who are just beginning to; or, in Ryan's father's words: between those whose ancestors came on the *Mayflower* and those whose parents docked at Ellis Island.

"They want to meet me and Jason. I won the contest!"

"Sweet." Tiffany sets the plate of eggs and a matching cereal bowl filled with a half grapefruit in front of Ryan, who sits at another one of Tiff's finds: the colonial maple table set—so sixties and Cape Cod-ee with its turned-leg captain's chairs that are scratched up big-time. Just like the ones in the small cottage in Falmouth where her family stayed when she was little. The kitchen set does go well with the red-brick vinyl flooring and the knotty-pine cabinets that, no matter how many times and with what cleaners Ryan scrubs them, are sticky. The white cotton café curtains trimmed in eyelet that Ryan's mother gave her are crisp and stain-free at least, but Ryan can't forget they used to hang in her parents' bathroom (a thought she finds as revolting as the dead skin color of the kitchen walls). There's a door leading to a fire escape where they barbecue on a hibachi in warm weather. The landing is filled with garbage bags that the upstairs tenants refused to take all the way down to the alley and that will now remain frozen in ice and snow until spring.

"*Mangia*," Tiffany, who is taking Italian classes at the Boston Language Institute, orders. Her parents rent a villa in Europe for a month each August; next year it's Bellagio, on Lake Como. Tiff has sliced a strawberry, so that it fans out from its bright green leafy stem and placed it in the center of the grapefruit. Even in her stunned state, Ryan resents the fruit that has come from Central America and that cost an arm and a leg in the barren dead of New England winter.

"Sweet? How do you figure?" The initial surge of elation from winning the contest begins to sink like rancid meat into her gut.

"Why'd you ever enter to begin with? Like you and Jason have been over for two years."

"Sixteen months."

"Almost time enough to give birth to two babies. More coffee?"

Ryan shakes her head and picks a hair off of her plate.

"Must be yours," Tiffany says about the hair.

"Nope. Yours," Ryan says, holding up a long azure strand. "I just entered on an impulse. It was a fluke. A challenge. It was right after we won that case against the polluted salmon waters in Maine."

"You took two days off to sober up after that celebration,"

"It made me melancholy."

"Six Dirty Martinis would."

"And a Mojito chaser, I was told."

"And it never crossed your mind you might win? You're a good writer."

"Why would I think I'd win? All my stories get rejected. Maybe I was in denial. I thought he would have come around by now."

"If you don't know what you've got until it's gone, you don't know what you want—or need. And why the hell did he enter the seminary in the first place? No one becomes a priest anymore."

Tiffany jumps up to the sound of the toaster announcing two English muffin halves as done.

"What do you know about priests? You're Congregational—whatever that is."

"I may have majored in sociology but I minored in religion. Besides, it's common knowledge that no one wants to buy into the celibacy thing anymore. Of course, there've always been priests who manage their way around that."

"Jason is not like that."

"No. Jason is more like Jesus Christ. Maybe he *is* Jesus Christ. Hail, Jason." Tiffany solemnly puts her palms together and brings them to her bowed head. "I'm surprised they didn't canonize him along with Mother Teresa."

"You have to be dead. So what do I do now?"

"Just tell them the truth. I'm sure they have a runner-up who'll be thrilled."

Tiffany lathers her muffin with strawberry jam and takes a bite. Ryan's half remains dry on her plate, where it will be left to harden.

Ryan hates that thought. Being runner-up to God was bad enough. All of her twenty-eight years she's been second: on the bubble to make the all-star Lassie League softball team, then cut; three-tenths of a point from being the high school salutatorian; placed on the wait list to her first choice college, then denied; magna—not summa—cum laude when she graduated. She takes another sip of the coffee Tiffany prepared from freshly ground beans in a glass-and-chrome coffee press. Burnt. She hates French roast. How come coffee never tastes as good as it smells?

"I can see the wheels spinning a mile a minute underneath that mop of copper coils. You're not going to tell them the truth, are you, Ryan? Either way you're screwed. It's the curse," Tiffany says, pointing a fork at Ryan.

"What curse?"

"The one you said your grandmother Toscano put on you when your parents didn't name you after her."

"Old World nonsense. My father says my grandmother has no power; couldn't even get herself arrested if she tried."

"My money's on the curse."

"Holy shit! They want me to *get acquainted* with *all* of these when I visit," Ryan says, opening up the attachment labeled "Chamber of Commerce Board of Directors." "It's like a football roster."

"Better print it out and carry it with you at all times. Memorize it in your spare moments. It's the key to being poised and composed when you meet them."

"Ace Auto Repair? Burns Accounting? Baby's Bar & Grill? Are they fucking kidding? Is that where we're having the wedding? Look at this!" She hands the phone to Tiffany.

"From your crimson cheeks, I'd say the only one kidding here is you."

Chapter 3

Wednesday, January 15

Welcome to Brackton, Vermont
Unrushed, Untainted, Unforgettable
Population 1,732

ERIC SLOWS DOWN as he nears the familiar sign and turns the bend where the Daffodil House appears from out of nowhere on his right, lit up like the Taj Mahal in the black of night. He stops short. The girl on the old two-wheeler stares into the headlights, her eyes wide and fixed like those of a scared rabbit. She's older—mid-thirties—than the childlike posture she assumes on the bike. Instead of pedaling out of harm's way, Bicycle Girl, as townies call her, cocks her head, unprotected from the single-digit temperature, to one side, red plaid scarf flapping around a brown leather bomber jacket, and continues to ride in circles on the snow-caked street. He waves as he maneuvers around her (he is late), drives a good half mile to the center of town, and pulls up to the one-room storefront where the Brackton Chamber of Commerce board of directors meetings—all town meetings—are held because the town hall across the way is in disrepair and has been closed for three decades.

Tonight, the chair of the Friends of Brackton Town Hall is making a pitch to the Chamber to soldier up and fork out a hefty pledge to restore the Civil War-period handicapped-inaccessible building that could pass as a small replica of the Roman Forum or the Supreme

13

Court, with its long flight of steps, row of stately columns, and handsome pediment, and which in its heyday hosted everything from vaudeville performers to spiritual meetings. But the merchants are tapped out, many claiming that another down year will do them in. That's why all of their energy has been focused on the Brackton is for Brides Contest and the big wedding that will take place in June.

The irritating screeching of rubber chair cups against the linoleum floor punctuates his late arrival as he takes his place at the banquet tables that form a U.

"We started without you, Eric," president Danni Pritchard says apologetically. The thirty-two-year-old owner of the ice cream shop that doubles as an antiques and collectibles store, and that in off-season serves breakfast and lunch, can't conceal the blush that washes over her face whenever her former classmate, Eric, walks into a meeting.

"Sorry I'm late."

"Business as usual," someone murmurs.

Eric has a habit of being late. He really tries to be on time, but he can't stand to waste a second, and so he undertakes some small task before leaving wherever he is at the moment, which turns into a bigger task and—voilà—he's late to everything. Tonight, while he waited for the clock to register the exact number of minutes needed to make it to the meeting, he decided to change the battery in a smoke detector that goes off whenever his mother puts something in the oven. Exhausted after having prepared the food, she lies down, leaving the oven unattended. This evening the alarm was wailing on account of two overbaked apples whose dripping butter and maple syrup had scorched the oven floor.

"Eric?" she called from her room. Her voice was always soft, but the cancer has rendered it feeble.

"Got it!" he yelled back, reassuring her that it wasn't a fire, and then proceeded to change all the units.

"Pick an anniversary date," the volunteer fire chief had told him, "and change every one of them at the same time."

Tonight was as good an anniversary date as any, but it took him a while to find the batteries he'd bought and saved to celebrate the occasion. He'd done only half of the units when he had to abandon the project and leave for the meeting in a distracted mood, because once he started something, he hated to stop until it was finished.

"Is your mother okay?" Danni asks.

"My mother's fine, thank you, Danni." He doesn't like her bringing up his mother in front of everyone.

"You missed the Friends of Town Hall presentation," Danni tells him, her eyebrows elevated just a bit in coy chastisement. "I'll catch you up to speed afterwards."

Eyes roll. The owner of Ace Auto groans. He's still wearing the grease-stained blue shirt with his name, Hank, and Ace Auto embroidered on the pocket, with matching encrusted fingernails that Eric's mother likes to say he could grow potatoes in.

"Here's the list of the board of directors." Danni passes out copies. "I sent you all an attachment in an email, but I wanted to save you the trouble of printing it out. I know *I* like to have a hard copy. It's already been sent to our winning couple. It's in alphabetical order, although I wasn't sure if I should do it by business or proprietor."

"Waste of taxpayers' money," the most senior member grumbles, though he's the reason everything has to be printed out in the first place—and in large type. He refuses to close his fix-it shop for small electrical appliances even though today patrons buy new irons and toasters when they break. He wouldn't even know how to repair them, and stays afloat with a few clogged vacuum cleaner hoses and well constructed but outdated models owned by fellow octogenarians.

Ace Auto Repair	Hank Wilson
Baby's Bar & Grill	Jimmy Goulet
Brackton Inn	Terry Stewart
Burns Accounting	Rob Burns
Cut Above Hair Salon	Maisie Billings
Chez Alexandre	Alex Dubois
Daffodil Inn	Mark Goldman

Dale's Appliance Fix	Dale Lapointe
Boulanger Photography	Eric Boulanger
Heavenly Bakers	Lisa Anderson
High Spirits Shop	Mother Twinkle
Jazz Man DJ	Richard Rinaldi
Licks & Relics	Danni Pritchard
Pine Willow Realty	Cary Clarkson
Plantasia Florist	Annie Chalis
Trousseau Bridal Shop	Fran Costantino

After scanning the list, Eric asks Danni where the phone numbers and email addresses are.

"The email addresses are in the email. I didn't blind-copy them," she tells him.

"We should still have them written in the directory, along with phone numbers. Otherwise, Danni," he says, lowering his voice, "what would be the point of the directory?"

"Okay. I'll send out a new one. Now that we're all here," Danni says, "I'd like to announce the results of the election of new board members for this year." She proceeds to pronounce each name slowly and distinctly. "And all officers were reelected to their positions. They are: Eric Boulanger of Boulanger Photography, vice president; Annie Chalis of Plantasia Florist, treasurer; Lisa Anderson of Heavenly Bakers, secretary, and me, president."

"You have to state your name for the minutes," the secretary says.

"And Danni Pritchard, president," she blurts out in one breath, looking at her as if to ask whether she'd made the correct response, but the secretary is focused on transcribing. "First on our agenda is the business of the Seniors' Monthly Dinner. The Elks have offered to take over the job of hosting for this year, so we're off the hook on that one. But if you remember, the Chamber voted to prepare the St. Patrick's Day Feast. I'll pass around a sign-up sheet, and I hope that many of you will be able to volunteer your time for the event. We need cooks and servers and a cleanup crew. The Grand Union in

Rutland has offered to donate twenty-five pounds of corned beef and the paper goods. One of the farms will donate the cabbage, onions, potatoes, and carrots. The Chamber will contribute soft drinks from our budget, since Ray's Country Market refused us again. I hope we can count on Heavenly Bakers for one or two large sheet cakes?"

"I don't think it's fair that Heavenly is always the one to contribute the baked goods. What about Tea for Two Bakery in Putnam? They never contribute anything," the treasurer and owner of Plantasia Florist says, continuing to work at some furry-looking piece of mint green wool with one circular knitting needle that puzzles Eric. Her defense of Heavenly Bakers also puzzles him, since everyone knows the two middle-aged businesswomen have been infamous rivals at everything since grade school.

"I'll look into it," Eric says. "And I don't think we should be so hard on Ray. We're lucky he's still open. How many of you do your big shop at Grand Union?"

"How many of you do your big shop at Grand Union?" a familiar voice bellows, as though he hasn't heard Eric. The owner of Burns Accounting has a habit of taking a joke, or suggestion, or significant point someone makes and repeating it much louder, so that it appears as though *he* initiated the comment.

"Jeez. Can't one of you girls bake something?" the mechanic asks, bypassing the comment about the depressed grocer.

"I'll make a cake. It's no big deal," the baker says, directing her statement to the hairdresser who has just stood up for her, as if to say: *Don't pretend you're looking out for me.*

"Thank you." Danni is relieved to have the matter of the cake settled. "The dinner will be in the basement of Saint Anne's, as usual. That's it for new business." Danni lets out her unwarranted trademark giggle that irritates Eric no end. "And now Eric will report on how the Brackton Is for Brides Contest is coming along."

"Well, the committee has selected our couple. They're from Boston—"

"Boston! I thought we were trying to reach out to bigger fish, like New York," someone says.

"We couldn't afford to advertise in the *New York Times*. The *Globe* gave us a deal." Eric has told them this before.

"Doesn't the *Times* own the *Globe*?" another asks.

"Not anymore. I think it's owned by the Red Sox," Danni says.

"That's impossible." The mechanic has begun cleaning his fingernails with a pencil point.

"The same guy owns both," Eric informs him.

"Whatever," Danni mutters. "What about the online advertising? Why did we have to advertise in the paper at all?"

"I linked our website to whatever wedding market sites I could find. And I ran it on Facebook and tweeted it once a week."

"Not enough," the loudmouthed accountant says.

"There's such a thing as desensitizing, you know. If they saw it every day, they wouldn't see it at all." Eric is having trouble not fixating on the accountant's inordinately large ears. He glances at those of the DJ sitting next to the accountant. The DJ is a big man, but his ears are normal and half the size of the accountant's—ears that appear better suited for a donkey.

"I disagree."

"Not everyone's on Facebook," Eric tells the accountant.

"Everyone's on Facebook," he says.

"How many of you are on Facebook?" Eric asks.

Three hands besides those of the accountant and Eric go up.

"There you have it. We haven't decided which hotel will host the wedding yet." Eric wants to get off the social network topic that's creating anxiety on the part of the older members, who have no idea what he's talking about. "Look, we're done for this year. We can discuss advertising for next year's contest in the fall. But we got a great couple. I hope you'll all be happy. They're gay."

"What?" The mechanic can't believe his normal-sized ears.

"At least we think they are."

"Couldn't you find out?" the hairdresser asks, twirling a pen like a miniature baton. "Not that I care."

"That would be discriminatory," Eric tells her.

"So why do you think they're gay?"

"Their first names are both male, so we are just assuming," Eric says. "Actually we're thinking trans—he was a flower girl when he was little."

"Oh my God!" the mechanic bellows, still concentrating on at his fingernails.

"Isn't that stretching it a bit, Eric?" the baker asks.

"I vote we find another couple." The mechanic is adamant.

"We've already notified them." Eric is trying to keep his cool.

The mechanic shifts in his seat. "This is supposed to bring business to Brackton, Eric. What the hell are you doin', turnin' this place into Provincetown?"

"As far as I know, P-town does a pretty good tourism business, " Eric snaps back. "Look, I think we've really got something here. We were the first state to adopt a same-sex civil-union law. Then what happened? Connecticut and Massachusetts—even Iowa—beat us to the punch by legalizing actual gay marriage. But now we can say not only that we've legalized gay marriage, but we actively stand behind what we preach by—"

"By what? By making poster children out of this young couple? And I'm assuming they're young." That's the heavy-set host of the *Jazz Man* show on the local public radio station out of Rutland, who also has his own DJ business and is the only openly gay man in the Brackton area to serve on a town committee.

"I'm surprised you feel that way," Eric says.

"Because I'm gay, Eric? That's the elephant in the room, isn't it? We're looking to be accepted as normal, not freaks. Face it. We legalized marriage because we have hardly any gays who've come out in this state." He undoes the top leather button of his vintage brown cable-knit sweater, heat rising within it.

"I know you're hot on a gay couple, Eric," the florist says, putting down her knitting needles. "But taking it for granted they're gay just because of the *name*? Isn't that wishful thinking? Someone could mistake a lot of our names for the opposite sex—Danni or Cary or Terry or Dale or—"

"As far as I know, *Oh Danny Boy* has a *y*," her antagonist, the baker, cuts her short. "Boys' names don't end in *i*."

"Thank you, Madam Secretary," the florist says, then purses her lips.

"On second thought, it's probably a great idea. It'll drive the governor—and Hank—crazy," the DJ says, glaring at the mechanic.

"Why do you always insinuate I'm homophobic?" the mechanic says, looking up from his nails.

"Gentlemen, let's not lose sight of our prime objective—making Brackton a destination for weddings. Revving up retail," Eric says. "Go to Cape Cod and you'll catch Lyme disease. Go to New York and get bitten by bedbugs. Go to Chicago and you might get shot. What's better than a pure, wholesome small town in Vermont?"

Eric couldn't look at anyone when he uttered that last statement; he knew he was overdoing it about the other cities, and Vermont's image of purity was a figment of the imaginations of lovers of the organic. As his mother always said, small towns have all the trouble any big city has—just in lower doses and secrecy.

There is murmuring of consent with no disputing the need to drum up tourism in Brackton. Its main industry of construction—mostly roadwork and renovation projects—has fallen flat on its face over the last few years, and because of it their children are leaving and their population declining.

"We've asked Ryan and Jason to come to Brackton early in February," Eric says. "That should give the vendors who volunteered to be part of this venture adequate time to prepare their presentations. It will also leave enough time afterwards to work out the details of the wedding with the couple. If we're going to do this, let's do it right."

"Or left," someone says. A few laugh.

"I think we're off to an excellent start thanks to Eric," Danni says, jumping in. "You have a question?" Danni recognizes the raised hand of Mother Twinkle, the owner of High Spirits Shop.

"I'm new here and just getting to know you all and having trouble keeping you all straight." She's wearing green velvet slacks and a black velvet cape with gold trim. Her voice, in contrast, is harsh like the *ribbit* of a frog, leading Eric to believe she was a heavy smoker back in her heyday, and of as much tobacco as weed. Her cascading waist length white hair is also coarse and dry.

"Just look at your list of members." Danni holds up the sheet of paper.

"I thought it would be easier to put a face to a name in a small town. That's why I didn't go to Bennington or Burlington," Mother Twinkle says. "But I'm still finding it difficult—as though I were in some sort of Lope de Vega play, like *Fuenteovejuna*, where the entire town is functioning like a single character." They stare at her, not having the slightest notion of what she's talking about. "You know, like in Agatha Christie's *Murder on the Orient Express*. No? Look, can we just take a moment for everyone to identify themselves so I can observe your auras and absorb you into my psyche?"

The mechanic lets out a groan of disgust.

"We're a little short of time tonight, Mother Twinkle, but we'll do a complete introduction at the beginning of each meeting until you, uh, absorb us. Won't we, Danni?" Eric says.

"All you gotta remember is Danni and Eric. They're the principals here, as I see it. They run the show," the vexed mechanic says.

"When the couple meets with you participating vendors," Eric says, "please try to give them some options so they'll feel like this wedding is really theirs."

The board wants to know if the couple will have to choose between the Brackton Inn and the Daffodil House for the reception. It's an awkward question for Eric to answer since the longtime owner of The Brackton Inn is sitting across from him. He knows the renovated Daffodil House is better suited to impress, but the owners are newcomers.

"Why don't we have the reception at one place and the rehearsal dinner and Sunday morning brunch at the other?" Danni suggests. "We can have equal number of guests stay at each inn and send the overflow to the smaller B and Bs and area motels."

"That can work," someone says.

"That can work!" the donkey-eared accountant says louder.

Eric can't help but marvel at Danni's brilliant solution. They take a vote, and the Daffodil House has the majority for the reception and the Brackton Inn for the other two events. The owner of the Brackton

Inn is not happy to play second fiddle to the Daffodil House as far as the reception is concerned but is relieved to be involved. Mother Twinkle suggests having an ice cream social for the couple when they arrive, with ice cream donated from Ben & Jerry's.

"Are you for real?" The mechanic jumps down her throat. "We got Danni's ice cream. This is about getting people to Brackton, not the Ben and Jerry's factory! Middlebury has the college; Stowe has the ski slopes; and Waterbury has frickin' Ben & Jerry's. Even Woodstock's got that damn covered bridge. What the hell do we have? We got crapola, that's what we got."

"Watch your mouth!" the hotheaded owner of Baby's Bar & Grill says, pushing back his chair.

"Oh, excuse me, I forgot. We got Baby's Bar & Grill." He raises his grease stained-hands as if to surrender to the restaurant's proprietor, who responds by taking a step in the mechanic's direction.

" All right, all right. Please. Forget the ice cream social, everyone, and let's take a cleansing breath." Mother Twinkle inhales and exhales. "We have a beautiful town nestled on the slopes of the Green Mountains, where a warm and gentle people await you, in the perfect setting for a couple in love to take their marriage vows and begin their lives together. That's what we have." She addresses the mechanic. "That's what drew me here from Pittsburgh, and that's exactly what I wrote in our new brochure, by the way. And that's what we'll be known for. Everyone will say Brackton is for brides."

"Straight to the dogs this town is going," the cranky appliance repairman mutters, making a racket with his chair and cane, and tottering out of the building.

* * *

After the meeting, Eric heads over to his friend Michael's house. Danni wanted to go over to Baby's Bar & Grill for pizza and a drink so she could get him up to speed on the Friends of Brackton activity, but he said he was in a hurry and to please send him an email. He almost said he needed to check on his mother, but he didn't like to lie—even little white lies gave him the uneasy feeling that his fabrication would one day come back to haunt him: in this case, his mother's cancer might return.

Yes, he was superstitious. In high school, he never washed his baseball jersey or cut his hair until the Grizzlies' lost a game. Senior year, they went on to win the state championship, and Eric's mother swore it was because no one could get close enough to him to tag him out at the plate, he stank so badly after losing only two games during their twenty-game season. She was surprised he almost never missed a ball in center field: "Even a ball wouldn't want to get that close," she liked to say. That was the year he broke the school record for stolen bases—a title he still held.

Danni had been at all those games. And while baseball didn't have cheerleaders, Danni, captain of the squad, had convinced her coach and the principal to let the girls cheer the boys on throughout the playoffs. It hadn't been a hard sell: The five-town school system rallied around the boys' success like bears to a honey pot, since the Division II Grizzlies hadn't had a baseball state championship in twenty-three years. They had gone to the playoffs Eric's sophomore year but got knocked out in the first round. After the big win, however, there'd been a parade in downtown Brackton, led by a fire truck and a police car from each of the towns. Baby's Bar & Grill, with its wide plank floors that reeked of stale spilled beer and its raw shiplap walls lined with rusted farm tools and nostalgic business signs, gave out free hamburgers and hot dogs and soda to the team for a week.

It was at Baby's on the night of the game, after Brackton's town manager, flanked by the other towns' managers and selectmen of the school district, had lauded the boys on their victory, that Eric committed his indiscretion. He'd been sitting in a booth with other players and riding high on adrenaline and a few beers a teammate's older brother had secretly provided, when Danni Pritchard asked him for a ride home. Danni, who'd always worn too much makeup for Eric's liking and whose large breasts and tight ass in a short but compact athletic body had compensated for her droopy eyes, wide mouth, and whiny voice, had never attracted Eric despite her obvious feelings for him since third grade. She wasn't stupid by any means, but she was plagued with insecurities that made her *appear* stupid, which bothered Eric.

She had changed out of her cheerleading uniform in the ladies' room and into a pair of jeans, sandals, and a button-down fitted V-neck sweater that advertised her infamous melons loud and clear. She slithered into the pickup, smelling like the sexiest spice Eric had ever taken in. He turned to Danni and kissed her, propelled by all the ecstasy he felt having scored three out of the four runs in the winning game, buoyed by his hero's welcome in the noisy darkness of a bar that now had one more excuse for a celebration, and prodded on by the raging hormones of a seventeen-year-old male. They sat for what must have been half an hour making out: tongues encircling each other; Danni's breasts wriggling against his hard chest. He was bursting.

He tore away from her, started the car, and drove, with all the anticipation he had experienced on the first Christmas morning he could remember, to Mount Misery, a popular lovers' lane in a secluded wooded area off of Mount Misery Road. There they continued their make-out session with the windows so steamed up no one could ever have known who was inside. He put his hands on her breasts—she let him. Then under her sweater and over her bra—she let him. Around the hard nipples and down to the snap on her jeans—she let him. He tugged at her zipper—she helped him. Then he slid to home. He was inside her panties, fumbling around a wet bird's nest of hair—sweet—slipping his middle finger into a moist pothole and tasting the spoils of victory, when he exploded within the confines of his jockstrap and uniform.

"It's okay, I love you," Danni said, putting her hand on his, guiding it and giving him permission to continue to touch her, but it was over for him, and luckily so, because embarrassment had jolted him from his testosterone-fueled insanity back to reality. He pulled away from her and hugged the steering wheel instead.

"I'm sorry," he whispered to the dashboard.

"It's okay," she repeated, acknowledging his premature ejaculation. "Next time will be better."

"No. I'm sorry, Danni. Really I am. I shouldn't have brought you here. I'm sorry."

She cried all the way back to her house, and at the prom he attended without a date, even though two other girls had asked him to escort them. He hadn't wanted to hurt Danni's feelings any further by going with someone else; besides, he no longer trusted himself with casual dates—monster that he was. And she cried in the ladies' room at Baby's for the next four years, whenever he came home from college.

From his car, Eric can see Michael sitting at the dining room table in the first-floor condo of the yellow clapboard two-family. Michael takes sips from a large mug, while studying a stack of papers in front of him. His black silhouette against the white walls mirrors Eric's photographs hanging on those same walls. The kitchen window frames Becca, statuesque and slender, with flaxen hair tied back into a ponytail, scrubbing a frying pan she holds up to inspect every few seconds while sweeping her long blond bangs out of her eyes. Michael and Becca never pull the shades or close the blinds. People who move to small towns from big cities think they've found Utopia—kind of like the college Eric went to where everyone was on the honor system and where people cheated just the same.

Eric's glad he hadn't taken his pickup, or maybe that was intentional: He likes it that his mother's Subaru doesn't idle as loudly and give away this Peeping Tom. In a few minutes, he'll shut off the engine and go to the door, and Becca will offer him something to drink or eat, and Michael will put his work aside; but for now he's happy just to observe and take them in, like a giant-sized happy comfort pill he wants to swallow whole.

Michael is calm and methodical as he works, perhaps on teacher evaluations or next year's class scheduling or résumés for the remedial-reading teacher position, whose funding was narrowly passed by the school committee. Disgruntled teachers at the high school, whining board members, and parents don't bother Michael. Eric, who was the community representative on the high school principal search, detected this trait about Michael the minute he met him, and he knew he not only wanted to hire him—he wanted to be his friend. You could be attracted to other males that way. You could love them. He loves Michael. And he loves Becca, who is hard and soft at the same time, a caring yet straight-to-the point bundle of energy that gets tempered by Michael's serene but no less engaging and ambitious personality. They have what Eric wants: They can pull out all the stops without fear of losing each other because, while their styles may differ, they're grounded by the same foundation of devotion they bring to everything they touch.

Eric is assistant baseball coach at the high school, and Michael, a former all-American épée fencer—tall and lean, with the classic left-handed advantage—would like to start a fencing team or at least a club, but it's not wise for a principal to be a coach, he says, especially a newcomer to the area, especially an African American newcomer. Parents might claim he's being partial—playing favorites with his kids—in academic and disciplinary matters. Although Eric knows Michael wouldn't, still it's better not to give people ammunition.

Even Eric thinks it's a little weird to watch his friends' lives unfold in *his* home among many of *his* belongings. On the other hand, it's as though their lives have melded. Michael desperately needed a place to live, and Eric's mom needed *him*.

Rebecca loved Eric's renovated duplex—everything white, like the backdrop paper Eric uses when he shoots ads or portraits, with sparse modern furnishing so different from his mother's cluttered taste of Vermont knickknacks and heirlooms. Eric likes clean straight lines. He likes order; it allows him to think better, or not have to think at all. It was only logical that he would rent his condo to Michael and Becca until they found something more permanent and that he would move back in with his mother in the farmhouse on the outskirts of town. That was two years ago. He could return to his place now; his mother's cancer is in remission. But why upset Becca and Michael? The extra income isn't bad at all, since work has been slow. Besides, Eric wants to make life as easy as possible for Michael, because he wants Michael to stay in Brackton. Yet it isn't always easy for Michael here. Then again, it would never be easy for him anywhere he went, and Eric hates that reality.

Eric's cell phone rings; he reaches under his parka, fishes it out of his pocket, and laughs at the caller's ID.

"Wassup?" he asks.

"Hey, dumbass, you gonna sit out in the cold all night like some pervert?" Michael says.

Chapter 4

The Holy Prostitute

Her face was red from the cold. Her head, with its tight-fitting woolen cap, looked miniature, out of proportion to the rest of her body, because of the oversized jacket she wore.

"I'm Daisy," she said, extending her hand. "You sounded a lot older over the phone—you know, gray-haired, running a rooming house."

Suzanne opened the door a little wider and gave a shiver as cold air filled the long bare hall. She held a thirteen-month-old on a hip while three-year-old Alyssa clutched at her thigh. She was embarrassed; it was January and Billy still hadn't taken down the Christmas lights that lined the rambling Victorian porch. He said they hid some of the chipped paint and broken spindles.

Billy had been dead set against renting out the extra bedroom. When she told him she had listed it with the Chamber of Commerce, he blew up and said he didn't like the idea of having a stranger in the house. Suppose one day an insane man walked in. Would she want to be alone with him? She promised to rent to a woman. No meals, just the room, just a few days here and there. It was a way for her to make money and still be home with the girls. She had to persuade him about everything; she never bought an article of clothing without his approval. When Daisy called, she was thrilled.

"Come in," Suzanne said.

Suzanne led her upstairs and pointed out the spare bedroom and private bath. Daisy unzipped her jacket but kept it and the cap on.

"This is great! I'll be staying until May."

"But I told you only three nights. How about until Sunday? Is that all right?" She included an extra day almost apologetically, hoping she hadn't discouraged her first customer.

R YAN LOOKS UP from her laptop and out her bedroom window at the last falling flakes. The block resembles a chalk model of houses and trees and cars waiting to be painted. The Greek man, who lives across the street with his wife in the white two-story with bright blue trim and who owned the dry cleaners on the corner, has already begun to shovel the foot of snow on his walkway. He is like Ryan's father, who never waits to attack a chore while her mother finds any excuse, from finishing a book she's just begun to searching for an item she lost years ago, before tackling dinner dishes.

It used to drive Ryan's father crazy when Ryan was little, but he seemed to have come to terms with it by the time Ryan was in her teens, loading the dishwasher or wiping down counters himself, or when he didn't have time, walking past a sink smelling of steak grease with his breath held and his eyes closed. Not unlike his clean-freak mother, who had made him pass a carpet sweeper under the kitchen table after every meal when he was growing up, Joe Toscano was so well trained he never left as much as a dirty sock on the floor, returned wet towels to their proper racks, and in nice weather even hung the wash out on a collapsible spiderlike metal clothesline in the backyard.

There had been that one time when Ryan was a very little girl and her mother attempted to put their living conditions in greater order. They had just moved into the neglected high ranch of a development on Long Island when, against her husband's better judgment (or what he thought was better), Lauren Toscano rented out a room in the hopes of earning a little extra money to spruce up the place. How, Joe had asked, did she intend to clean up after boarders when she couldn't manage to dig her way out of the mess one three-year-old made? Lauren insisted that Joe just didn't want to bring strangers into the house: His family was secretive and weird that way, she said.

Ryan didn't remember much about Lauren's first and last boarder (the lady had seemed nice enough to Ryan, but apparently she'd been psychotic). Yet somehow, over the years, Ryan had come to take her father's side whenever the incident came up, ridiculing her mother's naïveté rather than supporting the woman for a gutsy effort.

Ryan saves the beginning of her new story and closes the cover to her laptop. She puts on her parka, hat, scarf, and mittens and heads down the stairs to the first floor hallway, where the landlord keeps a shovel next to the basement door.

"I don't understand why you're doing that," Tiffany calls down the stairwell. *He's* supposed to take care of it."

"Yeah, well, he doesn't." Like Ryan's mother, the landlord is a procrastinator where manual labor is concerned.

"He does, but not on your timetable. Our super always cleans our sidewalk."

"That's the Upper West Side for you."

"I'll be down in a minute."

"Sure you will."

Ryan knows Tiff has every intention of joining her. She'll just let a number of things delay her, as though her privileged upbringing were holding her captive until the unpleasant deed is done. Ryan believes that Tiff can't help herself, just like Ryan's mother can't. Just like the landlord can't.

When Ryan was growing up on Long Island, young boys went around looking for driveways and walks to shovel to make a few dollars. Nobody comes around here, probably because their parents think it isn't safe to be out alone, pounding on strangers' apartment doors. Actually, she doesn't mind shoveling by herself. She doesn't even mind that Tiff and the two female med students on the first floor and the hippie-looking couple with the baby on the second floor don't pitch in: After all, it really isn't their responsibility. She likes the exercise and being alone. She also likes the stillness of the usually busy street that's been muffled by snow. Besides, the cold air will help clear her mind, which has begun to suffocate in the steam heat of the radiators and the thought of the email she received a week ago from Brackton.

She sinks the wide curved shovel into the drift and it goes nearly all the way to the sidewalk, the snow is so light and dry. Some weight applied, a big push, and she scrapes the pavement in front of her like a human plow, leaving the thinnest coat of white as though it's been dusted with confectioners' sugar. But even a foot of light snow proves too heavy to remove with just pushing. She'll need to chip away at it.

She's halfway down the sidewalk when she notices a man plodding up the deserted street. His pumpkin-colored down jacket is deflated and worn, with a few feathers straggling out of holes in both sleeves. The black hood of a sweatshirt is pulled down over his eyes; he has no gloves or cap. As he gets closer, she can see black hair on the backs of his hands. His acne-scarred face is dehydrated, his lips chapped. He slows down as he approaches her.

"Can I give you a hand?"

"I'm almost finished, thanks." She does not make eye contact with him. Her heart flutters with a rush of adrenaline.

She can hear that the Greek man across the street has stopped his meticulous removal of snow from his stoop. Out of the corner of her eye, she sees him leaning against his shovel, facing in her direction, taking in the situation.

"This your car?" the stranger asks, indicating the mound in front of the building.

"Yes." It's the car she needs dug out by tomorrow so she can get to the nursing home in Newton Highlands.

He begins cleaning off the snow from her windshield with big swooping movements of his arms.

"I have a brush for that," she says.

"But it's in your car, and you can't open the doors until you've cleared the snow off." The way he pronounces some vowels tells her he's a local, probably from Revere or Dorchester.

"You don't need to get all wet. Really, I can do it."

The Greek man resumes his work, alternating his shoveling with casting vigilant glances across the street at the stranger and Ryan.

"I like to shovel snow," he says. "I like being out in the cold air."

"Me too," she answers too quickly. She doesn't want to encourage him.

"Do you know anyone on the block who needs shovelin'? I'm in between jobs, a little down on my luck. I like to work. I just want to make a few bucks 'til I'm back on my feet. I was in construction but I got laid off a few years back. Still not much work in buildin' these days. Been in and outta work. I'm stayin' at the cot shelter at the church around the corner. But just for a few weeks. I'm hopin' to work with a buddy down in Jersey. Let me give you a hand with that."

She gives him the shovel and he rhythmically works his way down the walk in no time, then starts on her car.

"I'll run up and get you something," she says when he's finished.

"Don't bother. It was my pleasure. Piece a cake."

"How about a cup of coffee? It's made." She'll bring it down, of course.

"That's nice of you. But I'm gonna keep goin' and see if I can pick up a few jobs. I don't care what they pay me. I just like to work. God bless." He smiles and continues down the street.

She feels bad for having pegged him as some sort of derelict. He's just another unemployed statistic in this struggling economy and proof that your luck can turn on you on a dime. Didn't hers? She should have insisted on getting him that coffee. Jason would have gotten it to him, and he wouldn't have speculated on the man's vices or worried about his own safety, particularly in the middle of the street in broad daylight. Okay. She was a woman and that accounted for some apprehension. Jason had been at the helm of social service organizations for several causes at the university: tutoring students in South Boston, collecting clothes for natural disaster victims, volunteering to build hospitals and schools in remote Peruvian hill towns. Tiffany might have been joking when she called him Christ, but Jason's nickname at school had actually been Jesus, and was genuinely bestowed upon him.

Maybe Ryan can make a flyer for the man and leaflet the neighborhood, or post it in supermarkets and cafés and have the church's number in little tear-offs on the bottom. But who to ask for? She doesn't even know his name. She should have been kinder to him. She should at least have asked his name, shaken his hand. He's disappeared from sight now. Maybe if she goes over to the cot shelter, she'll find him and advertise for him. She envisions him owning his own pickup, with a plow attached to the front and cleaning big box-parking lots; in summer he'd be a landscaper.

Chapter 5

B Y MORNING, SHE'S all but forgotten about the stranger. He did say he might have work with a friend in Jersey. In her high laced-up black suede boots and black tights, short black skirt and black fedora, she's overdressed for an office where the lawyers prefer to dress down, making business casual more like barbecue casual, with jeans and T-shirts the typical attire. She tried to start a dress-up day, but was voted down five to one. They were a nonprofit in a dingy office above a pho restaurant in Downtown Crossing and didn't see the need to formalize their wardrobes when they weren't litigating. It's crossed Ryan's mind that the absence of a dress code rather than any moral or social obligation was why they had chosen to work for this organization.

She makes an effort not to think about Jason and the contest she won and the hole in her heart, but no matter where she turns, something or someone reminds her of him. Almost a year and a half, and she still can't shake him. This morning, it's the damn sign in front of the old stone church across from the T station: Taizé Prayer Today at 7 p.m. When had they started that practice? A ridiculous event, she concludes: people deep in meditation, lighting candles, singing verses. Might as well be a Pentecostal service with followers jumping up and down and speaking in tongues like lunatics.

That wasn't how she had felt at the Taizé Prayer she attended at Driscoll University. She had gone to the basement of Loyola Chapel on a mission: to emblazon her memory in the heart of Jason McDermott. The chapel was unilluminated, and she could barely see in front of her. She had taken the first empty pew she came upon, and as luck have it, when her eyes adjusted to the darkness, she saw that she was sitting two pews behind and a little to the right of Jason, affording her a perfect view of him. He was alone, kneeling, eyes closed, head bowed and cradled in the palms of his hands. With his fingers spread apart, she could see the intensity of expression that signaled he was deep in meditation, far away. What was he praying for? A date with her? She knew even then the answer to that, and she questioned getting involved with a boy so drawn to religion.

Numerous unlit candles lined the simple wooden altar rail. To the left was a trio of two guitar players and a singer who also led the service, assuring everyone they could either participate in the chanting or simply meditate. Ryan had to admit it was a bit intoxicating, or maybe it had just been the proximity of Jason. Still, the strumming of the guitars, the flickering candles people had begun to light, the chanting from Exodus was transporting and so different than a Mass, where you were preached to, asked for money, commanded to stand up, sit down, kneel, form a line for Communion. Here you were free to speak, to walk up and light a candle wherever you wanted, to remain silent. The young woman in front of her, like several others, had her arms outstretched, palms up, thumb and forefinger touching; she didn't utter a syllable throughout the service. Ryan tried not to let her mind drift, to be in the moment just the way her mother had urged her to when she had given her *Be Here Now* by Ram Dass for her thirteenth birthday or taken her to yoga class.

After the last reading, the singer began to extinguish the candles, which by then numbered at least forty or fifty. One by one the flames went out until the entire chapel grew dark again. Slowly, students gathered their backpacks and made their way out into the balmy spring evening. Some ran off, others lingered to talk. Jason was the last to awaken from a contemplative state. But when he did, he emerged refreshed, as though he had just showered, had a cup of coffee, and was ready to begin a new day. Smiling, he spotted her on the bench, where she was pretending to be searching for something in her book bag.

"Ryan! I didn't know you went to Taizé Prayer."

"Occasionally," she said. Nothing like coming out of a religious experience and lying right off the bat.

"I got the things you put in my box," he said, referring to the cross of palm fronds and the Hebrew calendar she had had the mail service place in his mailbox after the seder she had invited him to. "I've been meaning to thank you, but I've had these midterms to get through."

"No problem. I just wanted you to have them." She was feeling stupid. Why would he want them? What kind of a fool had she taken him for? She was as transparent as plastic wrap. But he surprised her by saying he was glad; he was not as naïve as other women imagined him to be. She stood up and was about to walk with him toward the upper campus when another student approached them. She was petite and much shorter than five-feet-four Ryan, with long wavy jet-black hair that fell down around her upper arms and heavily shadowed deep-set eyes that sucked you in. Her straight nose widened at the tip. Her lips were on the thin side, thank God, or else she would have been perfect. No matter how long Ryan walked around with whitening strips on her teeth, they would never dazzle the way this woman's smile did against her dark complexion.

"Wasn't that amazing?" the woman said to Jason.

"You two know each other?" he asked.

The two women nodded as if to say: somewhat. Ryan Toscano and Rutvi Thapar had met three and a half years before in a freshman orientation group that had been arranged alphabetically. They'd had little or no contact with one another since.

"I'm going to Espresso Royale. Want to come?" Rutvi asked.

Ryan was quite sure she was inviting Jason alone, because those searing midnight eyes were fixed on his face. Jason turned to Ryan, who didn't know if he was asking her permission to go with Rutvi to the off-campus coffee shop or asking her if she'd like to join them. Ryan answered them both with one gamble of a reply. Should he have opted to go with Rutvi, it would have been too late for Ryan to join them.

"I'm off to the library. Got a midterm tomorrow," Ryan said.

"Me too," he told Rutvi, apologetically. "Got a paper due."

"Well. Okay. See you at the dorm meeting later, Jason."

"Right. See you there," he said with genuine enthusiasm.

That was what made Jason one of the most sought-after guys on campus by men as well as women. He was not only smart and hot, with his curly black hair, milk-white skin dotted with brown speckles, and blue eyes (*black Irish, cream of the crop* is how her roommate Jenny Sullivan described him), he was genuine and humble, and seemingly unaware of his physical attributes. Now, having come face-to-face with one of his pursuers, any qualms Ryan might have had about getting more involved with Jason vanished. Rutvi was the nail in the coffin: There was no way he was going to belong to a woman who was probably Hindu and not taken with the Old Testament any more than Ryan was.

"She lives in Holden?" Ryan asked, referring to the modern high-rise where Jason was a resident assistant.

"Rutvi? Yeah. Two doors down from me."

Ryan had her work cut out for her with only six more weeks until graduation.

They continued over to the old Gothic library that was lined with long oak tables and high-backed, elaborately carved mahogany chairs. Two rows of chandeliers and tall stained-glass windows depicting biblical images gave it a solemn atmosphere like that of a church. This was where students went when they really wanted to study and not run into everyone they knew, the way they did in the modern library. And if someone was craving greater solitude, they went downstairs to the stacks, a dungeon of dusty volumes, where they entombed themselves in one of the carrels that lined the walls.

They found two adjacent empty seats: She took out a paperback and a pocket English/Spanish dictionary; he opened his laptop and set a pile of printed-out articles next to it. He typed from time to time while he attempted to interpret highlighted paragraphs. She read a page of the first story in Julio Cortázar's *Final del Juego* (*End of the Game)* over and over. If she was going to pass this midterm in Survey of Latin American Literature, she was going to have to stay up all night, because although she had come to the serious library, she had brought the biggest distraction with her. She was not alone. After half an hour, the cover of his laptop came down with the finality of a theater curtain.

"Let's grab a cup of coffee," he said. "It's going to be a long night."

"At that new Hillside Cafe under the parking garage," she said, making certain they would not wind up where Rutvi had gone. And she closed the book on Cortázar. End of the game? This was only the beginning.

* * *

A crystal chandelier and an enormous lily arrangement grace the spacious wainscoted lobby of Laurel Manor, where a pianist at a shiny black baby grand turns out show tunes like *Everything's Coming Up Roses* and *Mame* from five to seven in the evening. It's as though they were hosting a bar mitzvah or a gala fundraiser; Ryan anticipates being passed a bacon-wrapped scallop and her glass of champagne. Then her eyes fall on several wheelchairs parked next to the wall. Hollowed-out bodies of indecipherable gender slumped to one side. Sunken eyes with whites yellowed like ancient parchment staring up at her or at nothing at all, waiting for visitors who may or may not come, give her the shivers. It's a premortem ball, she concludes. Luckily, Faye, her grandmother, is at the nursing home only to recover from a fractured hip she received from falling off a bicycle.

At the entrance to the rehab unit called Golden Meadow, Ryan passes a round table with a blue cloth hanging to the floor. Its only purpose is to display a gilded, framed copy of today's dinner menu: herb-encrusted salmon, pork tenderloin with cherry glaze, garlic roasted potatoes, asparagus spears, mesclun greens with bits of poached pear salad, fresh baked popovers, and fruit and assorted pastries for dessert. All that's missing is neat rows of table-seating cards.

She finds her grandmother in the activity room, already digesting the 5 p.m. dinner, and she knows Faye will try to entice her to visit more often by offering her things she's saved all week from the dining hall: small containers of rice pudding, decorative place mats, or even centerpieces she's persuaded the staff to let her take away. There aren't many people Faye can't persuade. Ryan enjoys being with Faye; a degree away from the parental unit, she is the perfect person off of whom to bounce things. While Faye is opinionated, Ryan can tolerate her in a way she can't her own mother, who is either indifferent to Ryan's dilemmas or attacks them head-on, devising strategies she thinks are innovative and foolproof. Her mother is mysterious and, not unlike Jason, cautious with her love. Ryan's father, on the other hand, is the emotional one who has one reaction to most things that involve change—a rise in the pitch of his voice, a nervous twitch of his left eye, and the question: What for?

At six fifteen in the evening Faye is still made up with rouge, lipstick, and penciled eyebrows. Her hazel eyes nearly obscured by heavy-handed clumps of black mascara and green shadow that weigh down her lids, she has difficulty peering up at Ryan as her granddaughter approaches the group of gamblers. Faye deals the last of seven cards face down and calls for the man with a pair of aces showing to make the final bet.

"A royal flush and that's it for me. My beautiful granddaughter is here," she tells her poker buddies, throwing down her colorful hand of cards, scooping up the stacks of nickels and dimes in front of her, and dumping them into a large red leather pocketbook the size of a small duffle bag. "This is Ryan," Faye says with pride.

The two women and one man smile and nod with satisfaction as they take in the girl.

"She has her grandmother's eyes," the woman Faye has introduced as Sylvia says, as though Ryan and Faye weren't there.

"She has her grandmother's good looks," the man named Harold points out with slightly slurred speech.

"A *shana madela*," Esther extols her beauty in Yiddish.

Okay, this is the Jewish table. No Kennedys here. It's also the younger table, because despite their wheelchairs, these seniors are healthier looking than others in this short-term unit. Ryan finds the man attractive. Too weird; he's so old. Yet he *is* handsome: clean shaven with high cheekbones, a sexy smile and mop of silken silver hair, fine features, erect posture, firm muscles covering these bones, except for the slight droop of the right side of his mouth that could be mistaken for a subtle smile. She even likes his aftershave. God, she must be desperate!

Ryan tries to avoid the stares from envious residents as she wheels Faye away. The plush hunter-green-and-beige geometric carpeting is reminiscent of a four-star hotel, but Ryan can't decide if the heavy floral scent is a by-product of genuine cleanliness or an attempt to mask urine and decay. When they get to Faye's room, Faye gestures for Ryan to take a leather-upholstered chair from the corner, where the wheelchair can't fit, and sit opposite her. The heavy institutional chair, so hard to push, confirms that this is not the Ritz-Carlton.

"So, darling. What's cooking?"

"What's with the garbage bag?" Ryan points to an oversized green plastic one in the corner. "Don't tell me you have to take out your own trash."

"That's not trash! That's what I bought from the Home Shopping Network. Bags, sweaters, shoes, jewelry. You should see my bargains. Look, I can't get to Filene's basement in my condition. What else am I going to do in here with all this deadwood? It passes the time."

"Faye, you know Filene's closed, don't you?" She frequently tests Faye's memory.

"Of course. But I can dream, can't I? And I don't dare say the word 'Macy's'. It's like the Empire State invasion of Massachusetts. Isn't it enough they took the Babe, the *Globe*, and now that cute outfielder Ellsbury? Didn't you just love him?"

"I'm a Yankees fan."

"Your father's bad influence again. I just can't stand the thought that Filene's is gone, that building standing empty. Now *that* was a department store. Talk about elegant. Stepping into that place was like diving into a plate of molten chocolate cake. Today I watch these women on TV play show and tell, and I call a number. But, hey, it serves its purpose. Where could I go for these, in my situation? Did

I tell you I dated the grandson of William Filene? I could have been rich, if his mother hadn't matched him up with that socialite. He had no balls. Did I ever tell you that story?"

"Yes."

"He was a milquetoast. But his store—ooh la la! Boy do I miss the Bargain Basement. That's where I bought your mother's wedding gown. Stood on a line that went all the way up Washington Street for three hours. I bought her a Priscilla of Boston for next to nothing. She looked like a million dollars in it, but with the puss she put on, you'd think it was a consolation prize I forced on her. And what does she do? She goes to Goodwill and buys a yellow floral cotton dress for ten bucks that made her look like Little Bo Beep and gets married at Jones Beach—not even the Cape, or the North Shore, mind you—we had to go to New York. I can go along with a lot, *bubeleh,* but the dress—that was like pouring a bottle of milk of magnesia down my throat."

"What'd you do with the gown?"

"My friend Pearl's daughter wore it. But it didn't bring her luck; she got divorced in a year."

"So let's see what you've got here." Ryan undoes the twist tie on the bag.

"Stop stalling. What are you up to, *bubeleh*?"

When Ryan tells her about winning the Brackton Is for Brides Contest, Faye raises her penciled eyebrows and lets out "Well, ain't that a hoot." Words like that often come as a surprise, because Faye's vocabulary is usually eloquent, as though she hailed from the best finishing school or Ivy League college and not an inner-city Boston public high school. She loves to dance and has never been able to sit still when she hears music. Right now she taps the foot of her good side on the pedal of the wheelchair to the beat of a swing number that can faintly be heard coming from the room next door: Faye's hearing is excellent.

"You know when your grandfather and I were courting, he used to take me dancing every night to the Bradford Hotel on Tremont Street. They had a nightclub on the top floor—The Cascades—with an open sky roof so you could dance under the stars. Glenn Miller, Benny Goodman, Harry James; we danced to them all. After we got married, he never danced again. I could have had the marriage annulled for misrepresentation. After fifty years of marriage he didn't know how I took my coffee or that I hated milk chocolate."

"You're not making a good case for marriage here, Faye."

"My Sidney did do the wet wash every Saturday before we could afford a washing machine," she reassures Ryan. "That's what we used to call going to the laundromat. Must have been some expression your grandfather got from the old country. Just make sure your husband dances with you after you get married. Get it in writing beforehand."

"That's the issue here, Faye. I'm not getting married."

"Why not? You just won this contest."

"Get serious, Faye."

"No, *you* get serious. If there were a doubt in your mind, you wouldn't be here today to discuss anything. You need to find a husband."

"I can't find someone and fall in love in five months." Ryan uncrosses her legs then recrosses them.

"Don't say can't, Ryan. Never say can't. You can do anything you want." She's getting excited and talking faster.

"What drugs do they have you on here?"

She waves the question away. "Where's your moxie?"

"My what?"

"Your creativity. Your nerve. Your balls."

"I carry them in my purse."

Faye laughs. "That's a good one, Ryan. You should use that in one of your stories."

"Is that why you tried to ride a bike at eighty-seven? Because you have so much moxie?"

"Well, it wasn't because I was on the drug of youth, was it? I used to love to ride my bike through the Public Garden every Sunday morning when all the gentiles were in church."

"How long ago was that?"

"'About seventy years."

"What were you thinking two weeks ago, Faye, when you landed in the hospital?"

"I was thinking I wanted to ride a bike. What did you think I was thinking?"

"That you'd give yourself a bone-density test. In the middle of winter, no less."

"It was a warm day. No snow."

"Whose bike did you steal, anyway?"

"The little girl next door; she always leaves it in the front yard. It's a small bike, a pink bike. I just borrowed it. They say you can always get back on, no matter after how long. *It's like riding a bike.* Isn't that what they say?"

"Oh, Faye."

"Look, I was trying to reinvent myself. Do you know the only magazine that talks about women improving themselves over sixty is *AARP*? The fashion magazines don't even mention women past fifty. It's as though the second half of your life doesn't exist. But let's not get off the subject. In my day, the women were the scheming, clever, conniving ones and men were the dummies. But it was the men who ran the world with those gutsy women behind them. *I Love Lucy. My Little Margie. Our Miss Brooks. Burns and Allen.* I can name a million of those TV shows."

"What's your point? Men are still running the world."

"But young women like you are moving up. They're all over the television now, not just giving the weather and in sitcoms. They're on the talk shows; they're giving the news. Trust me, Ryan, you can do anything you want. But it's all about knowing what you want. Your grandfather and I met in the movie theater and got married a month later, before he shipped out overseas. Of course that was wartime, emotions ran high; but where love is concerned, it's always wartime."

"You crack me up, Faye."

"I know. I'm a pisser. That's what your mother used to say. Your grandfather used to say, 'Faye, you're hot stuff.' But that was when I embarrassed him; it wasn't a compliment. Listen, Ryan, it's not fun being alone. Even now. It's not the sex you miss. It's the hugs. The closeness."

"I *was* engaged."

"Forget that Jason!" Faye discounts the statement with a wave of glossy red-tipped fingers. "I got over Billy Filene, didn't? I told your mother she should have raised you with some religion. Maybe if you had been more religious, Jason wouldn't have gone looking to marry God."

"He doesn't want to marry God. That's what nuns do."

"Men probably do now too. Times are changing. Speaking of which, how's your roommate, Tiffany? I like that girl. A little kooky, but I like her. Bring her around sometime."

"You like her because she caters to you. Sometimes I'm uncomfortable around her. She tries to be like us but she's filthy rich, you know."

"Money doesn't make a person, Ryan. You can be a lady at a bar and a tramp at the Astor."

"What's the Astor?"

"It was a grand hotel in New York built by the Astor family. You know the Astors—you saw *Titanic*. The husband went down with the boat. Like I said, money can't buy everything."

Ryan nods.

"You know, when your mother wanted to marry your father, I was opposed at first. Not just because he was Catholic, mind you. But he took her to New York. They got married barefoot in the sand—no priest, no rabbi—just some bearded guy with a white turban. Come to think of it, the dress was macramé not cotton. 'At least they got married,' your grandfather said."

"Now, what's your point?"

"If you know what you want, it'll work out."

"My parents separated."

"It was a phase. Your father just lost his mind for a little while."

"When he left my mother, you said he should have been shot with shit and sent to hell for stinking."

"I said that's what your grandfather would have said if he had been alive. Look, your mother forgives your father; even I forgive the bastard. They're working things out. Everyone deserves a second chance."

"Is this coming from experience?"

"I'm not talking."

"Since when?"

"I'll admit to this: Sometimes I thought marrying my Sidney was the best thing I'd ever done; sometimes I thought it was the worst. All marriages are like that. As my Sidney used to say, 'Take two and hit to right.'"

"Do you even know what that means?"

"It's baseball talk. Do *you*?"

"I played softball, remember."

"Something like: You can't keep stalling. Eventually you have to take a stab at it and hope for the best. All marriages have spells that are like a chronic illness: The symptoms subside and you feel good; they flare up from time to time and you feel bad; occasionally the illness is fatal. The question is: What do you *want*, Ryan?"

"I thought I wanted Jason."

"You were confused. I don't know why your parents ever sent you to a Catholic college."

"It offered me a scholarship. It needed diversity."

"Look, do yourself a favor. Go on the Internet. That's what all the young girls who work here do. You have a computer. There's this JDate for Jews. It can't hurt. I used to tell your mother, 'Would you just try it?' about dating a Jewish boy, and she would turn her nose up as though I were offering her gefilte fish that had been sitting in the refrigerator from two Passovers ago. She was like you—always with the gentiles. Always contrary."

"Can't imagine where she got that from."

"Why don't you put on some makeup? You're such a pretty girl, but everyone can use a little help. You never know when Mr. Right will show up. You could be throwing out the garbage. And wear a few pieces of jewelry, Ryan—to attract a rich guy: money goes to money. By the way, when I'm gone up here"—she points to her head—"make sure my nails are done and my hair is colored. Clairol Nice n' Easy, 101, Ash Blonde. And pull out any black hairs you see on my chin. Do I have any now? I left my magnifying mirror at home."

"You're good, Faye."

"When you were a baby, I never took you or your cousins Emma and Jake in a car when I babysat."

"Why not?"

"Because I was afraid," she says, as though Ryan should have known the answer. "Now I won't hold a baby unless I'm sitting down. I'm afraid I might drop her. You see what I mean?"

"No."

"Come on, Ryan. You're a bright girl. The longer you wait, the worse everything gets. Fear overtakes you. That's why I got on the bike—I was tired of being afraid. Get on the Internet. I want to come to your wedding."

"You'll be there. I promise."

"But I want to *know* I'm there. Your mother and your aunt say I should move into an independent living place with access to assisted living when I get out of here. What do you think?"

"Do you want to?"

"I like my house, my garden, though I can't work in it anymore. I keep busy with the few friends I have left. We play cards once a week. Sometimes we go to the theater. Well, we used to."

"Then stay."

"But they're dying." She sighs. "And it's getting harder for us re-mainders to maneuver. We've managed up until now, but something's bound to bite you in the ass. And so this question nags me: At what point do you stop listening to yourself and start listening to your children because your own logic is flawed? And if your own logic is flawed, how do you know it is?"

"I don't think you're there yet, Faye. I mean, you might have been bitten in the ass, but not the other thing."

"Why? Because of what I just said? It doesn't work that way." She waves her long red nails in Ryan's face. "One day you're on; one day you're off. At first you know you're missing something. Soon you don't know you're missing anything at all. I see the ones who live in the building next door—the *independent* living building. They leave their cars' key rings dangling from their hands like a teenager who just got his license, daring anyone to take those jewels of freedom from them. But then they'll blink, and the only thing they'll be driving is an aluminum walker with a license to linger because it's also an assisted living unit."

"You said it's about knowing what you want."

"There comes a time when what you want might no longer be good for you."

"Do you have to decide today?"

"Of course not. I'll be here for a good while. But hopefully I'll be out in time for your wedding. When's the date? I need to put it in my calendar." She points to a calendar book with the picture of a brass band on the cover.

"June twenty-eighth." Ryan goes over to the calendar. "This is pointless."

But Faye directs her with a pointed finger and Ryan makes the notation.

"Plan to go home, Faye. I'll tell you if I don't think it's a good idea when the time comes."

"Oh, I wish I could go with you."

"You'll be out soon enough."

"No. I mean to Vermont."

"I *am* curious."

"Tough to fold a winning hand, isn't it? Think of it as an adventure. See where it leads you. You can always tell them it didn't work out between you and your fiancé. But I'm optimistic something positive will come of this. And if it doesn't, it's material, Ryan. You can always write about it."

There's a knock at the door. When Faye responds, a young man with spiked blond hair and wearing blue scrubs pops his head in. "Can I get you settled for the evening, Faye?"

"I suppose, Louis. Come meet my granddaughter, Ryan. Louis is here to put me to bed." Faye winks at Ryan.

"Would you like something to drink? Coffee? Coke?" he asks Ryan.

"No, thank you. I was just about to leave."

"Take your time. I'll come back in a few minutes."

"Adorable," Faye says when he's gone. "Don't you think?"

"Please. He looks like he's ten."

"He's twenty-four and a great poker player, but he's a little too short for you. Listen, before you go, take something from the bag. Maybe there's a necklace you'd like. Consider it a party favor."

"Jeez, Faye. You haven't even been here two weeks."

"I like to keep busy."

Ryan pulls out a small padded envelope and holds it up for Faye to see. "What's in this?"

"A headlamp for hiking in the dark."

"Ooh, this is nice." Ryan examines a rectangular red faux-alligator purse with silver chain handles.

"The outside comes off. It's magnetic. There are two more covers— plaid and zebra. Three purses in one!"

"There must be a magnifying mirror in here somewhere."

"Take the watch in the skinny gold box, darling. It comes with six different colored bands to coordinate with your outfits."

Ryan puts everything back and closes up the bag. She walks over to her grandmother empty-handed. "Don't worry, Faye," she says kissing her on the cheek. "I'll be back."

"Whatever you do, *bubeleh*, make sure he dances," Faye calls after her.

"Faye—" Ryan turns around. "What's for breakfast tomorrow?"

"Buckwheat pancakes with bacon, stewed prunes, and a soft-boiled egg. I can't wait."

Ryan smiles with relief. "By the way, your poker buddy Harold is hot."

"Who?"

The worried look returns to Ryan's face.

"Relax. I was only kidding. Stop the testing. I know who you're talking about. Nothing wrong with my frontal lobe. At least he's not like the *mishuggah* on the third floor who goes up to every woman and says: 'I'm looking for sex.' Every day it's: 'I'm looking for sex.'"

"I think he likes you. I mean Harold. Can he dance?"

"I think he likes *you*. Didn't you see the wheelchair? Actually, he had a stroke, but he's improving off the charts. And you won't believe this, but he was an Arthur Murray instructor on the side. You know: *Put a little fun into your life. Try dancing.*"

"No way!" Ryan's never heard of Arthur Murray but puts two and two together.

"Specialized in the rumba. *Arthur Murray. A great place to be somebody.*" She attempts to shimmy her torso. After Ryan has left, she grimaces with pain.

Chapter 6

JASON MCDERMOTT KNEELS in a small chapel in a southern Catholic college. It isn't even really a chapel but a room at the college turned into a chapel for the novices like him. The walls are painted white; the flooring is oak; the altar is a rectangular oak table with a cloth draped over it; a life-sized image of Christ on the cross dominates the wall behind it. There are no longer enough men aspiring to become Jesuits in America to warrant the upkeep of the old seminaries, and so Jason and others like him have been relegated to one of a handful of Spirituality Centers carved out of universities. Here, through rigorous prayer, dialogue, and observation, he goes through the discernment process of discovering his Jesuit identity and of confirming that God is calling him and that his desire to serve is pure and not some misguided notion.

Jason grew up next to a defunct Jesuit seminary in a small New York State hamlet. The large modern brick building, built in the nineteen fifties, had stood vacant for as long as he could remember; today it's a yoga and meditation retreat center. As young boys, his friends found throwing rocks at the many twelve-over-twelve windows a favorite summer pastime. While Jason couldn't deny the rush he got from shattering glass with his perfect lobs, he hated it when one of the boys suggested going over to the seminary. He didn't mind peeking into the windows, though, trying to catch a glimpse of a ghostly sacred life through a broken wooden blind or the slit of a ripped green shade, but when it came to destroying property, he recoiled and often made excuses, like his arm was hurting, to avoid joining in.

His mother used to talk of how young seminarians had strolled in groups of ten or more—the way college freshmen now go out on the town in packs—along the hilly winding road, through cow pastures, down to the river. Always so handsome, his mother said, shielded behind the armor of those black cassocks, aware of how their smiles and winks titillated even little girls like her.

He remembers the dining hall at the seminary, lined with black-and-white class photos of those young seminarians, and the enormous chapel with the marble floor and stained-glass windows and the life-sized image of Christ with one foot extended off the Cross, looking as though he were about to step down and join the other young men in singing the *Regina Caeli* that Jason swore he could hear. He used to imagine every pew filled with these ardent worshippers, their heads squared off with the same crew cut, wearing the same long black cassock and white collar, and their eyes filled with the same wild desires, the same fears. They may as well have been marines or West Point cadets finding comfort in solidarity as they prepared to give up—no, trade—privileges, a terrifying yet at the same time exhilarating experience. In the heyday of the priesthood, several hundred seminarians would have sat in every chapel like this one across the country. Today, all the seminarians put together couldn't fill a single chapel. There are eleven other novices here at the Spirituality Center with Jason.

In one of his theology classes at Driscoll, Jason learned that the only thing separating man from other life on this earth was the God-given gift of free will. And while Jason entered the novitiate of his own free will, he cannot but help worry that in doing so, he surrendered that gift to its distributor. On the contrary, Father Curran, his spiritual father, tells him God has given Jason the grace to exercise his free will in an extraordinary way. Like the marine, Jason thinks. Like the cadet. Father Curran should know; he's been exercising his free will in this same way since he became a novice seven decades ago. Supported by an African carved cane, his free will is pretty much useless now except for when it comes to choosing between cognac and dry sherry at bedtime.

Jason could have done his first two years in Boston, but he requested a different part of the country, figuring that the farther away he was from Ryan, the farther out of his mind she would be. Tonight, however, sitting alone in the modest chapel, his thoughts wander—really wander, to Ryan. He remembers the day they met in The Writings of Teilhard de Chardin. Both were seniors, he with a double major in theology and philosophy, she fulfilling a philosophy requirement she had postponed for three years.

She invited him to a chocolate seder she was preparing for her suitemates and friends: chocolate-covered matzo, semisweet chocolate soup, brisket with Mexican chocolate *poblano* sauce, chocolate macaroons. She had liked being the only Jew, or half Jew, in the group, and she played up that aspect of her heritage, he later learned, not because she had any more affiliation to Judaism than to Catholicism, but because it set her apart from the others. And because she liked to have what no one else could have. This he understood about her right away.

The seder was a blast. They were all drunk before they even got to the permitted first sip of wine (the only non-chocolate item) in the Hagaddah. He fell asleep fully clothed in her warm bed, breathing the fruity scent of her long strawberry blond curls into which he had buried his nose to avoid the stench of vomit coming from the common room where several others had collapsed before making it to the bathroom.

He'd dated one other girl in college, but she'd broken his heart, and so he was cautious now, had been for a year. He left in the morning before she awoke, having scribbled a thank-you note on a Post-it and sticking it on the Jewish calendar she said her grandmother had sent her for Jewish New Year that hung from a bulletin board over her desk—next to the cross of palm that her Catholic grandmother had sent her after Palm Sunday.

"I like having them fight over me," she told him. On the cover of the calendar was a long, white-linen-covered table around which men with thick bushy beards, top hats, and spectacles sat studying texts in a room lined with bookshelves. *And they shall make a sanctuary,* the caption read in English. Everything else was in Hebrew. It reminded him of the seder table, and so he stuck the Post-it in the center of the table in the picture. *Thanks for the sanctuary, Jason.*

He thought it was a stupid thing to say, but he really didn't know what else to write. He was clumsy around women, and yet they were always around him, clinging to him like a piece of gum to the sole of a shoe on a hot summer day. He enjoyed them—especially witty and gutsy ones. He admired them. But he enjoyed being around men too. He just liked people. Two days later, he found the cross and the calendar in his box in the school mailroom. Then she showed up at Taizé Prayer, and he knew there would be no forgetting Ryan; *she* would see to that, and he was glad.

That night, as they sat side by side in the old musty library, the familiar scent of the mass of ringlets that fell around her like a whimsical drape drifted over him, overpowering centuries of dankness. When he glanced over at her from his laptop and she back at him, he was mesmerized by her big green eyes, as iridescent and glistening as the shiny coated lips and the porcelain complexion she said she had inherited from her grandmother and that, in the months and years to come, he would observe redden in the cold of winter or from a burst of laughter or outrage.

She would become like a kaleidoscope that was forever changing, becoming more and more interesting to him in every way. She, nevertheless, would continue to work hard to pursue him, from anointing her body with intoxicating oils to planning events that would bring them together, because what she hadn't suspected that night in the library was that he was already a goner. And all that stood in her way of knowing this was precisely the problem with Jason: his elusiveness, the difference between the feelings that lived in his head and those he revealed.

After they went for coffee, they took a walk by the reservoir. They talked about their plans for a career in law. All they both really wanted to do was touch: first hands, then arms wrapped tightly around each other, then lips. Standing outside in the chilled air that night was far better than being hung over in her bed. Kissing her, aware that he was growing hard against her, was enough. It was nirvana, paradise, the beginning of an odyssey. He was in the only place he wanted to be. He forgot about the dorm meeting he was supposed to run, and he didn't care that he would have to stay up all night to finish his paper. He was in love.

Chapter 7

Wednesday, January 29

RYAN IS LATE to her date. She should never have agreed to meet this guy way out in Natick on a rainy Wednesday night. Let him come to you, Faye would have said, even though Ryan does like the idea of being the one who *comes to* so she can be the one to *leave from* whenever she chooses.

She met the last prospect, an education consultant, at Pho Pasteur on Washington Street during her lunch hour. The only problem was the noodle soup was too hot to down quickly enough. He was certainly "built," as he had claimed, but in a way that resulted from having frequented too many restaurants and not enough gyms.

"I said my body type was average. I never said buff," he said when he saw the look of surprise she tried to mask.

He also said he was thirty-five. The man who could be a contestant for the Biggest Loser reality show and who stood up and insisted on kissing her on the cheek was at least fifty. Who would ever trust a man who used vintage photos? Honesty was a must, claimed the girl who had won a contest based on false pretenses. Still, this evening she's on her way to meet a venture capitalist who had suggested the food court at the Natick mall (his sincerity already in jeopardy since he'd stated he was a foodie) because that was where he was picking up a tux for a charity event and was concerned about wasting good dating time.

Ryan had taken Faye's advice and tried JDate this go-around, but she'd been in a car accident and was running forty minutes late for her rendezvous. It was hardly even a fender-bender. Her secondhand hybrid had ever so gently tapped the SUV that hadn't slowed down but stopped abruptly at the Natick exit tollbooth on the Mass Pike. Ryan couldn't detect a scratch on either vehicle when she got out to assess the damage and to apologize to the female driver, who was already talking hysterically into her cell phone, telling 911 that she'd been in a bad accident and couldn't move. Wailing sirens announced the arrival of two cruisers, a fire truck, and an ambulance.

"*This* is an accident?" The trooper demanded an explanation from Ryan who was leaning against her car, having pulled it over to the shoulder.

"*I* didn't call you. *She* did." Ryan pointed to the woman who sat as motionless as an inflatable doll at the tollbooth gate, rush hour traffic backed up behind her a quarter of a mile, cars zigzagging to change lanes. The officer told the woman to move her car.

"Can't. My back hurts." She did not look at the trooper but kept her sleek black-haired head immobile and facing the windshield.

"So does mine," he replied, poking his head into the window to get a better look at her. "Now move your car."

"I need to go to the hospital."

"Good. Go."

"I need to call my lawyer."

"Call ten lawyers, lady, but move your car first. By the way—you shop at Whole Foods?"

"No. I never shop at Whole Foods."

"Yeah, right." The trooper walked back to Ryan's car.

"I think I picked her up for shoplifting a few weeks ago. You sure she didn't back into *you*?"

Ryan's date is even hotter in person than in his profile photo—like a swarthy Rob Lowe. Sitting on a white wire mesh seat, he tells her that tardiness is something he won't tolerate: his time is valuable, and the time allotted for their date has expired. Picking up a black plastic garment bag, he ends the date before it begins and marches off, leaving a wake of Metro cologne that she will never gain find irresistible.

"Asshole," she mutters. Foodie indeed. She was half Italian; her people were born with a foodie gene.

A small Chinese woman stands on a chair behind the counter at Ming Dynasty and offers Ryan a chunk of Kung pao chicken on a toothpick, a gesture Ryan interprets as some form of consolation for the scene the woman witnessed. Ryan thinks the little square bits of chicken are mushy, so she turns down the offer and moves towards Cajun Grill next door. The Chinese woman grows aggressive, beckoning to her with her skewered chicken in hand.

"No, thank you," Ryan says, and places her order for coconut battered shrimp. Fast food aside, she's starving. She's also hypoglycemic, which means that not only her energy level but her mood (about to explode in a most unpleasant expression of irritability) is directly correlated with her blood sugar level.

"That not real shrimp," the Chinese woman calls out. Ryan ignores her. "Señora, Madam, Lady, you want shrimp? You like spicy? You like sweet? Sesame?" She stabs another toothpick into a pan of shrimp dripping with orange sauce and waves the crustacean in the air. "Señora, take it!"

"She doesn't want your shrimp!" the Hispanic Cajun Grill lady shouts back.

"She no want yours either!"

The air in the food court grows oppressive to Ryan, now at the head of a line of customers who seem to have appeared out of nowhere. Her armpits are tingling beneath her woolen sweater, already soaked from an overdose of the day's drama as she becomes the object of bickering between the two vendors. Without a word, she walks toward the escalator.

"And what am I supposed to do with this?" the Cajun Grill lady, holding up the plate of coconut shrimp and dirty rice, calls after her.

"I tell you, try my shrimp, crazy lady." The words of the Chinese woman, still perched on the chair, carry over the crowd and land on Ryan's ears as she is ever too slowly lifted upward on the moving stairs.

As she scurries toward the exit, a glamorous Israeli woman at a kiosk grabs her hand and urges her to try an anti-aging miracle cream.

"I have makeup on," Ryan says.

"Put it between thumb and forefinger."

Before Ryan can escape, the woman is rubbing a pink dollop on Ryan's fingers, which she won't let go of.

"Now look at other hand and see difference," the woman tells Ryan.

"It looks exactly the same."

"Is smoother."

"Of course it's smoother. You just put grease on it." Ryan pulls back her hand.

"Sometimes it takes a while," the woman calls after her. "Your lines will disappear."

"I don't have any. I'm twenty-eight!"

* * *

She opens the apartment door, anticipating the solitude of home, only to find Starr's hiking boots in the foyer, dripping onto the Persian prayer rug Tiffany's parents cast off on them. Starr, with her raspy know-it-all voice, jerky hand movements that startle the tattooed snake on her arm, the watermelon-gel-plastered crew cut she pats with the palm of her left hand every other minute as if to make sure it's still there. Ryan is about to make an about-face when Starr, her muscular body hidden beneath a plaid woolen jac-shirt, picks up her boots and storms past her. A few heavy footsteps down the stairs and she's gone.

"She's a happy camper," Ryan tells Tiffany, who's sitting on the sofa, down in the mouth and alternating puffs from a cigarette in one hand with swigs from a quart bottle of pomegranate juice in the other.

"It's over," Tiff says, moaning.

"I can see that—you're smoking. Get another girlfriend fast, because I can't stand secondhand smoke. I hate your breakups." Ryan swats the air around her.

"This could be a tough one."

"That's what you always say."

"I mean it. I thought she was the one." She takes a drag on her cigarette.

"Too bossy, too nervous, too rude—"

"Okay. Okay. You didn't like her."

"What are you doing this weekend, Tiff?"

"Starr was going to take me ice fishing. Now I'll be sitting around trying to get over her."

"I've decided to go up to Vermont. I feel I owe these people an in-person apology. Want to come?"

"To tell them you're a fraud?" Tiffany perks up.

"Maybe. Maybe just to check it out."

"Still keeping your options open. I admire your optimism."

"A road trip. What do you say?"

"I don't know, Ryan." She sinks full body into the couch. "I like to really get deep into my depression after a breakup. Works better than trying to ignore it and have the pain linger indefinitely. But, you know, I've never been to Vermont. My parents did take me to the von Trapp house in Salzburg."

"Of course, they did. Well, I've never been to the von Trapp house in Salzburg—or Vermont."

"Okay. You're on!" Tiffany sits back up, takes one last drag, and drops the cigarette into the bottle of pomegranate juice. "How about we order in Chinese and watch some rom-com with a happy ending? Then I'll have a good cry, go to bed, and feel better in the morning."

"I'll go down and pick up Mexican or Cuban or Ethiopian or anything else your broken little heart desires, but tonight, do me a favor—no Chinese. And on the ride tomorrow—no smoking."

Chapter 8

WHAT'S LEFT OF the last snowfall has already turned into gray slush in Boston, but the farther northwest they go, the whiter the landscape as they wind through the small towns and stretches of open fields of New Hampshire, then the dairy pastures and rolling hills of Vermont, with white colonial homes with black-paneled doors and American flags.

"I like the birdhouses, especially the ones in the shape of wind-mills that spin," Tiffany says. "There's one in the shape of a pelican."

"They *are* creative—or tacky."

"*Wilderness Taxidermy*," Tiffany says, reading and giving a shud-der. A pair of giant shellacked grizzly bears carved from tree trunks wave from the porch of a log cabin.

"They're everywhere," Ryan says, pointing to more bears in front of Victorian clapboard houses sorely in need of a paint job. "Two guesses as to what the major occupation of this town is."

"I don't see any doctor's office or medical building. Maybe people don't get sick here. Like it's Brigadoon or something."

"I wish this fucking car in front of us would pull over." Ryan is try-ing not to tailgate, but the blue Ford Focus with the ski rack and New York plates keeps braking.

"Let's stop for a while and put some distance between us. Maybe it'll turn off," Tiffany says. "Besides, I have to pee."

Ryan pulls into Ernie's eatery, with the big cup of steaming coffee painted on the sign of the renovated barn from which two bearded guys have just exited. Their work boots leave a trail of giant footprints leading to their pickup as they sink into the crunching snow.

"They smiled at us," Tiffany says. "Maybe you can bring one to Brackton."

"Go find the restroom. I'll be over in that Maple Museum." She points across the road.

"Coffee?"

"Thanks. Cream and sweetener."

The museum is a room behind the shop in this red cinderblock structure. There's a white screen on a stand, like the one onto which her grandfather used to project slides of her mother's childhood: images of her mother looking bored beside her sister Robin, and Faye at the races in Saratoga Springs; bored in a poufy hairdo—white-gloved, and boxy purse dangling from her arm—on High Holy Days; bored in front of the Washington Monument; crying at all her birthday parties, overwhelmed by all the attention of a dozen little kids in cone-shaped party hats singing as Faye presented her with a blazing cake.

There are a few folding chairs set up in the museum.

"When's the next presentation?" Ryan asks the young woman (dirty blond bangs covering half of her eyes and long wavy ringlets weighed down with too much product) who's standing behind the counter and looking as bored as Ryan's mother did in all the slides. A little blush would render some life into her cadaverous-looking complexion.

"Whenever you want. It's free," she says in a monotone voice.

Ryan waits for Tiff and the coffee. The film that depicts the process of tapping maple trees and collecting the sap in buckets or in a series of connected tubes that empty into a large vat, followed by a description of the tedious boiling and bottling process, takes under five minutes.

"Forty gallons of sap for only one gallon of syrup. That's amazing," Ryan says.

"Yeah," the woman lacking enthusiasm, confirms. Hopefully it's only a weekend job and she hasn't quit high school, Ryan thinks. "Ever been to a sugarhouse?" the woman asks.

Ryan shakes her head.

"Nothing like the sweet smell of sap when they're boiling. Come back when the sap's running."

Ryan fears it's a full time job, and the line—void of any punch in its pitch—been uttered thousands of times before.

"When's that?"

"Depends. Warm days, freezing nights. Maybe late February, if we're lucky. Maybe March." She picks up a brochure from the counter. "List of sugarhouses. You'll know they're boiling when you see the steam coming out of the roofs."

"My parents used to have that kind." Ryan points to a bottle of Log Cabin, one of many in a collection of syrup bottles that line the wall behind the cashier's counter.

"We have the vintage tin." She points to a pint-sized can in the shape of a log cabin, complete with red curtains on the paned window and a potbellied stove visible through a partially open door. "The red cap on the tin is supposed to be the chimney. That's where it poured out. Cute, eh?"

"Mine used *her*." Tiffany, who has just arrived with Ryan's coffee, points to a brown bottle in the shape of a well-endowed buttoned-up lady.

"Neither brand has any maple syrup in it," the shopkeeper says. "The rest have a very small percentage."

"Then why do you have them here?" Tiffany asks.

"It's an educational display."

"We"—she motions to herself and Ryan—"only use real maple syrup. And we pay extra for it in restaurants in Boston where we live. We're roommates."

Why did Tiffany have to profile her life for everyone she met? Ryan preferred to be discreet, blend in with the surrounding culture or at least be mysterious, not an open book inviting prejudgment.

Always leave something to be found out—desired. "Never go to bed naked with a man; at least keep your hat on," Faye once told her. It was a joke, but it wasn't, really.

"We only serve the real thing in these parts. No extra charge."

"How lucky," Ryan says, paying for a tall slim bottle of syrup infused with habanero peppers.

"You know, my uncle has a two-hundred-acre maple sugar farm in Pennsylvania," Tiffany informs the woman, who is unimpressed.

"I didn't know you had an uncle with a farm in Pennsylvania," Ryan tells Tiffany as they walk back to the parking lot of Ernie's Eatery.

"I don't. I just wanted her to know that Vermont isn't the only state that produces maple syrup."

"Why do you care about these things?"

"What things?"

"What people know you know and what they don't know."

"I hate smug."

"You could have fooled me. Now *I* need to pee. I'll meet you in the car."

After using the toilet in the café, Ryan goes to wash her hands but the automatic faucet doesn't stay on long enough for her to get the soap off. She's surprised this hole in the wall even has an automatic faucet—talk about smug. She removes her hands from under the spout then returns them. Three seconds later the water shuts off again. Three seconds: This is how long she has to wash her hands. Four more pain-free days left in this month's menstrual cycle. Eight years to safely conceive a child. Five months to get a husband. Everything in her life is timed.

* * *

Eric sits at the counter at the Tandem Café in Peterbury where he likes to go some mornings. It's almost like getting away: only eight miles outside of town on the road to Middlebury, yet far enough away not to draw a Brackton clientele—no big-city transplants here either.

Unlike the well-kept Brackton establishments that beckon to tourists, no one stops in Peterbury, where town planning seems to be a dirty phrase. Six one-story buildings with run-down wooden porches missing spindles in the railings and loose shingles constitute the single commercial block on either side of the Peterbury Common. A Chinese restaurant, a gas station, a Rite Aid pharmacy, a barbershop. The sad-looking lace curtains in the window of Lil's Salon frame a bald mannequin head, and its red-satin-papered interior makes the beauty shop look more like a saloon with a sign made by someone who couldn't spell.

There's a For Sale sign in the window of the Tandem Café. It's been there for at least fifteen years. The proprietors are a father-daughter team. It used to be the father and his wife, but she died. Before them it was the wife's parents, and before that Eric has no idea, except that there have always been two—thus tandem. He doesn't know much about the daughter, who is older than Eric, except that she was married to some guy named Curtis who seems to have gone dark and who gets talked about some by customers in the café.

It's quiet this morning as Eric dips his last piece of biscuit into the brown sausage gravy and wipes his plate. In fact, it's so quiet, every time he takes a sip of coffee and sets the thick white ceramic cup ever so gently on the saucer, the clang echoes through the eatery. Why does he care if he makes a noise? Because he's not from Peterbury and has been away from the county for a while, which has made him a minor source of suspicion. Not until a lumberjack the owners call Teddy comes blowing through the bell-jingling door—his face so raw from the cold you can hardly tell orange beard stubble from skin, his eyes tearing and nose running, his long honey-colored hair glistening like a surfer's—calling out for his eggs, steak, and biscuits with sausage gravy as though it were a mantra, and accosting father and daughter, who are behind the counter, with lively banter, does Eric relax some.

Or maybe it's the fact that the Boston couple who won the contest is coming today that's made him uncomfortable. He's reserved a room for them at the Daffodil. Not the deluxe suite where they'll stay during the wedding weekend, but one of the standard rooms. Should he have reserved two? Do any couples sleep in separate rooms in this day and age? Certainly not gay guys. Still, he doesn't want to appear presumptuous, yet not an ignorant country bumpkin. Maybe he should have asked. No, he shouldn't have asked.

"I haven't been here, Jesus, for ten, twelve years," the lumberjack says, sitting two stools away from Eric. "I had a lot of breakfasts here when I was a boy."

"Darlin', you remember Teddy," the father calls to his daughter who's already begun frying Teddy's steak and eggs.

"Sure do," she yells, as though competing with the sizzling sound of the grill.

"Where you been, Teddy?" the father asks."

"Workin' up north mostly. Holy smoke! That's a lotta sausage gravy!" he tells the daughter when she puts his order in front of him. "Where's the cot?"

She points to the clock on the wall.

"No! Cot! Where am I gonna sleep after I eat all that?"

"We got a booth for you." She laughs.

"Where are the pillows?"

"How is it?" she asks when he takes a bite.

"I'm impressed."

"Good."

"I hate it when people cook better'n I do."

She laughs again and refills his cup.

"I ain't holding nothin' against you, but can you order half a serving of sausage gravy? This is way bigger 'n my belly."

"That's 'cause you ordered a *full* egg breakfast with it." She draws out her statements that are equally laden with some sort of anticipation.

"I don't really like sausage gravy. I make it, but I don't like it," the father says, amused with the flirtatious dialogue between his daughter and the returned native, maybe even hopeful.

"I gotta give you our phone number so you can call us to let us know if you make it home," the daughter tells Teddy.

Eric smiles at the way the conversation is going. Time to leave. Just as well, since he doesn't want to be late meeting the couple. He slaps a five-dollar bill on the counter and tries to get the attention of either proprietor (he likes to say goodbye to servers and show his appreciation) but they're wrapped up with the lumberjack, listening to his tale about a big fir that nearly fell on him earlier that morning. When Eric stands up and puts his parka on, the father nods in acknowledgment, then he goes right back to Teddy.

He told Danni he'd pick her up and they'd go together to the Daffodil, which he knew pleased her. He could have booked the couple at the Brackton Inn, on the Common, but he really wants them to stay at the Daffodil, even though it's on the outskirts of town, because he believes the Goldmans, burned-out stockbrokers from Greenwich, Connecticut, know what city folk expect. That's why he couldn't be happier that the Chamber board of directors agreed with Danni's suggestion to hold the reception at the Daffodil, which is set on several acres, with winding garden paths and waterfalls.

He's heard that the Goldmans even iron the sheets at the restored mansion, built in the style of a Newport "cottage" (though much more modest in size), with creamy yellow clapboards and dark green shutters and a circular driveway that leads to a massive front door with leaded-glass sidelights. Its interior has been updated with pastel painted walls, unlike the dark floral wallpaper of the Brackton Inn. The Daffodil boasts white marble fireplaces, soaking tubs, and a glass-enclosed conservatory with French country and India-print cushions, fashionable touches that are mixed with the latest conveniences. (Eric knows all this because it says so in the brochure.) Eric would have described it a bit more succinctly, like: *Here at the Daffodil, WiFi meets wicker*. And their catering service is top-notch, second only to the cuisine at the new French restaurant in town, but nobody expects authentic French food at a wedding with 125 guests.

Eric pulls in front of Licks and Relics. In the summer, there's an antique ice cream maker on the porch and a wire rack filled with copies of the local weekly newspaper and the Vermont Country Store catalogue, but during the winter they're tucked away inside, along with the Depression glass, butter churners, crescent-shaped porcelain chicken bone dishes, funky salt and pepper shakers shaped like cars and animals and things unrelated to condiments, and whatever else Danni acquires from estate sales. Danni's been watching for Eric behind the wavy-glass-paned door. When she sees him, she runs out, pulls her white fur-trimmed hood over her head, and jumps into his pickup.

"This is so exciting! Our first winners! I couldn't sleep last night thinking about it. You know, *Brokeback Mountain*. That was so sad."

"Focus, Danni. This is Brackton. It's a happy day."

"You're right. You're always right. I thought you might stop here for breakfast but I saw you drive straight through town."

That she monitors his behavior is beyond annoying and not the least bit flattering.

"I ate at the Tandem. A late breakfast."

"Yes, you like sausage gravy."

She has a habit of rationalizing everyone's actions, especially Eric's, and offering explanations and extraneous information she's unable to keep to herself. If someone says they forgot the almonds for the green beans they brought to a potluck, Danni will nod and say, "Oh, yes, *amandine*," demonstrating that she knows the proper name for the dish. If they have traded heavy drapes for sheers, she will say, "Yes, nice and light for summer," when the person has no intention of limiting the curtains to one season. If she brings flowers to a gathering, she never fails to tell the host where she got them. "Grand Union," she'll confess for no good reason, even though she's betrayed the more expensive local merchant. Now she's making Eric aware that *she* knows why he frequents the Tandem Café.

"Maybe I should add sausage gravy to my menu," she says.

"You shouldn't, Danni. It's a Tandem specialty. Nobody makes it the way they do."

"I could learn to make it," she insists.

"No, Danni."

"Do you think it's okay that I'm wearing jeans? I thought about a skirt, but it's so cold today. That's why I wore my long coat."

"Unlike the heat wave we had yesterday?"

She giggles.

Eric shakes his head. Danni's whiny voice drives him crazy. *She* drives him crazy. It's so easy not to be nice to her, especially when he can feel her trying to get close to him, which is just about all the time. Occasionally he's downright mean to her, at least from *his* perspective. She rarely gets offended, except when her mouth takes a downward turn and follows the droopy outer edges of her eyes, like an apologetic dog with its tail between its legs. Then he feels bad about the way he's behaved, but at the same time satisfied. It's as though Danni is his ingrown toenail and bottle of Outgro all in one. Just when he's feeling insecure, along comes Danni—a shitload of insecurity—and he settles back into taking the upper hand. You're despicable, Eric Boulanger, he tells himself.

* * *

"They're upstairs settling in. My wife took them some tea." Mark Goldman is soft-spoken and of slight stature, with thinning hair and horn-rimmed glasses. In a collared shirt and vest he looks more like a stodgy academic than a successful Wall Street dropout. "Can I get you anything? Coffee? Shot of Jack Daniel's?" The wry smile on Goldman's face makes Eric suspect he should take him up on the whiskey even though it isn't even noon yet.

"I wouldn't mind a glass of white wine, Mark," Danni says.

"And you, Eric?"

"I'm good, Mark. Thank you. Was I right about the room—you know, the number?"

"Oh yes, they're fine. We gave them the Lady Wentwerth. They loved it."

"I bet they did," Eric says as Mark hands Danni her chardonnay. "You and your wife have transformed this place."

"Ah, here they come now." All three turn their heads toward the curved rosewood staircase. Right train, wrong track, Eric thinks as he takes in the lesbian couple—very attractive ones, he can't help but notice. He feels Danni's tension ease at the sight of the women in jeans.

"This is Danni Pritchard," Mark tells them, "owner of the ice cream shop and café. She's got the scoop on everyone, so to speak. And the handsome guy is Eric Boulanger."

"It's nice to finally meet you." Ryan extends her hand to Danni, then Eric, where it lingers a moment.

"And you must be Jason," Danni says, turning to Tiff, and for once Eric is grateful for the way Danni jumps mouth first into everything, saving him from taking the first stab at figuring this out.

"Oh, no," Ryan corrects her, laughing. "This is my roommate, Tiffany. Jason—couldn't make it."

Tiffany's eyes open wide with surprise at the ease with which Ryan perpetuates the lie, and so early into the meeting.

"Well, I guess we've got it straight now," Danni says, elbowing Eric, who feels like a damned fool that Danni had it right from the get-go.

"Yeah, straight," he says. "How was your trip?"

"Piece of cake, except for the forty miles behind the Ford Focus," Tiffany answers, although Eric had addressed Ryan.

"With Vermont plates?"

"Uh-huh. Wasn't the only time we were behind one."

"May have kept you from getting a ticket. The speed limit is strictly enforced here, and the cops love to nab out-of-staters." Eric, spokesperson for the Chamber of Commerce, cannot believe he just said that.

"You know the new pope uses a Ford Focus," Danni says.

"I thought he rode in a Popemobile," Ryan says.

"In the crowds, but in Rome he has an old blue Ford Focus. He's very humble and energy conscious."

"How do you know this, Danni?" Eric is astonished.

"I read about it. Didn't you? I think he's adorable and refreshing. And I'm not even Catholic."

"Have you had lunch yet?" Eric asks. "I thought we'd grab a bite before we meet with the vendors." He prefers sticking to the old rule of avoiding discussions about politics and religion when swimming in uncharted territory.

"Sure," the women agree.

There's a cleanliness about Ryan—not painted up like Danni, yet she glows like a match in the dark. He can see her in black-and-white, maybe even sepia. Her face is full, like one on an ancient Greek or Roman sculpture. His eyes frame her and impose her in the memory stick of his brain.

Ryan and Tiffany go for their shiny down-filled jackets—one red the other lime green. With their skinny jeans, they look like psychedelic lollipops.

"I know it's hard to imagine an outdoor wedding in the dead of winter," Eric says, helping Ryan into the sleeve of her jacket.

"Do we need a key to the front door?" Tiffany asks Mark.

"Not unless you plan to be back after midnight."

After a few smiles and Danni giggles, they're out the door. Only then do Eric and Danni realize they can't all fit into the pickup.

"I thought we'd walk into town," he says.

"Nice save," Danni whispers. "What were we thinking?"

"I like to walk." Ryan takes a crumpled tissue from her pocket and gives her nose a good blow.

"How long have you lived here?" Ryan asks Eric as they stroll; the narrow shoveled path has funneled them into double file, with Eric and Ryan leading and Danni and Tiffany falling far enough behind to engage in their own conversation.

"I was born here—but I left for college. Then I moved to Providence for grad school. I came back to take care of my mother. She's been sick."

"I'm sorry."

"Oh, she's better now. In remission."

"Tough stuff. And Danni?"

"We've known each other since kindergarten," he tells the white ground. He's afraid if he stares into those iridescent green eyes, he'll get lost like Alice down the rabbit hole. "Look, I know it's hard to imagine, but it's really beautiful here in summer and fall. It's a perfect place to have a wedding."

"It's pretty beautiful *now*."

"Yeah." Eric nods. Who's convincing whom?

"I always like the quiet during a snowfall," Ryan says. "It's like a big blanket that muffles the whole city, slows everything down. Of course, once the storm stops, it's all over. The city comes back to life and so does the traffic and noise and exhausts. Soon it's gray and black slush. But you've lived in a city, so you know."

"Well this is pretty much how it is here all winter. But in summer there's the farmers' market on the Common, and of course the leaf-peepers in the fall." He's pushing too hard. The couple has already entered the contest and won; let the place speak for itself.

"We initially thought we'd let you choose the vendors," he says, "but then we didn't want to create hard feelings in town or make you feel awkward. After all, this is supposed to make life easy for you and Jason. So the vendors are already designated, but you'll have the final say on what they present to you. There'll still be decisions to make."

"Do I hear a beggars-can't-be-choosers theme here?"

"Not at all. But I have to admit that the parents of the bride must be pretty happy about your winning."

"Actually, I haven't told them yet."

"You haven't?"

"It's a little complicated. One reason I came up here was to tell you in person that Jason and I—Jason and I are of different religions."

"No problem here. The Unitarian church is nondenominational. Or you can get a JP or have a friend get a license online. That's what some of my friends have done. Do you have someone in mind?"

"Yeah, the groom." She is, like Faye, almost cracking herself up.

He looks at her.

"I mean the groom will decide. I really don't care." She attempts to be serious.

"But your parents are not thrilled with the idea?"

"They'll need a little getting used to it."

"Inside or out?" He has to move her along. He doesn't understand how she and Jason could have come this far, concealing their wedding from their parents.

"Out of what?"

71

"Of a church. Or a gathering place. The ceremony. Indoors or outdoors?"

"Oh, maybe outside, weather permitting."

"You got it. Maybe on the Daffodil's grounds? Make it easy on the guests."

"Maybe."

All this vagueness is unsettling to him.

"Guess you really aren't bothered by snow," Ryan says, as a young girl appears from out of nowhere on a rusty old bike. Head to one side, plaid scarf flapping around her brown leather bomber's jacket, she stares straight through them, performing figure eights in the middle of the road and ruining Eric's picture-perfect landscape.

"It's Bicycle Girl," Eric tells Ryan. He can hear the wheels of her brain turning along with those of the bike, wheels he guesses are accustomed to working overtime, along with a tongue that's probably used to straining hard to hold back. At least she isn't transparent like Danni.

"Bicycle Girl?"

"Another time."

Ryan shrugs her puffy-down-shoulders.

"So what do you do, Ryan?"

"I'm a paralegal for a nonprofit environmental organization. I started out there to test the legal waters, but here I am five years later, still contemplating law school."

"What's the drawback?"

"Not really sure I'll like it for the long haul. Lame, I know."

"Not at all. My father was a lawyer. Can get pretty ugly."

"And boring a good deal of the time. I'd really like to write, but haven't had much success there. The arts are tough. What about you? Are you the mayor?"

He laughs. "Hell, no! We don't have a mayor, just selectmen, and I'm not one of them either."

"Seems like you'd be good at it."

"I'm not big on politics. The Chamber of Commerce is about as entrenched as I care to get."

"Why are you in it at all?"

He can't believe she's asked that question. He hasn't even asked himself that. He puts his hand over his mouth to hide a smile.

"Another time?"

"Yeah. Another time. I'm a photographer, so I understand about making it in the art world."

"Will you be doing the wedding?"

"No. First of all, it would be a conflict of interest, since Brackton Is for Brides was my idea. Also, I don't do many weddings anymore—too competitive. The portrait scene pretty much dried up with digital, but it opened the way for events."

"I don't follow."

Was she really interested in all this?

"If you take a hundred photos with a digital camera, you're going to get at least one good one, so anyone can do it. But for events, you need someone outside of the family, because guests just want to have a good time. Fewer portraits. More events. That's why it's become more competitive for us again."

"So if you're not shooting portraits or events, what do you shoot?"

"You mean how do I make a living?"

"Well—"

"I studied at RISD."

"I *love* their museum. I love museums."

"I had a show there this fall—not just me, with a few other alums from the grad program. I only had three pieces. I also do theater work—you know, the shots you see of live drama for brochures and newspapers and playbills. I do a lot of the live theater around New England. Sometimes I travel farther, but not much lately because of my commitments here."

"What kind of camera do you have? I'm thinking of taking up photography—just for fun."

"I'm a dinosaur, love my 35-millimeter for black-and-white. And I've begun working with a Hasselblad XPan—a panoramic. That's what I used for my show. But in the theater I usually use a traditional digital. I'm using a Nikon D810 now." He's getting impassioned explaining his work. No one outside his field talks about it with him. "It lets me capture high-resolution images in the really low-light situations you can come up against when you shoot actors onstage. But in a lot of situations, I most likely will use my iPhone."

"No way!" She looks up at him in wonder.

"Less conspicuous. You can produce images that are more contemporary in feeling. There's a kind of immediacy to taking and processing a photo on a phone. But with limitations, of course."

"So I'm already ahead of the game."

"I guess so." He feels his cold skin ache as it stretches into a broad grin.

"Wish I'd known about your exhibit."

"I can show you some of it while you're here, if you'd like."

"Absolutely."

By the time they reach town, it's snowing heavily, the air opaque, the gazebo in the center of the Common whitewashed like a familiar piece of old furniture, everything and everyone losing definition. He knows Ryan's hands are as numb as his, even in the thick snow-caked woolen mittens she's been trying to wipe her nose with. Hair like strawberry swirl soft-serve topped with whipped cream cascades out of her cap. God, he'd love to take a photo.

"Is it a holiday?" Ryan asks.

"Not that I know of."

"Why the flags?" She refers to light blue ones bearing the town's name and "1765" on every telephone pole.

"Oh, those. I don't even see them. They're always there. Guess Brackton is proud of its founding date."

"Where do the wreaths go in holiday season?"

"Lampposts."

She nods.

He likes her attention to detail.

"I know it must all look stark to you right now, but you really have to imagine it in summer: sunny, everything in bloom, window boxes and urns overflowing with petunias and geraniums. Blue hydrangea bushes everywhere. Summer roses."

"You know your flowers."

"I'm a photographer, remember. Geez, I forgot how far the Daffodil is from town. I think we've lost the others. I hope Tiffany's okay." He's worried about having left her to fend for herself with Danni.

"It's all good. Trust me, Tiff can take care of herself. Here they come."

They appear at the bend on the edge of town, laughing, arms interlocked like two old women who have been friends for ages, trying to keep each other from slipping.

* * *

"So, Ryan, what does Jason do?" Eric swallows a large bite of Baby's Supreme: a burger smothered in cooked onions beneath a layer of melted Roquefort and topped with a sliced tomato and pickles. He washes this down with pale ale: He wants to relax some but keep his wits about him. He would have liked to take them to Chez Alexandre, but it isn't open for lunch, so Baby's Bar & Grill had to do.

Ryan, sitting opposite him and Tiffany, and next to Danni, is crunching her way through a Cobb salad when Eric's question shifts her into low gear. She runs her tongue over her teeth to sweep up any stray greens, takes a sip of hot cider, and plucks a few napkins from the dispenser. She speaks slowly, more carefully and more quietly than the bubbling conversationalist she'd been on her way into town. She's either OCD about her hygiene, suffering memory loss, or stalling, Eric concludes.

"He's an investment banker," she announces, which nearly causes Tiffany to choke on her Vermont Reuben oozing local cheddar instead of Swiss. "He was in law school but changed his mind."

Eric thinks it odd she didn't mention him when they talked about law before.

"What house?"

"A small one. He works for a private firm."

"More of a broker?"

"Yes."

"A hedge fund?"

She nods, but the way she casts her eyes downward when she

answers makes him think she isn't even sure what a hedge fund is, or maybe she disapproves of his occupation. He's not sure, but something is off.

"Actually, he's in between jobs right now. Interviewing out of town. That's why he couldn't come."

"So you might be leaving the Boston area?"

"Yes."

The prospect of his finding a job out of the area is probably a source of tension between the couple—clearly makes her uncomfortable, Eric thinks. Better move on to another topic. Why did he do what everyone else does and ask what Jason did? What did it matter? So many of his friends struggled—were still struggling—to find a way to support their art. He himself doesn't like to respond to the question because it makes him feel inadequate, as though he were way behind in the achievement time line for his age. Yet their careers had been the first topics they broached after they met.

A friend of his mother's once told him that this was an East Coast thing, and that on the West Coast you could converse for hours on meeting a person before the subject of how they earned a living came up—if it ever came up. It was the person they were interested in, not how much money their career might bring them. He's never gotten the opportunity to check that out, never been to California or Oregon or Washington. Maybe that concept was all pre–Silicon Valley and Microsoft. Maybe nowadays they ask what you do out west too. Given the tight job market, Ryan and Jason are probably more thrilled than he'd imagined to have won the wedding. He feels redeemed, good about being able to provide something worthwhile.

"Can we see your artwork?" Ryan asks, changing the subject.

"Well—if you'd like. After we meet with the vendors."

"What artwork?" Tiffany looks over her corned beef.

"Oh, Eric's the best! He's so talented. He's a photographer," Danni says. She leans toward Ryan and whispers, "Do you have a tissue?"

"Yes," Ryan answers as she reaches for her bag. "You need one?"

"No. You do."

* * *

In the same plain room where they hold Chamber meetings, the vendors have already set out on red-cloth-covered tables the brochures, photo albums, and whatever else they've brought to promote their businesses. A few have lined the walls with easels that hold large photographs of brides and grooms wearing the proprietors' wedding rings or hairdos, gowns or tuxedos. Eric is pleased with their displays. They make the drab headquarters come alive.

"I wanted pink or mint-green tablecloths, but Alex loaned them to us and the restaurant only has red," hairdresser Maisie Billings tells Eric.

"It's fine, Maisie. Really."

"Looks like a high school football banquet or a steak house."

"Maybe that's why I like it." He smiles. "A guy thing."

"And maybe that's why I don't."

He likes Maisie. She's pretty, dependable, no nonsense yet considerate. Pity she's too old for him. Her son played football with Eric, and to the team she was the MILF: mother I'd like to fuck. Not only was she cool and attractive, but she was younger than all the other mothers, having given birth to her son in the spring of her senior year of high school and having had to marry her now ex, the captain of the 1985 football team.

Yes, there was often a population increase after those postseason revelries, and he was lucky to have avoided one with Danni. He used drop in at Maisie's shop with the excuse of having to see his mother about something while she was having her hair done. And petite blond Maisie would smile at him with those blue eyes—he was a sucker for eyes—and he'd swear she was in love with him. He'd still like to hook up with her—just one time. And he's pretty sure she'd go for it. He refrains because he's adult enough to know he might not satisfy her. Better to keep it a fantasy.

Ryan is polite to the vendors, with a certain restraint to her cordiality. She tentatively leafs through photo albums and collects pamphlets as though the images on paper might jump up and eat her if she were too aggressive. Tiffany, on the other hand, is all enthusiasm as she oohs and aahs over wedding gowns, tiered cakes, bouquets and centerpieces and white-lily-and-voile-draped arbors, lists of favors, and massive scrapbooks of invitations, bringing everything that grabs her to Ryan's attention, including whispering (with a hand-shielded mouth) that the fabric on the arbors is tacky. She pulls her over to the easels and points out bridesmaids' dress colors and hairstyles, and even notes how the women in the photographs have their nails done: "You see, not everyone has white polish or a French manicure. Look how iridescent green brings out the leaves on her bouquet."

"Yes. Okay. Not bad. Uh huh. I don't think so," can be heard in response from the not quite blushing bride to be.

"Everything is lovely, really. But I'm a bit overwhelmed. Do I need to decide today?" Ryan asks Eric.

"Not at all," he says, though he's eager to have everything nailed down as soon as possible. "We just wanted to give you a taste of what we offer. Why don't you take info on what appeals to you and share it with Jason?"

"Of course, I have to talk it over with Jason," she says, as though he's not only brought the notion to her attention but given her an out as well.

"Too bad he couldn't be here, but you can get in touch with the vendors anytime with questions or requests for more options. I know Danni sent you their contact info. Some of them have websites, but not all, obviously." He's embarrassed about that. "And you've got some calling cards, I see."

"Do you do upsweeps?" Tiff asks Maisie the hairdresser. "*Good* upsweeps?"

"Actually I do." Maisie smiles. "Just bring photos of what you'd like if you don't see anything in our stylists' magazines."

"And of course you'll have to come back to try on wedding gowns," Danni says. "Probably a few times. Are you thinking white or ivory, strapless or halter, mermaid look? And you'll need to discuss the music with the DJ. He couldn't be here today; he has a radio show at this time."

Ryan holds up his card.

"He *does* have a website," Eric is happy to tell her.

"I will. *We* will."

"I love weddings! Don't you?" Danni turns to Tiffany, who smiles, as do the vendors. Ryan appears to have a case of premarital jitters.

"By the way, Ryan. We were really touched by your essay," Lisa Anderson, the baker, says.

"Straight from the heart." Florist Annie Chalis has to one-up her.

"And it's so cool that you do invitations *and* you're a florist," Tiffany tells Annie. "Makes it easy to coordinate the theme. Something botanical on the invites would be perfect."

"If you don't see anything you'd like in the books, I can have one of our local artists design something special."

Eric shoots her a look that reminds her they have a budget.

"But I'm sure you'll find something from these selections."

"I'm sure she will," Tiffany says. "We'll be in touch."

Eric senses that Ryan wants out and is surprised when she reminds him about seeing his work. Danni suggests they walk over to Licks and Relics and offers to drive them all over to Eric's house, but Eric tells her it's not a good idea for a crowd—even a small crowd—to show up unannounced because his mother might be napping or want to fix them coffee and cake and get all stressed out.

"I understand. Maybe next time," Ryan says.

"I could take *you*, Ryan, just not a crowd."

"If you think it's okay."

"Danni can drop us all off at the Daffodil House, and if Tiffany doesn't mind being alone for a little while, we can go on in my truck. It won't take long, really. There's not that much to see. A lot's in storage."

"Would that be okay, Tiff?" Ryan asks.

"All good with me. I've got some emails to catch up with."

"And I need to prepare for the Chamber meeting tonight," Danni says, and for once Eric can't believe how easily he's gotten rid of her.

* * *

Eric's mother isn't home; he knew that. She's gone to a mindfulness session at the Cancer Patient Support Foundation in Williston and won't be back for another two hours. He worries that the house smells like a sickroom even though she's in remission. It doesn't. There's nothing in there that ever made it smell like that, even when she was undergoing treatment. Yet he recalls the ointments his father needed to apply every morning and night to ease the stiffness and pain that plagued him in the years before his death, smells that the air and upholstery and wallpaper absorbed and, in his mind, never exhaled. "What's that smell?" his grade school friends asked. "What smell?" he would answer in his father's defense and his own discomfort.

Ryan follows him down basement steps covered with worn olive-green carpet pads they should have removed years ago and that never bothered him until now. When he turns on the light, it's like being in a gallery in the midst of an exhibit turnover.

"Wow! I don't know where to begin." Her eyes scan the walls where photos are hung in tiers that reach the low ceiling, then down to the floor, where others—some framed, some just matted—are stacked against the wall.

"I thought you said there wasn't much."

"I've been at this for some time."

"How long?"

He has to think. Photography is such a part of him that he can't really remember when he first took it up.

"I mean there must have been a beginning ..."

"My parents gave me their old 35-millimeter camera when they got their first digital. Is that good enough for a beginning?"

"How old were you?"

"About ten. My dad liked to shoot and develop—just a hobby—but he had disabilities, and it became too hard for him to work his camera, even to change film on an automatic. Digital saved him."

"He's gone?"

"Going on twenty years."

"I'm sorry. And it was love at first touch? With the camera?"

"No. I was more interested in sports, doing something with all that energy boys seem to be overloaded with at that age. But that's not entirely fair. I really did like looking at the world through that lens: adjusting what I saw, bringing what I wanted into focus, fading out what I didn't, making what was important to me prominent. The camera's a powerful little tool. Lets perverts like me do their thing. It covers your face; you can hide behind it."

Oh boy, that was a really smart thing to say, because now she's looking at him with apparent misgivings in the cellar of an empty house. Where are the bodies? Where's the bulkhead door she can run to?

"I didn't mean it that way. I just mean, I've always liked to observe people, especially through windows. Not lewd scenes. Just everyday scenes." He was strangling himself with explanations. "Imagine what their lives are like within those frames, how they're different from my own. So the camera is my window. You just reproduce what you've seen, or imagined you've seen, because you're trying to capture a story, an emotion, a life, but you also have that power to tell it raw or give it a slant just by using a device, lighting, angle, et cetera. Give it that special emphasis. I don't know if you know what I'm talking about. Maybe *I* don't even know what I'm talking about. It's not the same with every photographer. That's what separates the good from the great, I suppose."

"No. I do. I really do. I like looking into windows, especially at night. Any apartment or room in a house looks better then—warm, interesting, no matter what the décor, or lack of."

"Now you know the secret of shelter mags."

"What?"

"Home decorating magazines. They don't look good only because everything's in place and new. To me, from the outside any house—or shack—looks good, and even better in lamplight. Light is so important. I like shooting in fog or with other techniques that can give you a feeling hope will arrive soon and something new will come from it."

He can tell by the way she's looking at him that he's impressed her. It's so easy. People are always fascinated by the arts, as though the artist were a sorcerer whose talent streams unbidden into his subconscious;

they never see him as the laborer who constantly searches for and never waits for his muse, who through trial and error, day after day, strives to perfect his skill.

"Which is real and which is the reality show?"

He cocks his head to one side and smiles. "That's up to the beholder."

But then she surprises him. "My mom's a painter. She's always struggling with light in her oils. So happy when she gets it right—at least in *her* reality."

"What does she do?"

"Landscapes and still lifes. Kind of somewhere between Chagall and Van Gogh. She teaches too. One course a semester at a community college. She's really good. Is that you?"

She points down at a photo hanging in the corner just above the floor molding where his grandfather had laid gray marbled Kentile flooring so long ago. It's a color picture of Eric with curly sandy hair that, unlike his present haircut—nearly buzzed at the sides and tapering to a longer straight-up scissor-cut on top—is parted on one side, with curls dipping over his forehead and down his neck, complementing a three-day beard. His skin is tanned and glistening—triceps, thick neck bursting out of a tight black tank top that defines his pecs and abs—against a bright blue sky. Head tilted, he smiles wryly, daring the person behind the camera to shoot. Sunglasses hide his dark brown eyes, eyes his grandmother used to call *the Gene Kelly smiling eyes*. When he first Googled the name, Eric saw no resemblance to the deceased actor whose eyes squinted, turning upwards at the outer edges, when he flashed a wry smile. Eric did see similarities in their builds. He read his bio on Wikipedia. Kelly had been intelligent, a hot educated jock turned dancer-actor, an athlete who, according to all his admiring costars, had loved his art and been secure enough to combine gymnastics with ballet and other dance forms and come out sexy. Such a nice guy he spent his last acting days playing a priest on TV. Yes, he liked it that he bore a resemblance to Gene Kelly. Too bad no other millennials knew the actor and could make the comparison.

In the photo, Eric's eyes sit above what Eric considers a crooked nose. His mother has told him it's not crooked, that it just takes a slight deviation in one spot where he had been hit with a chunk of ice during a snowball fight when he was five. His mother wanted to take him to the doctor, but his father insisted there was nothing they could do with a broken nose. It gives you character, he'd said. His parents viewed every hardship that came their way as character building. By the time his mother got cancer, Eric decided that both she and he had developed more than enough character.

"When was this?" Ryan has again become the enthusiastic woman on her walk into town earlier that day. Eric knows the photo flatters him.

"About eight years ago."

"Where?'

"The Whites."

"Who took it?"

"An old friend."

"A girlfriend?" She continues to study the picture.

"Yeah."

"A photographer?"

"That's correct. She was."

"And the photo was a gift." She finally looks up at him.

"Very good, Sherlock."

"I can tell by the frame. It's different from all the others. I'm glad I saw it."

"Why's that?"

"You're playful and open. Relaxed. Content." She turns her attention back to the photograph.

"And now?"

"Like the rest of us," says the girl who is about to be married, and Eric can't help concluding that talk of the impending wedding does not reveal a happy heart. "You do that a lot, don't you?"

"Do what?"

"Cock your head to the side like this." She mimics the photograph. "You just did it a few minutes ago."

"Guess I do. Is that bad?"

"Not at all," she tells him, and he swears she's coming on to him. "For what it's worth, I like your hair better the way you used to wear it."

I don't remember asking your opinion, he wants to tell her.

"What's behind that curtain?" She points to a ratty black velvet cloth hanging on a curtain rod.

"*That* is my darkroom—when I use one."

"Can I see it?"

* * *

She is not horrified by the condition of the darkroom hidden behind the curtain Eric's mother had sewn when his father first enclosed the five-by-seven-foot area for his own hobby so many years ago—the hideaway with its raw plywood floor installed to better maintain the warmth given off by the small space heater in the corner, the stained sink, plastic gallon jugs of chemicals, crude shelving that holds boxes of fiber paper, clothespins clipped to the clothesline that await photos after they are developed, the safe lights whose wildly strung wires look anything but safe, exposed copper water pipes running along the ceiling, the second-hand enlarger, an old beige wall phone, the timer, the grain enlarger, the pegboard filled with small odd tools, the collage of photos tacked up on the walls, giving the room the appearance of a crime lab. It is unattractive chaos to a neatness fanatic, antiquated to those who crave state-of-the-art, incomprehensible to the laity.

"I dry the negatives and film here. The fiber photos get pressed in this press. I like analog."

"What's that?"

"Film. I still like to use black-and-white-film on occasion. Don't get me wrong, there's great advantages to digital: You're never aware of film problems, like having to change it; you just shoot away and then edit and get rid of the crap."

"I thought you used a phone sometimes."

He laughed. "There's that too."

He goes around the room from the wet area to the dry, explaining the developing process, the machines he rarely touches anymore, the ones he still does, trying to make the sequence understood.

She steps closer to a black-and-white 8 x 10 matte photo of a couple, though the position of the subjects does not make their human qualities apparent at first glance. She studies it. The man and woman are naked and sitting on the floor, but the way their legs and arms are entwined hides any private parts. The sleek blond head of the woman rests on the smooth black shoulder of the man, whose face can be seen only in profile. But that's not all. There's another arm, another leg, another head, another body there—darker than the woman's, lighter than the man's. He's between them, his head arching around the woman, his torso around the man. It's as though they're melting into one another and can't be separated. A sculpture of unity. A lyrical, never-ending story.

"You can almost see them breathing," Ryan says. "I want to touch their skin, there's such a soft quality to the photo. How did you do this, and what's it doing on this wall with a pushpin in it?"

"How?" He's pleased with her reaction.

"How did you pose them like this? Who are they?"

"Friends. Honestly, it was easy. It's who they are. They kind of posed themselves."

"They must be pretty close friends to let you do that. It's as though the photographer is part of the picture. It's so intimate."

"He is."

"Oh my God! That's you!"

"I was taking a portrait class when I foolishly thought I could sustain my bread and butter with them while I worked on more creative stuff. One day the professor asked to see my self-portraits, and I told her I didn't have any. 'You're a fucking portrait photographer and you don't have any self-portraits?' she said. 'Get naked and take some.' I was used to a controlled photo session, where I set up every aspect. Self-portraits loosened me up and opened my eyes to getting something I didn't know I was going to get. It's been a great help in my new project—and in photographing actors."

"I should feel like I'm intruding on them but I don't. It's like they're drawing me into their private world. Is that a contradiction?"

She's moved closer to him, their bodies purposely touching as they examine the portrait, and again he can swear she's coming on to him. Or is he coming on to her?

"I suppose. But that's the beauty of art, isn't it? I wish everyone saw into images that way."

"Were you happy with it? I mean, is that what you set out to do?"

"Sort of. When the end result surprises you some—surprises your audience—I guess that's what you were striving for."

"Well you killed it. This is amazing."

"Thanks, but you're way too complimentary."

"No I'm not. I can see why you want it here. To remind you of what you're capable of."

"And who and what you love."

"It makes me want to take up photography even more," Ryan says. "It also discourages me. I could never do this."

He shakes his head. "Do it because you love it—or at least like it. Because it brings you pleasure. See what happens."

"Maybe."

"Put it on your gift registry—a camera, a class. I'm just talking. Do people do that?"

"I don't know. Guess I should get back to the inn."

Her mood's changed again with the mention of the wedding.

"Come on. I'll take you back."

"Wait! Where are the pictures from the show?"

"Still packed away."

"Can I see?"

"Sure." He wants to keep her here, and it seems she wants to stay, as long as he doesn't bring up the wedding. He's about to leave the darkroom and lead her to the carton with the three wrapped-up photographs, but instead he bends down and does what he's been wanting to do—he kisses her. And she kisses him back, putting her hand on his chest. He wraps his arms around the small of her back. She moves her other arm around his thick neck. And now they too are in some fashion entwined, as though seeking to replicate the photo. He's a good kisser; at least that's what women have told him. Maybe they lied, though she seems to be enjoying it. He can feel himself growing. Shit! He can feel her body temperature rising, her breath becoming heavier. They pull away at the same time, as though they had set the developing timer and it just went off.

"I'm sorry," he says, wiping the sweetness from his lips.

"Don't be." She combs her hair with her fingers. "Just don't be sorry." But they have already turned away from each other and are heading for the black velvet curtain and the long flight of stairs without mentioning the carton of photographs from the show.

Chapter 9

The Holy Prostitute

"Morning." Daisy stepped barefoot into the kitchen where Suzanne was giving the children their breakfast. "That quilt was so warm and cozy. I had one like it. When my father was dying, I left for two weeks to visit him. When I got back, my roommate and his girlfriend had taken all of my things and thrown them in the street. In the street!"

"Why?"

"Sick." She pointed to her head. "You should have seen it. Everything in the gutter, thrown every which way. I like things orderly. Neat. And do you think my father cared what happened to me? He kicked me in the face. Almost broke my jaw. Then he called the police."

"Your father?"

"No. My roommate. He had me on the floor. Even the policeman said he didn't like to see anyone down and out like I was."

Suzanne wondered if Daisy's father had died. She had lost both of her own parents early: Her father when she was ten and her mother when she was eighteen, just before she married Billy. Alyssa lifted up a piece of toast and held it out to Daisy.

"*Thank you, sweetie, but that's your breakfast.*" Then she took it just the same, and eying the jar of peanut butter on the counter, asked if she could have some.

"*Go ahead.*" Suzanne shoved a spoonful of cereal into the baby's mouth. Daisy began to open all the drawers. "*What are you looking for?*"

"*A knife. Don't get up. I don't mind. Actually, I'm enjoying going through your things. So neat and orderly. You're like me. Neat. You know what that shows, Suzanne? Good upbringing. Right?*" She drew out the last word in a sing-song manner. "*I have a lot of dishes like these—somewhere—I think. Is nine-thirty too early to call someone who's been up late at a party?*"

"*I really don't know.*" The company of another adult—even a bizarre one—was a welcome change from being alone with the babies. Billy managed a gas station during the day and was finishing up his third quarter at the university in the evening. He wanted to be a lawyer.

"*I told him not to stay up all night. John, my boyfriend. He'd better have listened. Does Billy listen to you?*"

Suzanne laughed as she began to clear the dishes. That was an understatement.

"*He's probably got a real hangover. But you know men. They go out and cavort, then they want to run home and make love to you. I don't mind. I like to think of myself as a prostitute.*"

Suzanne straightened her back and squeezed the sponge in her hand.

"*Oh not that kind. I mean a holy prostitute, like they used to have back in Ancient Greece, in Mesopotamia, in Egypt. They were women in the temples. You know. When men came back from battle, they would go to these temples and screw these prostitutes. Entering them was a form of cleansing after their barbaric behavior. Like confession. But, of course, that was before the great misogynists took over.*"

"Who?"

"Misogynists. You know. Women haters. Right?" She said, drawing out the word again and taking a slice of bread from the package on the counter, then slathering it with peanut butter.

CONFESSION. THERE WAS a handy little sacrament that washed away evil thoughts and deeds with a few Hail Marys. Ryan could use a good confession now, sneak behind the curtain into the dark box of the local church (because she isn't allowed since she has never been baptized) and spill it all. That way she wouldn't have to admit any deception to the Brackton Chamber of Commerce. It had worked for her first college roommate who chose the religious practice over therapy to deal with her nymphomania. And how nifty was it for those ancient warriors who derived pleasure while receiving absolution? How arrogant of them! Men, like her father, still came crawling back in the same manner, only now they called it makeup sex.

Ryan is making good progress on this story. If she stays at the office for an extra forty-five minutes, she can write a page a day. In a month, she'll have the first draft down—sooner if she puts in time on the weekends. In a year, she could write a novel, though every book she's read on writing says it takes at least two. She doesn't at all mind staying late today and waiting out the rush hour traffic before she picks up her car in JP and heads over to the nursing home. She can't wait to go to Laurel Manor. She's dying to tell Faye about her naughty weekend in Brackton.

* * *

She finds Faye lying fully clothed on her bed, eyes closed, mouth open, left arm hanging over the mattress. Ryan's heart sinks, adrenaline rushes.

"Faye!" She clasps the limp but warm hand.

An annoyed Faye moans in protest. "I was having the most delightful dream. I was in Venice. Marcello Mastroianni and Rossano Brazzi were fighting over me in a gondola."

"How come it wasn't Paul Newman, Miss JDate? Or have you crossed over to the world of gentiles?"

Faye's eyelids fly open.

"Ryan! I thought you were one of the little nurses here. Always waking me up for one thing or another. Pains in the neck."

"You scared the shit out of me, Faye."

"Now it even costs to dream?"

"You didn't answer the phone when I called you an hour ago."

"I was out."

"Excuse me?"

"Probably in physical therapy, or the *gym*, as they call it. I call it physical torture." She pushes herself up and rests on her elbows; Ryan adjusts her pillows. Suddenly Faye's mouth droops to the left, then to the right. Her eyebrows rise an inch. Ryan reaches for the buzzer.

"What's the matter, Faye? What's wrong?"

"I'm doing my facial exercises. I always do them when I wake up, no matter how many times a day. You should too. And will you please relax already? You're becoming as nervous as your father."

"I thought you were having a stroke."

"Don't be ridiculous. I take an aspirin a day."

"Should I do that too?"

"Not until you're fifty." Ryan helps her sit up. "So tell me, *bubeleh*, how did you make out on the Internet?"

"I didn't. But I did go to Vermont."

"Vermont?"

"Remember the contest? Or are you still in Venice?"

"Of course I remember."

Her thin penciled brows work hard, meeting together over the bridge of her nose. Then the smile of recollection.

"I don't know, Faye."

"What don't you know?"

"Why I'm pursuing this marriage thing at all. Some of my friends are already getting divorced. What's the point?"

"You and I wouldn't be here together having this conversation without it. That's the point."

"This contest is creating too many problems."

"If you're not cut out for problems, Ryan, you're not cut out for life. I look at it this way: You can be happy or you can be sad; the glass can be half full or half empty. I choose to be an optimist. Now, tell all."

Ryan begins to recount the weekend's events to her grandmother. She takes a long time to tell a story; her descriptions are detailed, her dialogues verbatim. When she was a child about to recount her school day at the dinner table, her father would look at his watch and ask if it was going to take more than five minutes, so he could go pee and then pour himself another glass of wine in preparation. Ryan has barely finished describing the vendors' presentation and is up to her visit to Eric's artwork (she'll leave out the darkroom episode) when there's a knock at the door. This time it's the CNA Louis whom Ryan met last time, coming to take Faye to the movie they're showing. Tonight it's *Pal Joey*.

"Louis, I'm so glad it's you. You remember my granddaughter."

"Forget it, Faye," Ryan whispers. "He still looks like he's ten."

"This Eric character sounds like he might be a prospect."

"Out of the question."

Faye challenges with raised eyebrows. Was Faye that clever or Ryan that transparent?

Louis helps Faye into a wheelchair and pushes her past Ryan.

"Sorry, *bubeleh*. I have a date."

"Let me guess. Harold the dancer."

Faye confirms with a smile. "We're working fast, since we're both short-termers here."

"Why? Your mother won't allow you to go out when you get home?"

"Cute. At our age, we don't buy green bananas. By the way, we've exchanged bodily fluids."

"Too much information." And in front of Louis, no less. Ryan waves away her grandmother's last statement.

"Orally, Ryan darling. For now. There's a slice of coffee cake wrapped in a napkin on my night table."

"I'll be *back*, Faye."

"Can you bring me a can of spray paint next time you come?"

"Don't tell me you're into graffiti?"

"I might be getting a walker soon."

"And you want to paint it."

"Metallic gold."

Chapter 10

F ATHER CURRAN'S OFFICE in the seminary is the size of the small foyer that used to lead to the secretary's large office adjacent to the tremendous oak-paneled president's office—the office from which Father Curran had once steered Freeland College on the Oregon coast, like a ship caught in a perfect storm of tumultuous times that roiled the country and threatened to veer out of his control daily. The youngest Jesuit president at the time, he lectured on the collision course that the country was headed toward concerning materialism and racial inequality. Having studied on the cusp of Vatican II, he was keenly aware of reform and revolution.

He found himself so impassioned about the Vietnam War that he marched with students, a step that caused the faculty to cast a vote of no confidence and the Board of Trustees to call for his resignation, but a step that also cemented student fidelity: No building was vandalized or occupied at Freeland; there were no administrative takeovers, no strikes. And it was Father Curran who was asked to address the student body after the murders of Bobby Kennedy and Martin Luther King, atrocities his religious peers ignored despite their order's commitment to social justice. And so by popular student demand, the Board of Trustees and influential alumni had no recourse but to uphold Father Curran's position at the helm, where he remained for thirty years.

When he was at last forced out to pasture at the age of seventy-five and urged to spend the rest of his years in some cushy old priests' community in the Midwest, Father Curran threatened to expose to the alumni the overspending engaged in by the treasurer and supported by several emeritus Jesuits who had continued to live on campus after retirement. He was given a choice: preside over a seminary for the diminishing order of American Jesuits or give last rites to his colleagues in that cushy rest home—but get off the grounds of Freeland.

Of course he chose to be rector of a seminary: He loved young people and abhorred stodginess, stultified thinking, and an opulent lifestyle. Too old to be a provincial superior or a rector any longer he was assigned the job of spiritual director to the small group of novices who were nowadays out in the field most of the time, fulfilling mission assignments during their years of discernment.

Seated in the cracked tan leather recliner that caters to his age (his vascular surgeon has ordered him to keep his feet up as often as possible), his ruddy and liver-spotted scalp with its white furry rim is nearly lost in the pilly beige afghan his sister knitted for him when he graduated from seminary and that he keeps draped over the back of the chair. The blue eyes magnified by wire-rim glasses get tired at age eighty-nine, and he needs to rest them, along with his veiny legs, from time to time. His laptop is propped up where it was intended to be—on his lap—with the screen open to an article from *Religions* when Jason's knock wakes him from a sound nap.

"Come in." The priest makes no attempt to sit up straight as he clears his throat of phlegm.

"I apologize, Father. I didn't mean to disturb you. I saw your light was on." Jason knows Curran is far from being done for the day: He's still wearing his black shirt and collar.

"I couldn't reach the switch and was too lazy to get up," Father Curran says, referring to the brass floor lamp beside him with its dusty yellowed shade. "Just kidding, Jason. Odds are at my age you're going to wake me up more often than not, so why turn out lights? I'm beyond embarrassment about it. I was trying to get through this article on fighting self-deception by means of the dramatic imagination. Should know better than to deceive myself by reading at this hour, since I haven't been able to make it past the first paragraph." He lifts his right hand as if to give a blessing, though it's merely to emphasize the inconsequence of Jason's interrupting him. As though obeying gravity, the hand floats back down to the armrest. "What can I do for you?"

"Can I ask you a personal question, Father?"

"All questions are personal, Jason. Even the most objective ones are clouded by perception."

Jason chuckles, his turquoise eyes cast downward at the cracks in the dull oak floor, at his too-long toenails, at Father Curran's thick white compression stockings. How generous is his license to speak candidly with his superior, to make assumptions about Curran's sense of humor?

"You don't believe me?"

"It's the fact that I do that I find amusing. You don't disappoint, Father. You always provide the expected, which is the unexpected."

"Sit down. Is it time for a Scotch?"

Jason, in khaki shorts, gray T-shirt, and sandals, sits in the wooden rocker opposite Curran. Hands on his hairy thighs, he leans closer to his advisor, as though he were about to give him a shoeshine.

"So let's talk turkey," Curran says.

"Okay. Why'd you become a priest, Father?"

"You mean you didn't come in to chew over Saint Augustine or Thomas Aquinas?"

Jason chuckles again, but this time it's a nervous laugh, and his gaze slips away from Father Curran. "Not today."

"I like to think of it more as why I became a Jesuit."

Talking to Father Curran is like talking to a human vegetable peeler. A crazy comparison, but that's the way Jason sees him—always shaving, further, further, further, until you've been pared down to some odd-shaped seed of truth that no one has ever noticed before.

"I went to Saint Louis University," Curran says. Jason sits attentively, like a child awaiting his favorite bedtime story. "I wanted to be a lawyer—like you. My dad was a first-generation Irish college graduate—an optometrist. He hated it. He wanted to be a politician. He was always involved with some political organization, from Young Democrats to city council. Even ran for mayor, but lost. Good for the family but disappointing for him. What I'm getting at is that I didn't want to be disappointed with my life, so I thought that if I started out in law, I'd be on the right road to politics, because as the only son in an Irish family of five sisters, aligning myself with my father to the point of fulfilling his ambitions was a given. Wouldn't *I* want what would have made *him* happy?

"But at Saint Louis, I got involved with this Jesuit business, and I started to think about what *God* wanted me to do. It wasn't terribly profound, but I had a feeling that I had the religious life thing going on and sort of liked—from a distance—those Jesuits. I liked the intellectual life and social questioning that I probably got from my father, and I liked the Jesuits' association with academia and teaching. Diocesan priests tended to be pious in a way that wasn't attractive to me. But I became anxious. Would I be getting into the pious nerd-type stuff anyway for the rest of my life? So I get to the seminary in Florissant, Missouri, and the director of novices, whom I didn't know, says to me, 'Ambrose, welcome to the novitiate.' And I'm thinking, how does he know who I am, and he says without my asking, 'Because you're the last one to arrive.'

"Well, that's how I got started: the last one to arrive. So here we are, forty-five first-year novices in my class, if you can believe that. Over two hundred in the seminary! That night one of the guys, Eddie Sullivan, a war vet, told a dirty joke at recreation time, and I went to bed thinking, these guys are all right. Not going to worry about being stuck with a bunch of pious nerds. I'm not saying that's the cause of my remaining a Jesuit, but it certainly was a contributing factor—this dirty joke, which I can't remember. I wish to hell I could remember it. But *you're* not worried about being with a bunch of pious nerds."

"No."

"You're not even worried about being with a *handful* of pious nerds, as the case may be."

"What was your father's reaction to your becoming a priest?"

"'Damn Jesuits!' But he came around."

"But how did you know, really know, it was right?"

"I've never thought about leaving, if that's what you mean. My coming in was problematic and whatnot, but it's been a done deal. Once I got away from the routine of the novitiate life—the daily order, the rising at five, the hours of silence, the constant cleanup, gardening, interspersed with meditation and prayer—once I got to the University of Michigan to earn my doctorate in political science, once I got into the world of academia—well, that changed my whole life.

"First I had to take on my theology studies for four years while being a hospital chaplain in Minneapolis. Oh, that was hard. You go around and try to console people. Then you go to bed, and at 2 a.m. you get a call about somebody dead on arrival—some guy on a motorcycle, the family there crying.

"Then I spent a month out in Pine Ridge, South Dakota, on the Sioux reservation. Total failure. I was supposed to give a series of talks, and I talked about the latest scripture criticism. Oh, I totally misjudged the thing." He laughs hard. "But I just loved being at the University of Michigan. I mean, I could stay up until 2 a.m., working on mathematics and economics. It was a luxury after going through the Jesuit thing, where you had to go to bed at a certain time. But I could stay up now until two! It was just about physical pleasure. They offered me a tenure track position, and I taught there for twelve years. I loved being a Jesuit in a secular environment. In a curious way, it made me more of a Jesuit. But then I got the call about the presidency, and I was back with the Jesuits."

"So that was planned—to be back with the Jesuits."

"I've never really planned anything. My life, Jason, has been blessed. Really, it has."

"Father, was there ever a woman? I mean in your decision."

"Hell, there's always a woman. From the minute we're conceived there's a woman. You didn't get here on your own, kiddo."

Jason smiles.

"That was the other problem I had, Jason. You see there was this girl I dated in college from a sister university—Our Lady of Fatima. A smart girl. A beautiful girl. I didn't think we were particularly serious, but she *was* my girlfriend. When I told her about going into the novitiate to try it out, I told her she could come and visit me. Well, that didn't happen. Like I said, she was a smart girl. A selfish girl, in the good sense of the word. She knew what she wanted, and she knew how to take care of herself. I learned a lot from that girl. Only at the time I didn't recognize it."

"What was her name?"

"Dorothy. Her name was Dorothy."

"Did you ever think about her after you entered the novitiate?"

"It was all a little easier back then. Out of sight, out of mind was the attitude you were supposed to adopt. *Modesty of the eyes*, my novice master recommended: control what you look at, close your eyes and grit your teeth, or else you'll have a hell of a time being a Jesuit. But that was before television, mind you, let alone the Internet. Nothing's out of mind nowadays."

Jason's next smile is guarded. He doesn't want to take privileges with his advisor. Ryan used to say he didn't allow himself to relax often enough; took too many things too seriously.

"Look, just because you're on a diet doesn't mean you can't enjoy the menu. I'm not saying this isn't serious stuff that's plaguing you, but don't forget you *are* Irish, lad. Lighten up a bit." Father Curran reads him well. The priest's eyes drift away from Jason on a moment's search into the past, then land back on the novice. "I thought about Dorothy a lot. But not in the way you're thinking about your girl. What's her name?"

"Ryan."

"A lassie!"

"No. Half Italian, half Jewish."

Curran gives a hearty laugh, then gets serious. "It's not about forgetting, lad. You never forget. It's about what file in your brain you put it into: Fond memories give me a thrill to remember, maybe even fantasize about, but wouldn't really want to exchange what I have for it; or the one that always sinks down into my gut, disturbs my meditation, makes me sick to wake up in the morning because I may be making a mistake."

The older and wiser of the two places his palms on his thighs to support his torso as he leans toward Jason and stares squarely into those pools of bluish green. "Do we need to put in for a leave of absence, son, to get that dramatic imagination checked?"

"Maybe. I think so, Father. Yes."

Chapter 11

Wednesday, February 12

"Y OU DID *WHAT?*" Michael hands Eric a bottle of beer and plops down alongside him on the sofa.

"I kissed her."

"What the hell's wrong with you, man?"

"It's not like we banged or anything."

"That's fucked."

"Okay. I'm a degenerate. What can I say? Becca's not home, is she?"

"Food shopping. Too late. She already thinks you're a player."

"Everyone's a player 'til they find the one. Besides, I can't even remember the last date I had, it's been so long. She's really hot."

"You wanna fuck up your big plan? You want some football hero to come and beat the shit out of you?"

"I don't get the sense he's a football player. Stocks and bonds type. She said not to be sorry. Really. She said that."

"Oh, that makes it all good."

"I liked it."

"Of course you did!"

"No. I really liked being with her—talking to her. She gets me, Mike."

"Nobody gets you, Eric."

"Seriously, she gets me."

"Well somebody already got *her*. You've got to hit the eject button."

"Yeah. For sure. But I think she has doubts about getting married, which scares the shit out of me about the contest."

"Whatever baggage this chick is hauling around is her business. You just better hope she's not crazy." Michael shakes a fistful of peanuts from a jar and deposits them into his mouth.

"She didn't even act like she has a man. You think she might not even be engaged?" Eric asks.

Michael's look indicates it to be a strong possibility.

"She liked the shot I have of you and Becca and me."

"Maybe she does have taste. Listen, not to change the subject, but this is Lambert's last season, as you know." Michael has turned the conversation to baseball and the longtime high school coach, who was Eric's coach. "You're going to put your name in, right?"

"I don't know, Mike."

"What don't you know?"

"If I'd be any good."

"You've been the assistant coach for two years. You want me to kiss your ass, Eric? You know you're good. The kids love you. Put your name in. Make my life easy. You know you're a shoo-in. I'll leave Brackton if you don't."

Eric looks at him. "Don't play like that! You know I don't like it when you talk about that shit. You're not leaving, are you?"

"Someday."

"Why'd you take the job, Michael? Seriously. I never asked you."

"You did. During my interview."

"I don't mean that bullshit answer. Why'd you really come?"

"I like to ski—why'd the search committee pick me?"

"There were two other finalists," Eric says. "One was decent. One wasn't on the same level. You were the best candidate."

"I was black."

"That too. You were good and you were of color. The diversity card definitely didn't hurt."

As he talks, Eric leans forward and passes his hand over the top of the Mission-style oak coffee table as though trying to detect any imperfections in the grain, any unevenness in the finish. He has a habit of examining the surface of an object in front of him in this way when he's anxious about approaching a topic. He moves his fingers back and forth along the lip of the table, presses the palm of his hand into the wood, around the sharp point of the right angle of the tabletop, as though he had made the object himself or is trying to determine how someone else might have made it.

"It's a pretty liberal town, always has been, but even more now than when I grew up, but I've been here a long time, Mike, and there's an old guard—especially in the surrounding towns. I never know how they think, or maybe I can't forget how they think."

"Don't worry about me."

"I've lived around here a long time."

"And I've been black a long time."

"You could have gotten something in a city. School systems are crying for principals."

"You mean in the hood?" Michael smiles and shakes his head. "I grew up in northwest DC. Far from the tough neighborhoods. My dad taught African American Studies courses at AU. We lived in Georgetown. One summer night when I was in high school and my parents were out of town, I went down to M Street to pick up something to eat. It was late. I was studying for a test. Here I am sitting on the stoop of our townhouse enjoying my pita pocket when a rookie cop pulls up. I had the key and money on me but no ID—had left my wallet inside. The cop wouldn't even let me go in and get it. It was absurd, but I stayed calm. Didn't put on a scene."

"Like Louis Gates at his door."

"I believe Gates made a scene, but then again, he's Gates."

"What happened?"

"Like I said, got taken down to the station."

"But you had the key."

"Now you're talking like a white boy. I was lucky. They finally got hold of my dad, who lost it on them and called his best friend, the dean, who also laid into them. The same cop drove me home." Michael shook his head, remembering the incident.

"You should get a Ph.D. and teach at a college like your dad."

"I like working with teenagers. And if I ever take a job in the hood, I want to bring everything I have to the table."

"So we're your guinea pigs."

"Basic training. There's something to be learned from everyone. And something to be taught." Michael goes into the kitchen and gets two more beers.

"You *are* the educator," Eric calls after him.

"I'm not under any illusion. I'm not trying to prove anything. And I'm not running away. If I was running away, I wouldn't be the only black dude in the heart of Vermont, would I?"

"So what are you?"

"I'm who I am and not afraid of that. Whatever it brings." He hands Eric a bottle of beer and resumes his seat on the couch.

"I don't know how you do it. Seriously."

"My parents taught me to forgive but not excuse."

"My mother's down with the forgiving part but I think she's excused too much."

"That's still you—*your* view of her. And that's what eats up your soul, man. Your mom's a beautiful lady. A courageous lady."

"'Cause I can't forgive *or* excuse? I know. I'm supposed to chalk it up to ignorance."

"Now, there's an excuse, if there ever was one. Another thing my father taught me was that no matter how much you try to teach something, there is always going to be some kid like you who will never get it."

"I'm not following."

"You're a smart guy. It's not hard. Think about it."

"Does Becca like it here?"

"I like it better than she does. She's a city girl."

"What do your parents think about Becca?"

"They're cool. As long as it's right."

"And you believe it is?"

"What do you think?" Michael asks.

"Don't look at me, man. I think it is. But that's only from my perspective, which obviously isn't worth much to you."

"Damn straight."

"What's your parents' take on you having kids?"

"My parents don't have to worry like white parents about what it'll be like for their grandkids to be half black. They already got a black kid to worry about."

It dawns on Eric that for the second time that day he's more than reluctant to let someone go. "Don't leave here before I do."

"Put your name in for coach. But no more fooling around with the contestants; don't screw up your coaching chances. You need to chill." Michael punches him in the arm. "This bride scheme of yours is taking you down. Have Becca give you a massage."

"I'll be fine."

"You're uncomfortable with my girl giving you a massage, aren't you?"

"I've never had one."

"Shit, you already got naked with her."

"That was different. *You* were there. It's not the naked thing. I don't like the idea of someone inflicting pain in places when and where I least expect it."

"It's her profession. It's what she does. She's not just poking around. You're a control freak."

"No, I'm not."

"Yeah, Eric. You are."

"I can't wait for draft day." Eric changes the subject because he doesn't like to think of himself as controlling—just organized. Controlling has bad connotations for a guy. He goes to the fridge and helps himself to another beer. He's talking about their fantasy baseball league. He's already begun to research the players' stats and his draft position—building a team takes strategy. He's not going to focus on on-base percentage and stolen bases this year, just home runs and RBIs. He's looking at a bunch of guys who swing hard and put up power numbers.

"Like I said, you're a control freak. But I'll let it slide."

Eric squirms with the discomfort of knowing that Michael sees through him, and yet he's glad for it. This won't be the end of the conversation. Michael just knows when to let up some on the pain and let the blood return to the trigger point before he presses again.

"I'll bet you a two-hundred-dollar lobster dinner my team beats yours," Michael says.

"You're on. Last season your team lost nine straight matchups. Or was it ten straight? It was embarrassing."

"We settled on March eighth for the draft, right?"

"March eighth it is."

"Too bad our league is all over the globe. Be fun to meet together in one place for a live draft," Michael says.

"Yeah. Like Vegas. Oh well, I'll be at your door March eighth with my laptop—or do you want to come to me?"

"Let's do it at your place. Becca likes her peace and quiet on occasion."

Eric opens the door to leave and finds Bicycle Girl making her figure eights in front of the house. Almost like a faithful puppy waiting for her master. But unlike that dog that hungers for human touch, he knows she'll ride away if he even approaches her.

"Ever wonder what it's like to be her?" he asks Michael as they stand on either side of the threshold.

"Frustrated. Confused. Out of focus."

"That's not how I see her. More like liberated," Eric says.

Chapter 12

The Holy Prostitute

Suzanne sat on the couch—the only piece of furniture they could afford for the family room—watching late-night TV and waiting for Daisy to return from her date. Suzanne didn't trust her boarder to lock the front door after herself. Earlier that evening, Alyssa had skipped into the kitchen with Daisy's nightgown draped over her own pajamas, the entire length of the gown bunched up in the child's hands.

"Where's the lady?" Alyssa had asked.

Billy demanded that she take the gown off, while a crying Alyssa said that Daisy had let her wear it. Shouting, Billy said he didn't want her touching anything that belonged to that woman. Then he got up and left. It was midnight now, and neither Daisy nor Billy had returned. At twelve forty-five, she locked the doors and went to bed. Why did she have to lock up, anyway? There was nothing to steal. "To keep out the crazies," Billy would have said. But the crazies already had keys.

Believing that Daisy had come in after she'd gone to bed and was in her room sleeping, Suzanne was astounded when, quivering on the front porch, Daisy rang the doorbell the following afternoon.

"Where's your boyfriend?"

"He took off somewhere on High Street. He's jaded like the rest of them. I met these guys. They said they would give me some soup and a place to stay. It was too far from here and too late to get back. They tricked me. They took advantage of me."

"Why didn't you use your key just now?" Suzanne asked.

"I lost it." She climbed the stairs and within seconds the shower was running.

God, don't let her have given my key to those guys, Suzanne prayed.

UNABLE TO CONCENTRATE on her writing, Ryan shuts down her computer at the law center a little earlier today and heads for the comfort of her favorite museum. Riding on the Green Line E up Huntington Avenue, she takes in the dark cumulus clouds, outlined in white, that float on a clear blue background. Still, the day is gray. How can that be? In Boston the sun resists appearing from winter to late spring. When it does show its face, it's only for a brief teasing moment and usually during the workweek when almost everyone is gazing out from their cubicles; then it retreats in a timely manner, as though frightened by the hordes of lunchtime foot traffic between twelve and one-thirty, only to reappear briefly around two, before winter's early dusk. Ryan photographs the fluffy clouds with her phone from the window of the trolley. She'd like to paint them, but she isn't like her mother; she doesn't know how to paint. And though her mother tried to cultivate any natural ability Ryan might have had, never demanding that she do it one way or another but urging her to let the brush explore—with circles and lines and broad back-and-forth strokes—to see what developed, Ryan became frustrated.

It looks as if it would be so easy now to paint the sky the way her mother does it: just make swirls—no blobs—of white with a few dabs of ocher, a thin outline of pink, then a thicker one of black. How hard could that be? She would try it one day, maybe even later that evening.

Then again, maybe she'll take up photography, like Eric Boulanger encouraged her to do. Or just stick to writing.

Ryan's parents' home on Long Island is filled with paintings and prints bought at charity art auctions or from hard-up artists on the streets of Greenwich Village, the Left Bank of Paris, the courtyard of Montmartre, the flower market in Nice, or a walkway along Lake Como. Her mother had worked as an art model in college, which intrigued Faye and at the same time made her a bit jealous. She envied everything that had been accessible to her daughter but denied to her: an education, sexual freedom, and above all—choice.

Ryan's mother, Lauren, used to tell Ryan that it had been difficult to sit or lie or stand still, barely breathe, naked, in the studio loft where the art professor, who had discovered her while she sipped coffee in the student union, made her assume a pose for half-hour intervals, with a few minutes to stretch during the three-hour class. But amid the smell of oil, the splattered clothes of the aspiring artists, the mess of it all, Lauren had found her niche. No wonder their house was always upside down; she had no penchant for order, in fact she thrived on disarray. At first she believed her only talent lay in her body and patrician face.

Unlike Ryan, who took after Faye's family, with their full and symmetrical round features, Lauren had inherited her father's Sephardic dark hair, olive skin, classic nose—nothing perfect, but taken together, strikingly different and captivating to the students who studied her in detail, as though she were inanimate—a well-preserved cadaver. In that bohemian loft and under Professor Lancaster's tutelage, she came to appreciate her form—her breasts, her vagina, her butt—as much as the artists and Professor Lancaster did. She thanked Professor Lancaster for her lack of inhibition during subsequent sexual encounters (he being one of them), for lighting the fire within her to study art, for setting her on the path to a fulfilling career. Whenever she thought of Lancaster, she thought of satisfaction. Too much information, Ryan told her mother, who in that regard was just like Faye.

While Ryan secretly loved to study the pastel drawings, charcoal sketches, and oil paintings of her mother that students had given

Lauren out of gratitude, or had simply discarded (Ryan would come upon them in the strangest places in their home—the laundry closet, beneath a stack of mismatched dishes in the basement, a bureau in the guest room), her mother's body, exposed for anyone who came upon these works, embarrassed her. Moreover, she resented her mother, who, despite her professor's criticisms of her first attempts to create her own art, persevered and succeeded. Whereas Ryan tried to make her profession fit her life—Jason's and hers—and as a result felt she was walking around in an oversized dress that had gone out of style long ago.

Ryan checks her coat in the new wing of the museum and heads straight down the corridor to the palace. Some days the city wears her down—the fumes, the noise, the odors—and she needs more than a park or a stroll in the country, she needs a *new* country. That's when Isabella Stewart Gardner waves an around-the-world frequent-flyer ticket in her face. *Need a trip to China or Spain? Italy or the Middle East? Come, I'll take you there and put you up in my villa to boot.*

After all, wasn't that Gardner's intention? To have a house just like one she had stayed at in Milan? To build a villa filled with beautiful pictures and objects of art and fauna, with delicate lace curtains that would make it hard for visitors to obey the *Do Not Touch* sign because they'd add a personal flavor along with other furnishings, large and small, that would make visitors feel as though they were going to bump into Isabella at any moment as she came down a grand stairway, or floated through the long gallery? To share her home was Isabella's dream, and the dream continues to delight visitors every day except Tuesdays, and very few holidays, for over a century. We are guests in her villa, Ryan thinks. Or are we intruders?

Ryan enters the Spanish cloister, with its green, blue, yellow, and white floral-patterned Mexican tiles that Isabella, working beside her craftsmen, spent hours arranging, along with the Moorish-style stone architecture of an alcove with cobalt blue tiles, the theatrical Andalusian tavern setting that hosts Sargent's *El Jaleo*. The gypsy woman's body is tilted back, defying gravity, one hand lifting her long shimmering skirt, the flamenco heels peeking from the folds, the other hand extended with a castanet. Ryan can hear the clicking—of the heels with their many hammered nails, of the small wooden hand-held instrument—and the strumming guitars of the musicians seated in a semicircle around her as one wails his mournful Gypsy lament. But Ryan has no time to stay in Seville. It's the courtyard that beckons her. It's the courtyard she's come to see today. Tiffany does her soul-searching at the dark cavernous Dirty Truth bar on Cambridge Street. Jason used to do his in church. Ryan does hers at the invitation of Isabella Stewart Gardner.

No matter the time of year or the weather, the greenhouse-glass-covered courtyard provides a refreshing contemplative environment, like a giant fountain of rejuvenation. Light, stone, water, exotic greenery. The sound of silence that only beauty of a bygone era emanates.

Sitting on a bench in the courtyard of the Venetian palace, with its stucco walls, arched walkways, fairy-tale-like windows, she is an outsider, a Peeping Tom straining for a glimpse of what the galleries hold. She's glad she got a chance to go to Venice before it sank out of sight—really got to go. When Ryan was thirteen, her mother had taken her on a whirlwind girls' Italian train excursion while her father was steeped in tax season. "Art," Lauren had said as they took in the masters at the Uffizi, of the mosaics of Ravenna, the Venetian architecture, "is the only lasting beauty in this world."

The intricately carved columns of the courtyard rest on life-sized stone lions. A glance in any direction is a feast for the senses. Every visit presents something new to her attention, along with the satisfaction of recalling something else. Three-story palm trees in each corner and strategically placed pots of plants and statues all render order in the garden, where everything is symmetrical. That's what she needs in her life right now: order. That's what she needs in her mind.

She focuses on the mosaic in the center of the courtyard; it becomes her meditative focal point, with Medusa at its core. Through her hideous appearance she had the power to ward off evil spirits, to turn anything she looked at into stone. Ryan remembers this from her Greek mythology unit in high school. She hadn't really been able to understand it back then. A boy who sat behind her told her that her coppery coils reminded him of the Greek goddess. He called her Copperhead. She had hated him for likening her hair to snakes. She hated snakes and couldn't even walk into the reptile house at the zoo. She'd wished she could command her curls to hiss at him, even bite him. She'd more or less hissed at him herself.

Looking back on it, she realizes he was paying her a compliment and was probably attracted to her. How many messages did people send that got misread? Had Eric misread her message of friendship when he kissed her? No way. She had clearly flirted with the guy. Now she's reminded every other day on Facebook that she hasn't yet responded to his request to friend him. How could she? Let him into her personal life so he can see firsthand she's a fraud? Maybe he's into two-timers, this Yankee and his tidy committee of nature lovers so unlike the ethnic misfits of her grandmother's Boston or the outspoken ones of her own Long Island. Wouldn't they be disappointed to learn the truth about her love life?

Is everyone a contradiction as she is? Her mother had called art's beauty a certainty; she had also said it was magic. Then how was one to extract reality from appearance? Truth from disguise? Even the magical Venice would one day sink out of sight. What could one depend on if not what went on in one's own brain? What made Ryan any different from the senile residents where Faye lived if she couldn't correctly interpret the codes others sent?

Whoa. All she had come here to do was to focus, tighten the reins and bring some clarity back into in her life. It shouldn't be that hard. Erase Jason from her mind. Come clean to Eric and the Brackton Chamber of Commerce. And move on, girl. Move on.

* * *

That night she composes an email to Eric confessing all, including how much she enjoyed their kiss in the darkroom. Adhering to her father's advice about waiting twenty-four hours before mailing an important letter, she saves it in her Drafts folder, where for much longer than a day it will patiently await a click on Send. She'll even stoop so low as to consider never sending it at all and ignoring the entire embroilment, leaving the Brackton Chamber of Commerce board of directors to fend for themselves. Surely they can get another couple.

Chapter 13

E RIC HATED RUNNING during baseball practice, whether for Little League or the high school team. Those were the times he wished he lived in Florida, where weather is baseball's best friend and spring training means just that and not fighting for time with or even running alongside the softball and lacrosse and tennis teams at the only indoor track in the district. It wasn't even that he hated running indoors—or in freezing cold if there was no ice on the roads. He just hated running. A former center fielder and receiver who everyone said had wheels but who didn't like running made no sense to most but perfect sense to him: He loved outrunning everyone to catch a fly ball or score a touchdown; it was running with no base or ball or goal line in sight that he abhorred. Unless, of course, he was running away. But even that had its purpose.

He runs now, however, during every practice. He runs with the baseball team he's helping to coach, driving his body to keep up with those half his age, while the silver-haired man who has been head coach for over three decades waits for them at the field. Eric enjoys feeling his heart pumping, his lungs expanding, his brain entertaining thoughts—pieces of conversations, striking images—that pass through it with the air he takes in and lets out in a high-speed meditation. He runs with Michael through the dark back roads of town on warm evenings, both of them closing their eyes at the approach of blinding headlights, sharing that familiar sweat of panic. And for an instant, they are the same: skeletons covered in light and dark, glistening with fear. But no matter how many cars slow down, no matter how much they let each other in, Eric knows he and Michael will never be the same.

It's been three weeks since I've heard from Ryan, Eric thinks as he runs today with the team, six weeks since her visit to Brackton. Her response to his earlier emails following their meeting were evasive: *too busy with work to really study the vendor options; Jason not feeling well; overwhelmed with family issues at the moment.* Then she went silent, failing to respond to his emails and texts, ignoring his invitation to be Facebook friends. He figures it must be on account of the darkroom incident, which neither of them has mentioned. Asshole that he is for that inappropriate action, though he doesn't blame himself entirely.

Gone dark after the darkroom antic. How ironic is that? He would laugh if he didn't sense he'd been played. But to what end by this couple who are like ephemeral beings, tempting and taunting with their absence? Any sense of grounding he experienced with her in that darkroom has sped by with incredible speed. Going, going, and soon she too will be gone.

Annie Chalis is on his tail about the invitations that need to be sent out two months before the wedding, with an additional month needed to place and receive an order, more if she needs to design something herself. Fran Costantino says at this rate Ryan will have to pick from one of the gowns Fran already has in stock and that will most likely need a ton of altering, because it's too late to put in for a different size.

"I'm not coming up with any unique wedding bands at this late date," Raphael O'Leary says. "Do they think they're the only ones getting married in June?"

While Eric was looking forward to spreading word of a successful Brackton Is for Brides Contest on Facebook, aside from commercial benefits, he's not a great fan of the social media, does not care if someone spent their Saturday fixing a leak in their toilet or baking a pizza from scratch. The over-the-top perfunctory compliments about photos of girlfriends and babies and selfies are the worst: *so cute, just adorable, gorgeous couple, lookin'good.* No one ever responds with: *Really? Are you serious? Who cares?*

Still, once again against his better judgment, if he has any, he sent a request to friend Ryan in an effort to learn more about her, to peruse her photo albums and see what she's up to, because he *is* interested in how *she* spends her free time, and, more important, what Jason looks like and how their relationship is revealed in their pictures together. Jason is not on Facebook or Linked-In or Twitter or any other social media, and is not even included in Ryan's thumbnail photo. In fact, Eric cannot find any info on or image of Jason McDermott except for several obviously impossible suspects with the same name.

Another Chamber meeting is coming up and Eric has no news for the vendors about the selections that Ryan said she had to pass by Jason. He should have listened to reason; he made a poor choice in insisting on this couple. At least he and Michael have set up their Fantasy Baseball teams. Right now that seems like a consolation achievement to him. Soon the entire town will see him for what he is: a foolish young man with little direction, one with misguided ideas— like his father.

He did manage to get the vendors listed in the *Vermont Wedding Resource Guide Book for Bride*s. Brackton is there in black and white under every category: historic Vermont church weddings; cakes; banquet and reception sites; beauty and spa services; florists; photographers and video; music and entertainment; bridal attire and formal wear; even bartending and transportation.

Brackton is there along with Middlebury and Burlington and Bennington and Killington, the contest revealed to every chamber of commerce, that is either laughing at the idea or has become insanely jealous they didn't think of it first. Brackton and all its vendors interspersed with photos of couples holding hands and kissing; grooms bending over brides tilted in backbends kissing; couples dancing and kissing; exiting churches and kissing; and standing by covered bridges kissing. If they aren't kissing, they display ear-to-ear grins and perfect sets of teeth that have no doubt been whitened, and in some cases even straightened, for the occasion. And without fail the words *beauty* and *perfect* and *idyllic* appeared somewhere in the ad: *the beauty of the idyllic rolling hills of Vermont; the perfect place for the perfect time; the perfect day.*

He's starting to believe what everyone else beyond the Green Mountain State holds fast to: What else was there in the cold northern state after the ski season ends? He knows what visitors think when they take in the welcome sign with the words *unhurried, unspoiled, unforgettable.* Unlivable, they mutter. It's what must have turned off Ryan and her friend, and now she's putting them off, not knowing how to back out. In all fairness, he wasn't the one who had seen to it that the Vermont Convention Bureau included the Brackton resources; it was Danni who had taken charge of that. He's been spending more time with his mother these days, ever since he came home from a photo shoot in the woods for his double exposure project and saw the same look on her face she had worn the day she told him his father had been beaten up.

Eric was eight at the time. Nothing like it had ever happened in Brackton, at least not in years recent enough for anyone to remember. His father was a trial attorney who had represented a rape victim and won, but the judge opted for a light sentence—sixty days—for the prominent citizen's son, citing the defendant's low level of intelligence and inability to receive counseling until having served time. Soon after, René Boulanger ran for state representative on the platform of revamping sexual assault laws by adding amendments that would clarify what constituted the offense and, in turn, allocate appropriate sentences (which in most cases would be heavier).

He was driving home from stumping one night when he was forced off the road and out of his car, beaten badly about the head with a tire iron, and had both legs broken. He was never right again: walked with a limp, slurred his speech, and was unable to properly process thoughts. After months in Massachusetts General Hospital, he returned home but never resumed his law practice. He spent his remaining twelve years refinishing old furniture he sold, along with rusty tools and other farm collectibles, out of the barn behind the house. The motive for the attack was never established. A message regarding the prosecution of sex offenders? A robbery attempt? Nothing had been stolen; the perpetrators were never found. They were thought to have been outsiders, but put up to it by whom? In Eric's eyes, everyone was suspect.

That was Eric's first lesson about what was and what appeared to be. Shock waves hit the county. How could something that only happened in congested inner cities happen in Brackton? And in this day and age? But, as his mother and his grandparents and other wise old-timers knew, anything could happen anywhere, anytime. All that was required was animosity, fear, and a bully mentality.

The incident sent Eric through a gamut of emotions. Fear that he would lose his father, who lay in a coma hooked up to machines in a hospital that seemed to be in another world. Anxiety about how he would relate to this new father if he returned home, this father who had fished, and played ball, and hiked, and biked with him. Anger when he did return and children laughed at him. Humiliation when adults pitied the father's son. And anger toward the father who had brought this down on them. And then there was the young unmarried minister at the Southern Baptist church that his mother drove over an hour to attend every Sunday, who tried to take his Catholic father's place as he mentored Eric while consoling Eric's mother to the point that Eric feared he would lose his mother to the clergyman. What had Eric felt toward him? Hatred might not have been too strong a word.

One evening while Eric's father was still in the hospital, the reverend stayed for dinner and offered to help Eric with his homework. Eric shouted that he was not his father, left the table, and went up to his room, where he threw a baseball so hard and for so long against the wall that all the plaster fell away from the lath. And to make matters worse, it was the minister who insisted that Eric help him put up and paint the wallboard replacement. The reverend's effort to have Marie Boulanger grow dependent on him was not lost on young Eric. Some, including his mother, might have seen the minister's attentions simply as earnest attempts to perform his duties where his congregation was concerned, but children have a keen way of decoding behavior, can sense sexual attraction and cut straight to intent better than adults, who often prefer to make excuses or look the other way.

During one of the cleric's visits, a snowstorm began, yet he waited until conditions deteriorated before taking his leave. Surely the minister had listened to the weather report before setting out for Brackton. Marie suggested that he spend the night in the spare bedroom rather than drive back to Burlington in the blinding storm. Eric lay awake all that night, baseball bat at his side, listening for footsteps to his mother's room, ready to leap out of bed and take action.

When his father finally came home from rehab, the reverend was transferred to a small town on the coast of Maine. Marie, busy attending to her husband, didn't seem to question the reason for the transfer or miss the minister's presence. So like a grown-up Eric thought, she pretended to ignore his disappearance, believing it the product of coincidence. But Eric maintained that the move was initiated by the reverend himself, out of fear of Eric and a principled and intrepid though broken man who had returned home.

Putting an end to the murmurs and looks, the overly solicitous attention, the obvious discomfort of others around his family became Eric's mission. All he had had to do was get some titles hung in the high school gymnasium to free the townspeople of their unease and give them something positive to talk to Eric's parents about, maybe even make them covetous. It's what drove him to get decent grades, make it into the end zone, hit the ball over the fence, and earn a scholarship to some place far away. What it never succeeded in doing was erasing the fact of the incident and the subsequent years of his father's pain. And Eric's sense of having been abandoned by him.

To leave Brackton, just like the family of the victimized girl had done, became his mantra as a youth, win trophies and leave. But what good is any of it now that his mother's cancer has metastasized, despite his having been faithful to his superstitions. And he can't bear the thought of watching her wither away painfully, of others pitying them yet again.

"There are ways, Mom. You don't have to suffer," he tells her. "We can help you ahead of time. You can help yourself."

"That's a sin," she responds, horrified at the thought of assisted suicide.

The woman who had grown her own organic vegetables, lined an entire kitchen shelf with immune-system-boosting supplements, concocted her own chemical-free sunscreen, downed a forkful of brine-free fermented sauerkraut daily, never smoked and drank only green tea, and whose body was attacking her like a sadistic turncoat stands firm in her belief in the natural order of things and has refused even to sign a DNR directive or a living will. She tells him she prays every day for God to take her in His own time.

"How is that any different, Mom? Asking God to kill you."

"Let Him do the dirty work," she says. "It's a violation of my free will to force yours or any doctor's on me."

And once again he finds himself a figure looking for acceptance in a place where he finds pain. A place where he is held captive not only by his mother's illness but the Michael factor, the solid voice of reason that knows what he wants out of life though it will never come without a fight. Maybe if Eric sits outside Michael's window and watches him and Becca long enough, he'll learn the secret. That's what he really wants to do—observe them forever. He's a voyeur. Shit. Still seeking the role model he lost years ago. His mother tried, but he never let her in the way he used to let his dad in. And to her credit, she understood this, because her love was greater than anything Eric had ever been capable of.

She lived without a man. She became the town clerk who worked every day in an office next to that of the director of public works—the father of the young man who, twenty-three years ago, raped a minor. She is the only townsperson to whom Bicycle Girl, the daughter of Marie's deceased friend, has ever gravitated, has made herself vulnerable, and sought refuge from, showing up unannounced at her whim for breakfast or dinner. People called Marie a saint; she maintained that saints were in heaven. Something—maybe faith—filled her will with steel, gave her a bottomless capacity to tolerate and pardon—to give.

He didn't see it as a child, but he sees it now. If she has a major fault, it's that she never asks for anything. Eric used to think he was like her, never asking, but he's the opposite. With every step he takes, every plan he makes, he asks, he pleads. He just isn't ever quite sure what it is he's demanding.

His confusion propels him on with this new double-exposure project that gives his photos endless possibilities, that allows him to control people coming and going at the same time, to have bridges and trees right side up yet upside down, and always a convergence of the two, with photographer keeping them there. So easy with this camera that has a panoramic format: shoot a roll, reinsert the film, and shoot again on top of the first images. He is even willing to try it using the digital format with a multiple-exposure option. His mother thinks it's brilliant. RISD thought it worthy. He's come to believe he's creating an exhibit depicting where he sees himself—stuck. But maybe if he sees everything simultaneously coming and going enough times, he'll be able to figure out which direction leads to the way out.

Breathing hard, he makes his way with the team back to Coach Lambert and the field, where he'll enjoy not thinking of anything but baseball for the next two hours.

Chapter 14

The Holy Prostitute

"Either she pays now or she's out. She's been here a full week!"
Billy told Suzanne.

"Maybe we should give her a little more time—"

"What is it with you and this woman, Suzanne? What have you got going with her that you're so concerned?"

"I just feel sorry for her."

It was too late to persuade him. He was already climbing the stairs, his big feet skipping every other step. She strained to make sense out of the shouting she feared would wake the girls. Then Billy came back down with Daisy, in her nightgown, stomping behind him.

"Call him," Billy commanded, handing her his cell phone. Hers was dead.

"Mother, put Daddy on. I don't care if you're walking out the door. Fuck your party! Put Daddy on! Daddy, I need money." Her voice bordered on hysteria, and when her father hung up on her, she began slamming the phone against the wall. "He's paying $500 a day for an institution, but he won't even pay for a motel!"

Billy wrestled the phone out of her hand when she began to slam it repeatedly against the counter.

"Don't' touch me!" she screamed.

"He won't hurt you," Suzanne said, although witnessing the tension in his jaw, the anger in his eyes, she could not swear to it.

"You don't know what it's like to be afraid. Do you know what fear is?"

Suzanne nodded. "No you don't. He came into my room and yelled at me while I was lying down. I was in a vulnerable position." Her face was red, her body rigid and trembling. "All men want is to do you, then take off."

"I'm calling the Crisis Center," Billy said.

"They'll put me away like they did in Dayton. You know why? They thought I was suicidal. You know why? Because I like the Grateful Dead." She was crying. "I have my period. What should I do?"

"I'll give you something," Suzanne said.

"Thank you. You're nice. You're a woman. He's mean." She glared at Billy.

"Oh, for Chrissake," he moaned.

"Men are jaded. Nuns are jaded too. So are monks. And lawyers. Shrinks. Nurses. They're all jaded. My mother's totally dependent on my father. You won't ever be like that, will you?"

Suzanne shook her head.

"I hate having my period. Men don't want to have anything to do with you when you have it."

When Billy had the Crisis Center on the line, he handed Daisy the phone.

"I want to talk to a woman! I don't care who you are. I want a woman!" She tapped her nails against the counter while she waited.

S UZANNE IS WAY too tolerant of Billy. Ryan knows this, but she must find a way to keep this young couple together: they have two small children. Can there be a happy ending without comprising Suzanne? No matter how much Ryan wanted her parents to reconcile, she couldn't help but feel that her mother had caved in too quickly, let her father off the hook without adequate suffering. When it came to her father, her mother—so combative in most situations—turned into putty.

Ryan has spent the afternoon at the office, despite it being Sunday. She does this on occasion, finding the quiet workplace free of distractions and a good place to write. She has to stop now; she's tired after having lost an hour of sleep to the arrival of Daylight Saving Time. The good news is that it will be light out when she descends the long flight of stairs at the law center and steps out into street, then heads over to a co-worker's house for a celebration of the impending vernal equinox. Yes, Daylight Saving promises that spring is around the corner. Soon buds will appear begrudgingly on trees and there will be no more snow. And if there happens to be, it will melt away in a day or so. Daylight Saving signals Easter is on the horizon.

She can taste her father's ricotta cheesecake made just the way his mother used to make it, and the *pizza rustica*—dough filled with layers of mozzarella and prosciutto and salami and chopped hard-boiled egg that they'll eat for breakfast for as long as it lasts. She can smell the lamb roasting—slivers of garlic stuffed in pockets—and the lasagne bubbling in the oven of the hot kitchen. She wonders if she will ever be able to carry on the tradition the way her father has since his parents died. She will. She'll make the little birds' nests that her grandmother made for Ryan and her cousins—the sweet dough dusted with powdered sugar that held colorful dyed eggs. She'll organize egg hunts for her children. And, of course, there will be church. Easter and Christmas were the two times a year her father, Ryan in hand, accompanied his parents to Mass at his childhood parish church in Brooklyn. His parents gone, he continues the ritual at a church on Long Island. The church is jammed—standing room only—with lit candles at the head of each aisle, baskets of lilies or giant pots of poinsettias depending on the holiday, incense, and glorious voices and piping organ music.

The priests are overjoyed on these days, though their mood masks an underlying sadness, the knowing that come the following Sunday, three quarters of the pews will once again be empty. The archdiocese of Brooklyn recently closed Joe Toscano's childhood church, and Joe was glad his mother wasn't alive to see it.

What Daylight Saving couldn't guarantee was that Jason would show after the sun and moon had changed shifts, his silhouette barely recognizable, sitting and waiting for Ryan like a shutout latchkey child on the steps of her three-decker. How many times had she imagined this scene or one like it: Jason returning from the seminary and telling her that he'd made a mistake, chosen the wrong one, that it was her and only her all along? And now he's there, tugging on the sleeves of his thin navy windbreaker to cover his cold hands like a repentant teenager who hadn't listened to his mother and worn a jacket unsuited for the weather: Jason with a sheepish grin that begs for a simple smile—an opening that will ease him into a justification for his sudden appearance.

Get up, she thinks. Don't sit there waiting for me to make the first move like always. *Get the fuck up!* And, as though he hears her, he rises like Jesus from the crypt, rolls away that heavy boulder between them, and meets her face-to-face.

"Hey," he says.

"Hey."

* * *

Jason didn't leave right after his talk with Father Curran. He didn't want to set his vocation back for nothing and admit, yet again, that he was wrong about his life's direction. And he certainly didn't want to hurt Ryan any more. He decided to plunge into religious life deeper than ever and try to file his feelings for Ryan into the appropriate sections of his brain Father Curran had described: fond memories was too vague; fantasize about—okay; not wanting to exchange what he had for her—he couldn't seem to locate that compartment, or maybe it just didn't exist.

At first glance, his fellow novices appeared a motley crew: JP and Holden with unruly curls, freckles, and wry senses of humor; Louis, Rory, and Clayton as hairless as Marines with necks and southern accents as thick. Ricardo and Amit, dark and exotic. Rob and Tyler, never without a tune except during meditation.

On the other hand, in their jeans and T-shirts they were as identical as a litter of kittens: eager, earnest, pious, gregarious, and at the same time loners. They sat together from morning until night: in the white-washed classroom bifurcated by a dark chair-rail, with its old wooden desks, small windows, and the ubiquitous crucifix above the chalkboard; in the library, plopped in comfortable but worn, mismatched sofas amid stacks of books; in the stark refectory seated on two hard benches lining the long oak table; and in the chapel.

At night they sat alone in their rooms. Most had old-fashioned mahogany dressers and two straight-back chairs, equally user-unfriendly. There was a desk with an attached bookshelf like the one he'd had in college, and a sink and medicine cabinet in the corner, a towel rack above the radiator, and an old brown iron hospital bed from which on the blank canvas of white walls he played out past scenes and envisioned new ones of Ryan. The drab green café curtains and plastic blinds made him long for the colorful and comfortable décor created by the woman who drove him crazy.

He thought about her when the seminarians gave each other haircuts, when they washed down the tub and shower of the avocado-green-tiled bathroom, when they prepared meals at the homeless shelter or tutored children at the local elementary school. "Don't cut it too short," he had cautioned her about his hair. "Use the large scrub brush," she had insisted when he cleaned the bathroom.

He thought about her in the weight room with its scraped red wooden floor. He played soccer and touch football on the lawn muddy from heavy rains—he and his buddies splattered with dirt, like hooligans out for a wild romp—all the while hoping the bodies crashing, the takedowns, the headers, would rattle his thoughts, shake them up like marbles in a pinball machine, until they dropped into holes and rolled to those secret compartments in his brain where they'd come to a quiet standstill. He formed a trio with Rob and Jared, and attempted some form of classical guitar since Rob was hot on Chopin and Bach. And he prayed—everywhere—that the thoughts would settle like dust on his dresser. But they never did.

* * *

On this first day of spring they stand speechless after their initial greeting: he in the anticipatory limbo of awaiting her next move, which he knows she carefully weighs.

"Aren't you going to ask me in?"

She hesitates. Even if he didn't look so pathetic standing there shivering, he could understand why she would hesitate. He wants to touch her—her face, her arm, her hand, anything—but she stands as impassive as the stone lions on either side of the steps, and he doesn't dare.

"Come on up," she finally says, leading the way to the apartment he has never seen and whose address he found online.

He settles for the warmth of the hissing radiators to welcome him as they step into the small foyer, where out of habit he removes his shoes. She does the same and lines up her tall boots alongside his sneakers on the colorful prayer rug. She's wearing black-and-white-striped socks on top of dark black tights or stockings or whatever she calls them. Then she unwinds the extraordinarily long scarf that's looped around her neck several times, takes off her coat and hangs it on a coat rack. He unzips his windbreaker and follows suit. Their actions are slow and deliberate, intended to kill time.

"You should have dressed better," she says.

"I know." He looks down at his outfit. "I'm sorry. I kind of picked up quickly to catch an early bus. I slept in my clothes. My nice stuff is probably all wrinkled now anyway, but I can change." He nods toward his duffle bag.

She purses her lips.

"I meant you should have worn something warmer. You came from Charlotte, not Aruba. You know how crazy the weather is here this time of year. Don't they give you gloves in the seminary?"

Damn, she could be cutting. But he's too literal, that's what she used to tell him. Takes everything too seriously. He's been in her presence for nearly ten minutes now, and all they have managed to talk about was the weather, and he's already messed that up. He's discouraged and nervous.

"Don't worry," she says. "Tomorrow's supposed to be in the sixties."

"Nice place. Why'd you leave Brighton?"

"Change of scenery."

"You live alone?"

He follows her into the kitchen, where she goes for the teakettle on the stove and takes it to the sink, as though determined to carry out some daily afternoon routine. But she freezes with the empty kettle in her hand and leans against the sink.

"You kidding? I couldn't afford this space on my own. JP's gotten even more popular since you left. I have a roommate who could, however, but chooses to have company."

Male or female, he wants to ask, but doesn't.

"She should be home in a little while." She reads his mind.

"What does she do?"

"Tiffany? Oh, what day is it? She's finding her true passion. She really doesn't need to work, but she does want to be instrumental in contributing to society."

"What's she leaning toward?"

"Probably some sort of social service. She volunteers for an NGO peace organization that deals with disaster PTS, but they can't offer her a position without an advanced degree, and, well, she can't seem to decide where she wants to get that."

"Wouldn't be too hard in this town." Now he's filling time, solving a problem for some woman he doesn't even know.

"You would think not. But Tiffany is particular—that's the part of her breeding she can't shake. She's thinking of Tufts School for Diplomacy or Georgetown's Institute of Politics and Public Service.

It's new. Tiffany likes new when it comes to education; everything else she likes is old. The fact that she's loaded doesn't exactly push the envelope." She finally spins around and turns on the cold water, letting it run.

"Sounds like a do-gooder. Maybe she should be a Jesuit."

"Have I missed something? Has the church reversed its opinion on women priests? You Jebbies now accepting us?"

He thought he'd made a joke. He should have known better.

"No. They're not."

That he said *they* and did not include himself in his last statement was not lost on her for a second. She stands with her back to him for a moment, the empty teakettle in her hand, before she fills it and places it on the burner. When she turns around, her face is as flushed as his own, for his statement has shocked even him. And they smile at each other for the first time.

Chapter 15

Monday, March 17

RYAN KNEW ALL along he'd come back. At least that's what she tells Tiffany the following morning when Tiff questions the cell phone on the coffee table and the blue windbreaker and white sneakers in the foyer. That he didn't charge his phone and left it in the living room was new: Jason was not a man one had to pick up after; he was like her father in that respect, rendering attention to detail. If the cap was missing from the toothpaste tube after he got up this morning, she might even be elated. She always knew he'd come back, but she didn't know he'd come back this different.

When Ryan ran or worked out at the gym after their breakup, she used to listen on her iPod to an old Beatles song her mother had played when Ryan was small. Ryan had liked to study the album jacket: individual portraits of the quartet wearing funny sideburns and mustaches, one looking happy, the others pensive, or maybe even sad or troubled. She thought two were cute and two were ugly. Her mother said it was the last album they made together. "The Long and Winding Road" had been Ryan's favorite song, probably because it had been her mother's favorite, and some days Lauren used to move the arm of the record player back and drop the needle onto that track over and over again.

That's when Lauren got into her nostalgic mode and recounted how the Beatles had begun, how she'd first seen them on some program called *The Ed Sullivan Show* when she was twelve, how Faye had

130

laughed at the ridiculousness of the lyrics of their first song and their bowl-shaped haircuts, and how Ryan's father had adored them in college and purchased every one of their albums as soon as it came out. Whenever things got rocky and her parents' arguing frightened Ryan, Lauren would play the recording and soothe the girl, telling her that the long and winding road would never disappear no matter how much her parents fought, that it would always lead them back together again.

Ryan used to picture her parents meandering along a serpentine dirt road amid a dense green thicket of trees and bushes. What road? Where had it started? Where did it end? How could she get there? Of course now she interprets the metaphor exactly as her mother used to, and it fills her with an undeniable hope—no, affirmation—that fate played a role in it all, and that destiny had put Jason on that road back to her.

She had had to control herself when she first saw him sitting on the steps last night. Suddenly there was a God; prayers were answered; life existed after death. Why hadn't she washed her hair that morning? He loved the smell of her shampoo. Then again, maybe he was there to tell her some bad news: Her father was dead; there'd been a terrorist attack in Charlotte she hadn't heard about. She wanted to punch him. That would have felt good. But at the same time she wanted to wrap her arms around his neck and welcome this prodigal son—of a bitch. She became aware of her every action; she heard her father: *Listen, Ryan. Stop talking so much and listen.* So, Jason, what do you have to say for yourself?

He was here because he had doubts. Why no notice? Because he did not want to be dissuaded by any negative words or vibes she might have spoken or given off. He wasn't that courageous.

"I think I may have made a mistake, Ryan."

He'd said it. Before the tea water even came to a boil. The words she'd been longing to hear for nearly two years. He'd fucked up. He wanted forgiveness. He loved her. Well, she was jumping the gun a bit—*that* he didn't say. But he did seek redemption and a second chance. Would she? Could she find it in her heart to allow him this time to explore? Was he kidding? Would she ever.

They had intended to go out to dinner. Something simple, like Pikalo's, the Dominican spot on Centre Street, but the night got colder, really cold, and Tiffany never showed anyway, affording them the privacy they wanted. The prospect of leaving the hissing radiators and comfy navy blue mohair sofa with all of Tiff's geometric throw pillows made them put off going out. And how could she interrupt his talk about the seminary?

"Don't get me wrong. I don't feel out of place there. But there's no place for you. No. That's not it. You're everywhere there."

"You always said I took up a lot of space."

She sensed him studying her out of the corner of his eye while she strained to understand the words she seemed to draw out of him, because for all his talk of envisioning of her in his mind in the seminary, he couldn't look her in the eye when he had her there in the flesh.

"Am I keeping you from anything tonight?" he said, as though it had just occurred to him that she had a life, one he hadn't been part of for quite some time.

"Zumba." She could have said she had a date.

"Don't miss it on my account."

"I pulled a hamstring last week. Better to let it rest. Besides," she said, looking toward the window with its chipped paint, "it's cold."

She scrambled eggs while he buttered toast and sliced an avocado. She apologized for not having much food in the apartment; it was Tiffany's turn to shop. He poured two glasses of wine from an open bottle in the refrigerator and they took their plates and returned to the couch, where she sat with her legs tucked under her and he stretched his out on the coffee table.

"You have jelly on your lip," he said.

She wiped the corner of her mouth.

"You missed. Let me get it."

He extended his hand toward her face, but instead of aiming for the spot of jelly, he pulled her face toward his and kissed her in an action that surprised even him.

"It's gone," he said.

Seconds later he was lying on top of her, kissing her hard, his tongue playing with hers.

"Is this allowed?" she mumbled, coming up for air.

"I'm on leave."

"How much time do you have?"

"As much as we need."

"I mean away from the seminary."

"I just told you."

Then his hand was on her breast, cupping it, squeezing it so hard she winced. "Sorry," he murmured, his face in her neck, his hand continuing to find its way under her sweater, over her bra. She was aching. He was moving so fast, yet not fast enough.

She hesitated to invite him. She hadn't shaved her legs in a few days; she hadn't showered since morning; she felt self-conscious of the body she wanted to offer in perfection after such a long absence. It didn't bother her that *he* carried an odor of perspiration and hormones, and it certainly didn't seem to bother him. And there were clothes on the bedroom floor; she hadn't done laundry this weekend.

"Let's go to my room," she said anyway. Tiffany could walk in at any moment.

They were almost naked before they hit the full-sized mattress, his mouth devouring every part of her, the considerate restraint he'd shown in the past nowhere evident. He moved so aggressively she barely touched him, merely responded as he sucked her nipples, dragged his tongue all over her, and pulled down her panties. No matter they weren't the sexiest she owned; he never looked. When he maneuvered his mouth between her legs, all he had to do was touch her with his moist tongue and she was in spasms. He entered hard then, with all the force of a man who was near death and had this night and only this night to play out his fantasies. His fingers reached for her hardened nipples as for reassurance that he'd really satisfied her and she hadn't pretended. In view of where he'd been for so long, she allowed him anything, even if it caused her discomfort.

Afterward, he lay on top of her, panting for so long she had to nudge him off because she couldn't breathe under his weight. She cuddled up to him—so close she could smell herself on him—not wanting him to think she had rejected him in any way; he wrapped his arm around her. She prepared to fall asleep, happy for the first time in so many nights, when he turned toward her and began kissing her body all over again. Never had there been a repeat performance like this in their years together. He had gone away a gentleman and returned a cowboy.

* * *

"Where you going?" he asks as she hands him a tall glass of orange juice along with his cell phone and heads toward the shower.

"It's Monday. I have a job, remember?"

"Right."

"What are you going to do?"

"Reacquaint myself with the city, I suppose. Meet for lunch?"

"Maybe. Still have my number?"

"Actually I deleted it."

She comes back to the bed, picks up his phone, and enters her number. "I'll text you when I'm ready."

"I might camp out on your doorstep all morning."

"I wouldn't make a habit of that. They pick up vagrants. Oh, and in case you're wondering, Tiffany's already gone."

She kisses his naked, snow-white body goodbye and flies out the door a happy woman before he has a chance to pull her back down onto the bed. She is higher than a kite. This was so easy. Too easy. What would he have done if she hadn't let him stay the night? Call up a friend? He never had *a* best friend; *everyone* was his friend. Did he have enough money on him? Maybe she should have given him some.

* * *

He walks the neighborhood, taking in the narrow renovated clapboard homes with neat fenced-in yards and the large white-pillared mansions on the corner. Nannies push strollers. Fathers mimic pregnancy with infant carriers strapped to their chests; they march hand in hand with mitten-protected toddlers, as though setting out to backpack the Yukon. He could see himself as a stay-at-home dad, or maybe dropping the kids off at daycare.

He used to think there were enough children in the world needing surrogate fathers, and so he rationalized a future that included another deprivation—fatherhood. But there is so much he could teach a child; so much he could learn. He is feeling reborn himself, reborn and free. He stops at a small Cuban grocery store and buys rolls and ripe plantains and a can of black beans. He'll make some rice and beans and fry the sweet plantains for dinner. Ryan loves them.

He thinks about the roommate he hasn't met and buys more of everything. He stops in a packy and gets beer and a bottle of wine. After he deposits it in the apartment he showers, finds the least wrinkled shirt in his duffle bag, and heads for the T. By the time he surfaces at Downtown Crossing, it's already nearly sixty degrees and climbing, and he's glad he hadn't carried that old windbreaker with him; he feels light—lighter than he's felt in months.

The homeless are on the steps of St. Stephen's Episcopal on Tremont, the warm weather having driven them outside their cot shelter and deposited them onto the steps of the Greek Revival church, where they sprawl out, some of them shirtless, heads up to the heavens like guests in a sauna at some spa. His experience working with outreach programs has taught him that you can find more people in church basements nowadays than in the sanctuaries upstairs. One of the men smokes a cigarette while he studies Jason.

"Morning," Jason says.

"Seen you before."

He's young and white, with matted dark brown dreadlocks and a scruffy beard. His jeans are torn but not in the fashionable spots. In fact, Jason can see a bit of his penis through a hole near the broken zipper.

135

"Oh yeah?"

"Shelter in Roxbury."

"Really?" Jason volunteered in many shelters during his six years in Boston but Roxbury wasn't one of them.

"Just fuckin' with you, dude. Just fuckin' with you. Why the fuck would *you* be in a shelter?" He laughs, then coughs.

Jason wants to give him money, but he hesitates; he doesn't have much with him and he's not going to live off Ryan while he's here. Yet he wants to give—always has this desire to strip himself of his trappings, pare down, make others more comfortable. Sure, the guy might buy a heroin fix. But then again, he might get a burger. One never knows, but one has to try. One has to hope.

"Can I buy you a coffee?" Jason asks.

"Already had my cuppa joe."

Where R U? Ryan texts.

He's saved.

Be there in five.

He is looking in the window of the jewelry store next to the building where she works, eyeing the price of diamond rings and feeling lucky to have had access to his grandmother's when she taps him on the back. He spins around and hugs her but not too hard—he knows he was a bit rough the night before.

"Where to, legal lady?" He kisses her on the forehead.

"What're you up for? Pho? Mexican?"

"How about we get a hot dog and eat in the park?"

"Well, okay. If that's what you'd like."

"You don't want to?"

"Sausage sub works for me. There's a great stand on the corner of Washington Street—the couple gives extra onions and peppers."

As they sit on the bench, Jason pinches small pieces from his roll and feeds the pigeons. Before long, there's a flock pecking around the walk in front of them, flying overhead, and swooping down around them. A woman on the next bench gets up and moves a good distance away.

"Do they bother you?" he asks Ryan.

"I can live with it."

"Yeah, but does it *bother* you?" He never asked before if that sort of behavior annoyed her. He just assumed it shouldn't.

"I don't want to get crapped on. I washed my hair this morning."

"Let's move."

"It's more like give up the roll and move, unless we want company."

"Right."

He breaks off a large chunk, drops it on the ground, and pops the rest into his mouth. He picks up her bottle of water with one hand and grabs her hand with the other. It's got to be different, he thinks. This time has to be different. *I* have to be different.

"I'm surprised you didn't want to be a Franciscan."

"Why? Jebbies don't feed pigeons?"

"I just always saw you more as the St. Francis type."

"I like to think of myself as the Ryan type."

He puts his arm around her shoulder and kisses her head. She isn't that far off about the Franciscan thing. Jason met one who was on his way to an Earth Day gathering while he traveled to the novitiate, and he was taken by their commitment to protect the environment as stewards of all of God's creation. The brother talked about a new book that blended three interrelated disciplines: scientifically informed ecology, theology, and the practice of reflective action. There is something so self-effacing about the Franciscan friars, a humility to which Jason is drawn. But he is also drawn to the Jesuit legacy of intellectualism; he grew up with them as instructors. Which order could help him reach others best, the classroom or the street?

He reminds himself that he's here in Boston to see if he can accomplish his goals in yet another way—as a lay minister. Not at all impossible. The religious order of Maryknoll has lay couples—some even with families. All other denominations certainly do, just as Ryan insisted when he told her about wanting to become a priest. He's getting excited, a warm rush filling him as he walks through the Common with the woman he professes to love, a spray of forsythia on the border of the winding path—a yellow brick road—guiding them.

"How'd you like to see Faye?" She breaks his concentration. "She's in rehab with a broken hip."

"I'd love to see Faye."

"Tonight? After dinner?"

"Sure." He squeezes her shoulder, testing to see if she's really there—or if it's he who is there.

* * *

"Well, well, look what the cat's dragged in, and on St. Paddy's Day, no less. Hopefully you didn't bring bagpipers with you."

Faye is in the Multi Room, with its dark blue rug, patterned pinch-pleat drapes, and wing chairs set around a coffee table to simulate a living room. She's like a queen in the gilded wheelchair she got the young CNA Louis to spray-paint gold. Her knight, Harold, is in his own wheelchair to her right, while her lady in waiting—a woman named Ida with a chalky stark-white face—is to her left. They are focused on the large flat screen above the fireplace.

"I told you it was Steinbeck!" Faye cries out with satisfaction at having guessed the answer to Final Jeopardy, when all three of the contestants got it wrong.

"I could have sworn it was Hemingway," Harold says. "You should go on the show, Faye."

"I couldn't press the buzzer fast enough. I'm only good for Final Jeopardy."

"Way to go, Faye! I would have said Faulkner," Jason joins in.

"And you would have been wrong. Come." She motions to him. "Give me a kiss."

Another grandmother would have sat and waited for the boy to pay homage to her, but Faye makes it her business to put everyone at ease (a little too easily this time); besides, she carries so much passion with so little time to express it that she jumps at any chance to unload some of it. Jason, still hesitant, crouches beside her and takes her hand in his; she uses her free hand to cup his chin, pulling his face to hers, and plants a smacker on his cheek.

"Is that your son?" Ida asks.

"I don't have any sons. Just two daughters."

"And this is your daughter?"

"No, dear. This is my granddaughter." Ryan has met Ida several times before.

"Where's Sylvia?" Ryan asks.

There's an awkward silence and Faye grows serious.

"Gone," she says.

"Home?"

"If that's what you believe."

"Oh—I'm sorry."

"We come and we go," Harold says.

"It's like I've been telling you, *bubeleh*, we're like ice cubes melting on a hot summer's day. So—" She is determined to be upbeat: "What's cookin'?"

"Well, Jason is back."

"I can see that," she says. Faye has no intention of letting Jason off the hook. "By the way, Jason, I'm forgetting my manners. Meet Ida and my boyfriend, Harold."

A bit surprised at the last statement, Jason attempts to be as cool as Faye and gingerly clasps first Ida's, then Harold's hand.

"Did you and God have a spat?" Faye cannot resist.

Jason chortles. "I'm on leave."

"Jason is a priest," she explains to Ida and Harold.

"Are you here to say Mass?" Catholic Ida lights up. By the looks of her ghost-like complexion she must be thinking he's just in time.

"No. I'm not a priest yet. I've been in the seminary."

"This is your son?" Ida asks Faye again.

"No. This is my granddaughter's friend."

To the relief of all, an attendant comes to wheel Ida back to her room and get her ready for bed.

"Yesterday, after her husband left, she was asking for an exorcist. She said he was possessed. Saw pink smoke coming out of his head. Today she's a Kabuki dancer—made her face up with toothpaste instead of powder. Why don't you write about that?" Faye tells Ryan, then wastes no time cutting to the chase.

"So you're just visiting?" She's still smiling, but the smile is frozen with expectation. "Are you here to torture my granddaughter? Pick at old wounds? *That* I will not approve of."

"I'm considering leaving the seminary."

"You're breaking up with God?"

"Enough, Faye," Ryan says, although she can't say she isn't enjoying the grilling.

Jason motions to Ryan that's it all right. "It's only been a day."

Faye nods, dissatisfied with the answer.

"Then we'll be seeing a lot of you," Harold says, jumping in for the save. A typical guy thing, and just when Faye had Jason's hand to the fire.

"I hope so," Jason says.

"I hope so too. Not many of us around here." Harold is referring to the scarcity of men at the nursing home.

"It's not like we're moving in," Ryan tells him.

"Speaking of moving, there's something I've been meaning to tell you, Ryan. As soon as Harold and I are back on our feet and can shed these spiffy accouterments, we're moving into the new independent living section in the building next door. We've already put down our deposit on an apartment. It's a lovely one bedroom with one and a half baths and a little den if you want to stay over, and a screened in patio. Your mother and father promised to help clean out my house in Newton and put it on the market. Harold is selling his condo in Brookline. And did I tell you we were getting married?"

Jason looks at Ryan wide-eyed. She shrugs her shoulders as if to say: *Who knew?*

"Should I get a dress?"

"We'll just do it simply, *bubeleh*. Maybe at Anthony's Pier 4. Just the family and a justice of the peace. Harold is an atheist."

"It closed, Faye."

"Anthony's? When?"

"Not too long ago. I think there are condos there now."

"Oh, no! That was the place to go. We went there after your mother and your Aunt Robin's graduations. We went there for *your* graduation! The view of the harbor was the ultimate—so were the prices. But it was special. Do you know there was a photo of my husband with the owner?" she tells Harold and Jason. "He was an Albanian immigrant and my husband helped him get a loan to open his first big restaurant. Anthony Athanas, a little guy. My Sidney towered over him. And he never forgot Sid. There he was up on that wall with Athanas, alongside the likes of Liz Taylor and John F. Kennedy and Joe DiMaggio."

She shakes her head. This has really thrown Faye, who usually rides the waves of change with a lot more grace. "Where will we go, Ryan? Jimmy's Harborside is also gone," she says of the other flagship eatery on the pier, and Ryan fears for Faye, who seems to have been tossed into her own sea of confusion with the loss of these landmarks.

"Don't fret, Faye, dear. There must be other good restaurants in town." Harold looks up at Ryan and Jason for confirmation, making it obvious that of late he hasn't gotten out much either.

"There are some great new places," Jason tells them. He turns to Ryan. "What's that one by the seaport we went to with my mother?"

"That closed last summer."

"Already?"

"But there's another one a block away."

"It's good?" Faye asks.

"It's really good," Ryan says.

"Will you make the reservation, darling?"

"Of course, but for when? How many?"

"When, Harold?"

"How about in a couple of weeks. End of April?"

"Yes," Faye says. "April in Boston. We should be in our new place by then. Just your mother and father and Aunt Robin and Uncle Jake, if they can come all the way from Seattle. Your cousin Peter is in India, and Emma can never get away from her residency, so they're out. And you and Jason, of course, assuming you'll still be here. But that's it. Oh, and my friend Pearl—and Tilly, if her doctor lets her."

"What about your family, Harold?" Ryan asks.

"My daughters are estranged from me, and my son was killed in a car accident a long time ago. Unfortunately, I've never had grandchildren. But I will now."

At least the news has shifted the conversation away from her and Jason.

"I thought you didn't want to give up the house, Faye."

"Let's be practical here. I've come to my senses. I really won't be able to go on in that big place much longer. Let some young family make memories there. Besides, the food's pretty good here, don't you agree, Harold? So go to the house some day, take what you want. I'll be bringing some of the furniture and a few paintings and treasures. The rest is going to the Salvation Army, or whatever your mother wants to do with it. It's the new way, that Japanese thing about only keeping what you love." She smiles at Harold. "So, Jason, what do you think about this Brackton affair?"

He's bewildered.

"I guess you haven't told him, *bubeleh*."

"No, Faye. We haven't gotten that far." Ryan does not find Faye's bringing up the contest amusing.

"I didn't think so." Faye is pleased with herself for having let that cat out of the bag.

A little boy about two or three and his mother have been sitting with an older gentleman across the room, taking in an earful. As they wheel the man out, the boy approaches Faye.

"What's this?" he says, pointing to the forearm that rests on her lap. With its deep dry ridges, it resembles a Yule log, and Ryan cringes for the appearance-conscious Faye, who smiles at the child.

"Just a very old arm, sweetheart," she tells him. "Just a very old arm."

* * *

O'Hanrahan's has turned into the Emerald Isle, with glittery sham- rocks hanging from the ceiling and servers dressed as leprechauns amid a sea of green-clad clientele jammed into the small establish- ment. Jason and Ryan stand—pints in hand—at the crowded bar waiting for two stools to become available, but the possibility is slim here and at every other bar in Boston on this day. A young woman who looks like a cross between Peter Pan and Little Orphan Annie in her black tights and a skimpy green outfit Irish step dances on a makeshift stage and serves as a distraction from the issue at hand.

"I can see sending the essay," Jason says, continuing the conversation he began as they left the nursing home. "I mean, you like a challenge. But this wasn't a game."

"I never thought I'd win. It was a fluke. I thought the whole thing was lame anyway, and I have to admit, I read the ad in a weak moment."

He gulps down the last drop of his beer, wipes his mouth, and motions for the waitress to bring two more, although Ryan has only drunk half of hers. It was her idea to go to O'Hanrahan's, their St. Patrick's Day tradition, even though the holiday has never been high on her list of celebrations. But what is also in keeping with tradition is the fact that they find themselves in a crowd with a hot personal topic simmering between them.

"I don't know why you're so upset," she says, watching the dancer's legs bending at the knee and straightening like a jackknife repeatedly opening and closing.

"Ryan, you used my name. You implicated me."

"Relax. It's not like they're going to indict you."

He shakes his head, astonished at her logic.

"Okay. It was unethical. It was dishonest, and irresponsible, and downright mean to the citizens of Brackton. Fuck, Jason! Do you know what I've gone through the last year and a half? You pulled the fucking rug out from under me without warning. Sorry if I cared so much I couldn't erase three and a half years of a relationship from my mind—from my heart." The dancer's mountain of red curls are bouncing every which way as she jumps.

"I'm sorry," he says.

"No, *I'm* sorry. I was wrong. You're right—as usual." She stays fixed on the dancer.

"I mean I'm sorry I hurt you."

"You already apologized."

"I don't think I fully understood the toll it would take on you."

"How could you not?" she says, returning her gaze to him.

"Selfish, I guess." Now *his* eyes move to the dancer. "Wishful thinking. Made it easier on me."

"And would it have changed your decision if you had taken it into more serious consideration?"

"No." He stares into his glass.

"So there you have it. You did what you had to do, and I did what I did."

They have whittled away enough at their defenses (and drunk enough beer) to confront one another face-to-face.

"So what's the plan for Brackton?" he asks.

"Tell them the truth. What else?"

"You're playing your hand."

"You think I'm bluffing?"

"If you were going to come clean, you'd already have done it."

"So I'm stalling, is how you see it."

"Of course."

"Can't blame a girl for trying."

"You like the place?"

"Brackton? It was sweet. Different from what we're used to. A funky pastoral nowhere. And everything was paid for—even my dress. Even my manicure! It was an offer that was hard to refuse, as they say."

"How 'bout the rings? Were they included?"

"Just gold bands from a local who makes handcrafted jewelry."

"No engagement ring?"

"It's not exactly *The Bachelorette,* where they give away three carat diamonds. Anyway I told them I'd be using your grandmother's. I *am* bad." Her speech has become thick as she starts on her second pint.

"Well, we've still got that. You were nice enough to give it back."

Ryan waits for the waitress, who's come to take Jason's order for another, to leave.

"What are you saying, Jase?"

"I mean, it's not like we just met. God, we've known each other long enough."

"Who are you talking to?" Her eyes follow his up to the ceiling.

"Cut the shit," he says. "Don't read religion into everything, okay?"

"Okay. But you've been back a day, Jason. One day."

"Happier than I've been in I don't know how long."

"You weren't happy in the seminary?"

"I was—at times. But there was always this unrest. I couldn't sustain the happiness, the peace."

"That's not necessarily because *I* wasn't around."

"That's what I kept telling myself. I prayed for clarity. What am I supposed to do when my prayers are answered? Say, sorry, no thank you, you're mistaken. Is that faith?"

"You're asking the wrong person."

"Now you're a nonbeliever?"

"I am what I've always been—a bit of a skeptic, a bit of an agnostic. Why would you even want to be with me, come to think of it?"

"What happened to: We're perfect together? We balance each other out?"

""I've had to do my own soul-searching."

"What do you think of the new Pope?"

"That's random."

"Not really. I've been reading up on him. I love that he's a Jesuit, with the ideals of a Franciscan. He's like Buddha and St. Francis of Assisi in one."

"He's the Pope."

"But he's different. You like St. Francis, right? I remember you brought your grandmother Toscano that statue of him back from Assisi when we went to Europe."

She smiles. That was a happy time for them both. Just out of college, working odd jobs to earn money to travel. They were in step on that trip, leading one another through metros and ferry rides, maneuvering in different languages, depending on who had the better command at the time.

"He understands the church has to change to survive," Jason says.

"He talks a good line, and I do like him. But when it comes down to dogma, he hasn't changed anything. Can he? Can he make the church accept LGBT?"

She is more like a Jesuit than he is at times, always asking for data to back things up. "He says he can't pass judgment."

"That's not changing anything."

"There are celibate straight and gay men in the church who want to change things."

"Really? That's good, because my boss's lesbian sister just got fired from the Catholic school she teaches at. You're more optimistic than me, but then you always have been—about everything."

"It'll take time."

"All the Catholic schools will be closed by then. The churches too. He doesn't give me much hope."

"You think I'm just talking myself into something?"

"Nothing I'm not guilty of myself at times," she says laughing and holding up her hands.

"So when do we go to Brackton?"

"Jason, can't we just be for a while?"

"This is a real turnaround. Getting nervous now that I'm actually back? Isn't your time running out?"

"Fuck Brackton. This is *our* life."

"Ryan, I'm here with you. I'm happy. And I'm willing to make compromises—and a commitment. Nothing's perfect."

"What?" she asks, because the college guys at the bar have begun taking Fireball shots. Holding up their glasses, they let out a deafening toast of "Heyyyyy!" every ten minutes when one of them offers to buy a round.

"Nothing's perfect!" he shouts, putting his face directly in front of hers, inhaling his breath like the air from an empty ale keg.

"You're on a schedule. You can't stand not knowing what comes next. You need a plan. And you can't keep the Jebbies dangling forever." She takes a sip of beer. She's getting hoarse from competing with the boys and the music and the clicking of the dancer's hard shoes.

"They don't want me half in," he says.

"Nor do I."

"Seems like you've left your own party dangling in Vermont, babe." He smiles.

"They *are* dying to meet you, Jason," she says, as though about to give him new information. "Faye is getting married."

"Don't change the subject."

"Why would Faye do that at her age?"

"Why shouldn't she?"

"Jason, maybe he wants her money."

"I got the impression he's pretty well heeled, with no survivors to speak of. Where's he going to go with Faye's money, anyway? And if they go together, good for them."

"But why marriage?"

"You talking about them—or us? Look, I'm not afraid to go for it either. I just wasn't sure which ring to grab, excuse the metaphor. But I know now. Let's not lose any more time. You still have over three months to back out."

"And then just crap out on Brackton like that?"

"Weren't you going to do that anyway? Cut the shit, Ryan. You haven't been sitting on this whole thing for nothing. Look, if you change your mind, Faye and Harold can take our place. She was so distraught about Anthony's being closed, she'd be happy to get married twice. I asked you once before and I'll ask you again. Ryan Toscano, will you marry me?"

"Can't hear you."

He goes down on one knee, drawing the attention of those around them, including the boys at the bar. Taking her hand and shouting, he asks again.

Damn, he's good. Pleased-with-himself good. They've both spent enough time around the legal world to know how to persuade. In college he even managed to talk the dean out of failing a friend accused of plagiarizing. He knows he can go the distance, and it feels pretty fine. He won't stop until he wins.

"You know I will." Her answer brings clapping and another "Heyyyyy!" from the boys, who are really messed up by now and lifting their glasses because they're here to celebrate—anything.

"How about I go to Filene's basement tomorrow?" he says. "I can use some new outfits for the north country."

"You're so out of it." She laughs. "You've never been a shopper. Filene's closed a long time ago."

"Don't tell Faye."

"She already knows."

Chapter 16

RYAN HAS ALREADY left for work when Jason and Tiffany meet for the first time in the bathroom while he's taking a shower.

"Do you mind if I pee?" she asks, though he can hear she's begun to take care of business without his permission. "I won't flush. The water will scald you if I do."

That's considerate of her, he thinks, but then she begins to brush her teeth.

"Can you turn down the hot water some?" she asks. "The steam makes my hair frizz."

Now he's getting cold. He rinses quickly and turns off the water, assuming that's enough of a hint, but water is still running into the sink.

"Will you hand me a towel? I've been using the blue one," he says, sticking his hairy black arm around the edge of the shower curtain. He ducks a pair of dripping pantyhose flung over the rod to hang; the towel follows. He steps out of the tub to find her still standing there in an athletic T-shirt that barely covers her private parts. Arms folded, she leans against the sink, wiping away wisps of gray hair with pink tips that spout from an elastic band on the top of her head like burning lava and ash from a volcano.

"Nice to meet you, Jason. I've seen your picture."

"I've seen yours too, Tiffany. The one on the refrigerator. Except your hair is blue in it."

149

She nods. "In the one on my dresser it's green." She continues to size him up. "I'm making French toast. Gluten-free. Coffee or tea?"

"Actually, I don't drink either. There's some OJ in the fridge. I bought it yesterday." He wants her to know he's no moocher.

"Gotcha."

And she's gone.

He was about to tell her to help herself to the juice, but it's apparent that she won't have any scruples about doing that if she so desires.

Dressed in a clean pair of jeans and a collared shirt that resembles graph paper, he is surprised to see the table neatly set when he enters the kitchen. Ryan was never particular about that, even when they had company. Like her mother, she never makes the bed either. He's relieved to see that Tiffany has put on a pair of leggings.

"Nice," he says. "Real napkins."

"They're cloth. All napkins are real."

"Right. But they're special. Nice flowers." He's referring to the sunflower print on the napkins, which he couldn't care less about.

"It's how I am, Jason. They match the flowers." She points to a tall green vase in the center of the table.

"Wow. Yeah. I see that."

"You should wear the shirt outside of your jeans."

"What?"

"You shouldn't tuck in your shirt. It's casual. You're not going to work. Or are you?"

"No. No work—yet." He starts pulling the shirt out of his pants.

"Do it quickly so it doesn't wrinkle."

"I'm afraid all my clothes are pretty wrinkled."

"It's a good length, though—you want mid-fly. But it's a little too relaxed; needs to be more tapered. Next time, buy a slim fit. The jeans are nice."

"My mother gave them to me."

"Great taste."

"That's what everyone says."

She pours herself a steaming mug of coffee and sits at the table. "*This* is real," she says, passing him a petite crystal pitcher of syrup. "From Vermont."

"Oh yeah. Ryan told me you went up there with her."

Tiffany smiles. At least his mentioning Vermont seems to have pleased her.

"So what'd you think?" he asks.

"About what?"

"The free wedding. The whole thing." He helps himself to two perfect triangles of French toast.

"My parents have a friend whose family was Scientologist. When he and his wife got divorced, he left the religion. That was the end of his family for him, because you can't have a relationship with anyone who leaves. Then the wife and daughter ask him to pay for the daughter's wedding: apparently that is allowed. He refused to pay. They wanted this free wedding."

"I see." Ryan has not nearly prepared him for Tiffany.

"My point is that money isn't everything. You were a fucking asshole. The fact that Ryan's been pining for you all this time has been painful to watch and very disconcerting. Do I have to go to confession for saying that to you?"

He swallows quickly so as not to choke on the laugh he can't hold back and shakes his head more in disbelief than as an answer.

"Good. Because I'm not Catholic."

"So, Jason—Father—what do I call you?"

"It's Jason."

"How long will you be staying?"

"I know it's an imposition, but if it's okay with you, I'd like to stay until I get a job and Ryan and I can get a place of our own. If that's what Ryan wants."

"Stay as long as you like. Like I'm in and out these days."

"Can I ask you something?" He realizes Tiffany and Ryan haven't known each other all that long, but women are quicker than men to share intimate information. "You think we have a chance?"

She looks directly into his blue eyes. "Jason, I'm a believer in fate—karma. Things will turn out the way they should. And I hope it's what makes Ryan happy." She carries her half-finished plate to the sink. "Have to get to my kickboxing class."

"I'll clean up."

"Thanks. I was hoping you would. Good talking to you."

It troubles Jason that she has doubts about his and Ryan's relationship. She knows things, this woman.

* * *

He uses his phone to check email: no word from Father Curran, no word from any of the other novices. Not that he expected to hear from them. That was the deal: no communication. They were putting up a fence. Some might say they were giving him space, but the Society of Jesus looked at it differently. It was the same way they had looked at the three-month technology fast inflicted on novices, which wasn't meant to eradicate modern technology from their lives, since each one of them owned a cell phone and had a computer in his room. It was understood that they could keep up long-distance relationships and watch movies other than the limited selection offered in the seminary. The fast was aimed at having them learn the *value* of those modern tools, while concentrating on what was essential and on forming new relationships.

Some novices complained that the fast was equivalent to being castrated, but Father Curran and other advisors looked at it as a form of education. They needed to learn to relish their prayer time as an encounter with God, an encounter more satisfying than any film or video game. They needed to give themselves in totality to new relationships, which would be more difficult if they continued to be too involved in their former ones. They had to learn that technology couldn't give order to life, but that it was life that had to order technology.

Now Jason was engaged in another fast, the inverse of the one instituted within the seminary. He was being urged to fully immerse himself in this outer world and use technology at his own discretion, to restrict relationships within his newfound religious family and dive into an old one. And he was being asked to decide, with every step, how to establish order in his life.

There is an email from his mother—the weekly one he's limited her to. She agrees with his taking a break from the novitiate and will support his decision either way; that's how she's always been. She has one question for him: Did he get ashes on Ash Wednesday? There's usually a method to her madness; she is one of the few whose vision is not limited to seeing things the way she would like them to appear. He makes an exception to his rule and calls her.

"Got your email, Mom."

"What about the ashes? Did you get them too?"

"Of course."

"And did you wipe them off afterwards?"

"Why would I do that?"

"Maybe you've become ashamed of your faith. Of having put so much on the line for something you're not sure of."

"I changed my mind about my vocation—not my faith," he says, trying to mask annoyance.

"So it's a done deal?"

"Pretty much." A long silence follows; she knows him better than he cares to admit.

"Are you anxious about you and Ryan?" she asks.

And now it is *he* who hesitates.

"It's all right," she tells the man who, as a little boy, suffered tummy aches about how he might have mistreated others, or not lifted them up when they needed to be lifted, or not listened to them enough. "One can always make a case for doubting. Whatever you decide— or *have* decided, Jason. It's OK. Thank you for calling. I'll email next week. Love you."

"Love you too, Mom."

No word yet from his brother, who is saving tortoises in the Galápagos and who is on the monthly (sometimes two-month) email plan. His brother has no use for social networking, does not do well with human networking in general. Nothing from his father; hardly ever is. He's only seen him annually since the divorce eight years ago. Once a year is okay. Any more and Jason would become too demanding, and his father (who finds Jason a bit soft) would probably stop seeing him altogether. His father is a loner, and Jason accepted that a long time ago.

There is a freedom in not having to attend 5 p.m. Mass, not having to meditate or read or play according to schedule. He's like a kid who at the end of June anticipates a lazy summer. He does miss some of the guys, but this isn't Scientology, and he'll be in touch with them again in time. He has no need to meet up with any old friends in the Boston area. As Ryan used to say, he was a friend to everyone yet intimate with no one—but her. Still, like that kid who has been programmed with seven hours of school, several more after-school, and a weekend of sports and other outside activities, he soon finds himself lost and guilty. It's as though he's wandering through that familiar nightmare, searching for the class for which he has missed an entire semester of lectures and now faces the final exam.

He picks up a bottle of Ryan's perfume from the dresser, closes his eyes, and takes in a deep breath. He meditates—on her—and he feels himself swelling and rising, threatening to burst out of his pants. A racehorse at the gate. Christ emerging from the tomb. He is sacrilegious. Pure animal. Everything is overlapping, blending. Keep moving, keep moving, he tells himself, like a freight train that cuts through the scenery, reducing it to a blur, and leaving it to fall behind in a new order. Keep moving. That's the mantra that allowed him to leave Ryan in the first place. Keep moving until it all falls into place. And so he heads to Downtown Crossing to lunch with Ryan, to a new store that she said has unbelievable bargains, to the neighborhood with the only church he knows that will be open at this hour.

The moment he enters St. Stephen's he's calmed with the familiar scents of snuffed-out beeswax candles; the sweet-smelling incense burned at high masses and benedictions and funerals; the stale cigarettes of the homeless who must leave their shelters in early morning and continue their sleep on the hard mahogany pews. Is there ever an end to craving what has gone before and no longer exists—out of sight, out of reach? He is worse than an addict: so many cravings that can't be satisfied beyond the moment. No sooner has he satiated one than another makes itself known.

Keep moving. Keep moving. He fixes his gaze on the crucifix hanging above the altar, mindful of the pulsing at his temples, the dryness in his throat. He closes his eyes. Images pass by him. He lets them flow, until he is unaware of the traffic outside, of the light shining through the stained-glass windows, of the elderly woman kneeling in front of the statue of the Blessed Virgin, fingering her rosary beads, muttering Hail Marys.

He drifts into an abyss of peace, and then the phone he should have silenced sounds like a doorbell with a text from Ryan: *Can't make lunch. Working on a deadline. Go shopping. U can do it. Okay,* he texts back, writing the word out in full. He doesn't like it when people use letters for words like okay and you. He wishes Ryan didn't. He scrolls the emojis to seal his text with lips, but he hesitates. How ridiculous is that? They've made love every night since he returned. Still he refrains and uses a smiley face. She didn't seal hers with a kiss.

At dinner that night, over the shrimp scampi and angel-hair pasta she'll make him, and the salad and garlic bread he'll prepare with his signature dressing (his only dressing), and the cabernet sauvignon he'll spring for and uncork and wonder about how long it should breathe, he'll tell her how he maneuvered through the second-hand designer discount store all by himself. He'll haul out his booty bought at unbelievable savings and put on a credit card. And he'll express concern about how little the worker in some Southeast Asia sweatshop was paid. And she will too.

They'll discuss the benefits and liabilities of a global market, pour themselves the last of the wine, and drop the subject. Sitting there together in a familiar domestic bliss, glad that Tiffany isn't there, they'll feel good, and so good he won't tell her that he went to speak with the people from the outreach program at Driscoll and not to the registrar's office at the law school. He won't tell her that he doesn't think he's likely to return to law at all; rather maybe get a doctorate in philosophy, which will prolong his studies at least another five or six years. He'll ask her if she minds going to Brackton without the engagement ring he's got to get back from his mother, who lives in Boulder now. He'll tell her this and, moving on, he'll take her to bed.

Chapter 17

T HANK YOU, GOD. Thank you for not letting me send that email to Eric Boulanger. She was referring to the contrite note she had written just prior to Jason's appearance on her front stoop. She says *Thank you, God* a lot when she feels saved by some extraterrestrial power, though she isn't really sure whom she's actually thanking. Yahweh? An enlightened being like Jesus or Buddha? The morning after their talk at O'Hanrahan's on St. Paddy's Day, she deleted the confessional email waiting in her Drafts and wrote a new one:

> *Hi Eric,*
> *Forgive me for not responding sooner. As I explained in my earlier emails, we have been experiencing many complications that have prevented us from setting a date to come to Brackton. You know how it goes: life happens. However, our path has been cleared some and we should be able to pinpoint a date to visit very soon. Once again, please apologize to the vendors for me, and do tell them we're anxious to finalize our plans. We'll be in touch again very soon.*
>
> *Warmest regards,*
> *Ryan*

Friendly yet respectful, but not legalese in any way: something her friends accuse her emails of being. She did use a colon and thought about rewriting that sentence, but, as a former English major, she was a stickler for good grammar. Apologetic, but not offering any concrete excuses or information. Casual (their indiscreet encounter had no negative effects) but not diminishing their new friendship in any way—made clear by the closing. She did not save this email to Drafts; rather, she could not click Send fast enough. Done. Let the chips fall where they may with Jason, but her intuition on this one was a good one—better than good.

His response was short and to the point:

Hi Ryan,
Great to hear from you. We've all been wondering how things were going for you two. We are also eager to set plans in motion. Let me know when you're coming as soon as possible and I'll reserve a room at the Daffodil. I look forward to hearing back from you soon.

Best,
Eric

If he was harboring ill feeling toward her, he didn't express it, although the one-paragraph email with no spacing clearly smacked of annoyance or carelessness. He might have closed it with *Warmest regards*, or maybe just *Warm regards*, or even *Best regards*. Why should she have deserved more? What did she expect? At least he used a closing *and* a greeting, and hadn't jumped into conversational speech or ended with the trendy *Cheers* she found so annoying: after all, they weren't in England.

It had taken her another two weeks to follow up on that email. This time she had to be sure, and when she wrote back, she was:

Hi Eric,
Forgive me for yet another delay, but Jason and I would like to set a date for us to come to Brackton. Hopefully the lapse between emails has given the vendors extra preparation time. How does April 12 sound? We plan to leave Boston early morning.
Since we'll only be coming for Saturday, no accommodations will be necessary. I'm sure we can decide on everything in one day and make up for any lost time.
Best,
Ryan

She used his closing this time. His follow-up came in less than ten minutes and nearly froze her computer with its brevity. He had probably been put off by their not staying over, but she really did feel somewhat awkward about seeing Eric again, and the shorter the time around him the better.

Saturday, April 12 it is. I'll meet you at Licks & Relics.
Text me when you're passing Rutland to give me a heads-up.
Eric

Chapter 18

Saturday, April 12

"YOU DIDN'T HAVE to wait for us outside," Ryan tells Eric as they step from their vehicles pulled up to Licks and Relics on this wet and chilly morning.

"Just got here myself. I appreciate your coming so early. You must have left at the crack of dawn."

Eric and Jason shake hands as they stand, rain dripping off the hoods and visors of their slickers and down their faces. Eric's eyes do a quick body scan of Jason. He's surprised, Ryan thinks, to find Jason a good three inches taller than himself. She's glad Jason has a strong handshake to match that of muscular Eric's grip.

"We have a lot of time to make up for," Ryan says.

"Yes we do," Jason says.

Eric takes a direct jab at Ryan. "Find us okay? Been awhile."

"The GPS knew the way," she says.

"Let's get you some coffee and breakfast first and discuss the itinerary."

She is heading for the door of the shop when Eric suggests they could go to the Brackton Inn, if they prefer.

"This is just fine."

She hopes Eric finds her more enthusiastic about the wedding than on her first rip. She might even detect a bit of regret on his part to see her so happy, but then again, she might be conjuring that up. Hadn't she told him not to be sorry?

"Here all right, Rochelle?" Eric asks, looking around and pointing to a café table next to the window. A teenage girl with chin-length hot-pink hair and her boyfriend are the only other customers in the small shop. Rochelle, a short, thin woman older than Ryan's mother, is wiping down the counter lined with vintage red-leather-cushioned stools. Her dry, over-bleached hair sits like a haystack atop her head—maybe for extra height. A barrel-gutted guy with a full gray beard is scraping off the grill in a stained white chef's jacket and black cap that resembles a bandana with ties hanging down the back of his neck. Ryan guesses he rides a Harley.

"Sure. Anywhere's good, Eric. Not too many coming out in this weather this morning."

He can no longer hold off asking. "Where's Danni?"

"You don't know?"

"Know what?"

"Broke her leg, the poor thing, in three places skiing yesterday. Had to have surgery."

Ryan hears him mutter "fuck" under his breath as he goes into the pocket of his jacket for his cell.

"Where'd they take her?"

"Rutland Regional."

"That's too bad," Ryan says, draping her raincoat over the back of the antique bistro chair that creaks with every move she makes. "She was very helpful." She is really kind of glad Danni won't be there. It was irritating the way she gushed over Eric, making sure to let Ryan know how well she knew him.

"She likes to take time away from the shop in winter, summer's so chaotic," Eric says. "Excuse me a minute."

He steps outside to where she has a view of him standing underneath the awning, talking on his phone. When he returns, he seems to force that seductive grin of his, but it doesn't match the distance of those squinting eyes.

"Everything okay?" Jason asks.

"Yeah, considering," he says.

"End of the season's a dangerous time," Jason says.

"Best time, worst time," Eric says. "We thought you might bring Tiffany to help. Will she be an attendant?"

Everyone was always asking for Tiffany. "No attendants, except my cousin for maid of honor. That's it."

Ryan hasn't yet asked Emma if she'll be able to get away from the hospital for several days, but she knows that if it's possible, Emma will make it happen. That's why Emma is a doctor and Ryan is writing someone else's briefs for fish farms.

"How about you, Jason?"

"My brother is best man—if he can get back from the Galápagos."

Rochelle stands beside them, no pen and pad in hand. "What'll it be?"

"I'll have a cappuccino." Ryan picks up the laminated one-page menu and studies the options.

"Oh, we don't have cappuccino. Just regular coffee, honey."

"That's fine. And I'll take two eggs scrambled with wheat toast. Do you have wheat?"

"Sure do. Bacon or ham?"

"Neither, thanks."

"Hash browns?"

"No, thank you."

"Comes with it."

"Take it, Ryan. I'll eat what you don't want," Jason says. "And I'll have a cheese omelet and orange juice, please."

"Bacon—"

"I'll take it all, thank you."

Ryan stares at him.

"Can't help it. I'm starving. We didn't want to waste time stopping on the way," he says.

Eric laughs. It's a generous pleased-with-Jason laugh, and Ryan is starting to feel like the only outsider.

"Just coffee—and a cinnamon raisin bun, Rochelle. Already ate at home," he says.

"Got that, Phil?" She yells to the cook as she collects the menus.

"Yes, ma'am."

"Hey Rochelle, I'm gonna shave off half my hair," the teenage girl shouts out. The boyfriend laughs.

"Do it while you're young, honey."

"I'm thinking of my right side."

"Oh, but that's your *good* side," Rochelle says and winks at Eric.

* * *

At exactly 10:15 Eric deposits Ryan at Trousseau Bridal Shop, where Fran Costantino has just opened her store that looks like a wedding venue, with beige-and-lilac-patterned carpeting and artificial flowers and bridal veiling draped over a white arbor that leads to the dressing rooms. Fran has several dresses in Ryan's size lined up on a rack, and Ryan has to admit that the gowns are way more elegant than the cheesy ones displayed in the window of Mirabella's Couture on Tremont Street across from the Boston Common. Eric offers to take Jason to Neat 'n Tidy Cleaners to pick out tuxedos to rent. Jason prefers suits or even just khakis and collared shirts without ties, but Eric explains the necessity of using as many vendors as possible, and ties really do make a statement. They'll be back for Ryan at eleven. "Not enough time," Fran says. They agree on eleven forty-five. Half a day already gone, but, as Fran says: "This is one of the most important selections you'll make."

"Are these my only choices?" Ryan asks as Fran pulls out gown after gown. "I was thinking of something plainer."

"A lot of women think they want a particular style they've seen in a bridal magazine and then end up with something totally different once they've tried a couple on."

And so she complies with Fran's help, but still isn't wowed: too frilly, too many ruffles, too revealing, too heavy, too much scratchy beadwork, too-too.

"Do you have anything that wasn't made in some overseas sweatshop or in a way that's harmed the environment?"

"I don't deal with fair-trade companies, if that's what you mean. Not that I wouldn't like to. It's just too costly for me. Not many brides are willing to pay the high prices. Well-made gowns are expensive enough. But I carry a lot made of silk and heirloom lace, which is sustainable *and* eco-friendly. Silk uses very little water and chemicals, unlike the polyester that so many cheaper gowns are made of."

"How about that one? Is it silk?" Ryan points to a dress on a mannequin in a corner of the store.

"It just came in. But it's used, and not your size."

"Can't it be altered?"

"Again, it's a secondhand. I thought you'd like a new one. After all, it's on the house. And there isn't much time to make alterations."

"Something old, something new, right?"

"I guess that works." Fran shrugs.

The gown is too large, which is a good thing because there's room for adjustments. Fran takes some clothespins and clips them down the back. Now the dress starts to take shape on Ryan's body as she gazes into the three-way mirror at yards of the palest blush-pink silk with a sweetheart neckline that reveals just the slightest mound of her white breasts. The skirt falls softly from a fitted bodice into a subtle flair. Straps of the most delicate lace extend at an angle over her shoulder into what Fran calls illusion capped sleeves.

"I love it!"

"Well, because of the simplicity it shouldn't take too much time to alter. My mother helps me out. How's the length?"

"I don't like the train."

"Good. Because the dress is a bit short, especially with any kind of heel, even a wedge. We'll cut the train off and attach it on the bias with a false hem. My mother and I will figure something out so it looks like it's always been part of the design."

Ryan can see that Fran adores her work—and her mother.

"All done, with time to spare," Fran announces after taking the final measurements. "How about a cup of tea? Earl Gray okay?"

"Perfect."

Ryan loves this lady. She takes a seat on one of two richly upholstered purple chairs. After Fran returns carrying a tray with tea and biscotti that she places on a bronze-and-glass coffee table, they discuss the headpiece. Ryan doesn't want a veil or hat. She doesn't want anything.

"You should have *something* on your head to finish it all off. Talk to Maisie the hairdresser about flowers when you decide on a hairstyle. Oh no! We forgot your maid of honor! What size is she?"

"A six I think."

"What color would you like her to wear?"

Ryan hadn't thought about it at all. "How about black?"

"Kind of passé, or better for a black-tie wedding."

Fran disappears into another room and returns with a long shimmering champagne dress with a draped neckline and spaghetti straps. "I have this in a six. You can go neutral all the way, with white roses for centerpieces, or you can bring a burst of different colors into the room. If she's got your hair, she'll be smashing."

"She doesn't, but we don't want her to be too smashing anyway."

Fran laughs. "If she needs any alterations, she'll have to get them done on her own. Do you want to take it to her, leave it here, or should I send it to her?"

"Oh, I won't be seeing her before the wedding. You should send it. That way she'll be able to find shoes in time."

"Done. Leave me her address."

"I'll have to email it to you when I get home."

By the time the men return, the rain has stopped and Fran's next appointment has shown up. Eric whisks Ryan and Jason off to Gold Mine Jewelers, where they quickly settle on an etched antique white-gold band for Ryan, to accompany Jason's grandmother's diamond, and a plain gold band for Jason. The jeweler, Ralph O'Leary, will engrave the rings with the date.

They pass on lunch, since Jason had stuffed himself at breakfast and Ryan had a snack with Fran, and head over to Maisie's A Cut Above Hair Salon, where another local photographer, Sarah Bentley, turns up with her albums and brochures to save them time. Ryan shows Maisie a photo she took of the wedding dress, and Maisie plays with her hair—lifting, parting, and pinning—and decides on a style that will best complement the shape of Ryan's face and the dress: an upsweep to the side, a deep wave across the forehead with tendrils around the face for softness, a strand of rosebuds intertwined in the chignon. Jason selects the photography package: one large album, two miniatures (one for his mother and one for Lauren and Joe), and two 8 x 10s (one for Ryan and Jason, and one for Faye).

"Would you like me to do your makeup?" Maisie asks.

Noting the thick layer of pancake that coats Maisie's delicate skin, Ryan says: "I can handle it."

Afterward, the guys go for some spicy wings and a beer at Baby's Bar & Grill, but Ryan prefers to move on to Plantasia Florist, since Jason has no opinion on flowers or invitations except for what they will say: *Together with their parents, Ryan Toscano and Jason McDermott happily invite you to celebrate their marriage with them on June 28th,* etc. That's the perfect way, he said, to honor their parents and not alienate anyone. Ryan chooses a white parchment card that has a vine running around the border.

"Plants and flowers are not the only motifs," Annie Chalis seems compelled to tell her. "Animals and insects also carry symbolic meaning. Birds signify wisdom and joy, hope and beauty; butterflies, transformation. The dolphin is a sign of love—"

"The dolphin? People have dolphins on their invitations?"

"Even horses. They indicate vitality and beauty."

"I'll stick with flora and fauna." Ryan can only imagine what Faye would say upon finding a horse on her wedding invitation.

One hundred and twenty-five guests—that's what she's allowed. Ryan likes it that the vine will also appear on the upper left-hand corner of the envelope.

"How about the seating?" Annie asks. "Some couples like their tables to have themes and not just numbers, something they identify with, like cities or national parks or ballparks they've visited, or mountains they've climbed. Two high school guidance counselors had colleges and universities."

Ryan can't think of anything that might distinguish them except MBTA stops, but that seems ridiculous for a wedding taking place in Vermont. "Numbers will be fine," she says.

"Let's carry the vine theme on the place cards," Annie says, "and trim the tabletops with a little ivy."

"That might be nice." Ryan doesn't want to offend her, but she fears the dining room may look like a jungle. "We're pretty short on time, so the guests can RSVP by email. I like the idea of saving postage and paper."

"Stick with snail mail. It's classier," Annie says, and winks.

When Jason and Eric pick her up at Plantasia, Ryan encounters two old buddies who have clearly had more than one brew, and as the day wears on, Ryan has to admit that even she and Eric have fallen back into an easy place, their misstep clearly a thing of the past. Jason, as expected, has made good on his promise not to let on about the seminary and expose Ryan. As far as Eric knows, he's been in between jobs even having tried law school on for size. He doesn't lie about his being in the world of finance; he just doesn't mention it.

They make a quick stop at Decadent Delights, where Claire Bellerose, who has offered favors for the guests, presents half a dozen chocolate samples cut in two on a doily-lined silver dish. Ryan becomes queasy after too much sugar on an empty stomach, and they leave undecided. As they walk to Heavenly Bakeshop, she babbles on about the tea rose and white rose bouquet, the rosebud boutonnieres to match the flowers in her hair, and the centerpieces of roses and irises, only to have Eric and Jason revert to their lunch conversation about the Red Sox: three weeks into the season and still riding high on last year's World Series Championship, they're growing concerned over the team's last-place start.

Out of the blue Eric asks: "Hey, what about transportation? A limo? A horse and buggy? A pedal rickshaw?"

"Transportation to where?" Jason asks.

Eric would never have thought about half of this stuff either if he hadn't been living and breathing this event with the Chamber for nearly a year and if he hadn't photographed his share of weddings. "To the ceremony and back to the Daffodil," he tells them.

They haven't decided where the ceremony will take place. Jason would like it to be in a Catholic church with a Mass, Ryan outdoors at the Daffodil, with a friend or her uncle Vincent officiating. They agree on the church without a Mass, and Eric is surprised at how fast they can come to an agreement.

"Hello, we've known each other a long time," Jason says. "If you can't compromise on the ceremony, what can you compromise on?"

"I'll let Father Rivera at St. Anne's know. That's it over there." Eric points to a high white steeple in the distance.

"He'll probably want us to do Pre-Cana classes," Jason tells Ryan.

"What?"

"Sessions to help you prepare for marriage. I don't know much about them."

"We're not taking any classes, especially from a priest. We did Pre-Cana for three years." Ryan is adamant.

Eric smiles and takes a few steps away. He appears to be relieved to see a bit of dissension that indicates they *are* normal after all.

"Some dioceses have them online."

"No, Jason. You see, I knew having it in church would create problems."

"Given the time constraint and the distance from where we live, I'm sure the diocese will make an exception. That's if they even require it. I'd like to stop in to take a look. Is the rectory there too?" he calls over to Eric, who has been checking his email.

"To tell you the truth, I really don't know. My dad never went to church, and my mother took me to a Baptist one out of town."

"We'll check it out before we leave."

Ryan has lost her appetite for choosing a cake and sulks all the way to the bakery, where Lisa Anderson is waiting for them with inch-sized squares that she keeps in the freezer for tastings and a large photo album of cake towers that Ryan vaguely remembers flipping through on her first visit. As they arrive, Jason is distracted by the young woman standing out front—the same girl Ryan saw on her previous visit. Her face is expressionless, her body ever so still as she stares into the shop window. But at what? Her eyes don't scan the long-stemmed caked dishes. She just stares at something that doesn't seem to be there, her hands resting on the handlebars of the rusty bike alongside her.

"Wait a second." Jason steps toward the girl, his hand already in his pocket.

"She's not hungry. Trust me," Eric says.

Jason searches Eric's face for an explanation.

"She's fine, Jason. We need to go in. Lisa's waiting."

It's almost 6 p.m. by the time Eric suggests that they head over to the Daffodil for dinner, a meal that will also serve as their sampling of the reception fare, but Jason urges Ryan to check out St. Anne's first. Eric offers to drive them, but Jason and Ryan prefer to walk.

"Call me if you want me to pick you up. It's a good way back to the Daffodil."

They are intent on meeting him there. This requires private time.

"We should have come earlier," Jason says, reading the schedule of Masses inside a glass case next to the whitewashed double doors. "There was a Mass at four. We might have caught Father." He is surprised to find the doors still open.

The bland white clapboard exterior conceals an interior that is surprisingly ornate. The dark wooden pews seem to have been carved out of the church itself, as though the building might have begun as a giant piece of solid wood. The effect is of a bowl that tilts downward toward the altar, more like a Victorian theater rather than a house of worship.

"I've never seen these in a Catholic church before," Jason says, pointing to the worn velvet pew cushions that once matched the faded crimson carpet. "We're way too into penance."

The clear beveled-glass windows contain intricate patterns but no religious depictions. There are four Corinthian pillars—two in the front and two in the rear of the little church—that Ryan imagines Annie Chalis will have a ball wrapping ivy around. Better than bringing in galloping horses, though releasing some butterflies in the church could be a nice touch. Several real wax candles—not electric ones—are flickering on a metal rack to the right of the altar.

"Must have been built for another denomination," Jason surmises. "The confessional looks like an add-on." He points to three plain wooden doors in the rear.

"Can you do that—go from one denomination to another?"

"Why not? Look what's been happening: one day a cathedral, next day a shopping mall."

"Ooh, people will like this!" Ryan has turned in a full circle and is taken with the choir loft, also bowl shaped, featuring an organ with ranks of tall pipes.

"But do you?"

She really can't decide. The timelessness of it all makes her dizzy and claustrophobic, yet there is a certain solemnity that draws her, that sanctions the step they are about to take.

"Maybe we should look downstairs for Father ... what was his name?" Jason says.

"Rivera. Let's not. We have to meet Eric, and I'm starving. We can call him."

* * *

Eric is waiting for them at the bar in the lobby of the Daffodil House, chatting it up with two sunburned young women with long blond hair. He must have showered, because he's changed into a black fleece, the collar zippered into a turtleneck, that gives him a more artistic look—like a poet or movie director—and his hair is shining and neatly parted to the side. It bothers her that the flirtatious women are into him. Crazy. When he sees Ryan and Eric, he excuses himself and heads over. He's wearing the familiar scent of cologne that reminds her of the darkroom.

"We don't want to interrupt," Ryan says, moving closer to him until their arms are touching.

"All good. Skiers. Mark and Karen couldn't be here tonight, but they've got a nice selection of entrees for you to try. Can I get you a drink?"

"Not for me, thanks," Jason says. "Long drive back."

"How about you, Ryan?"

"I'll have a glass of red wine. Jason likes to take the wheel."

"Make yourselves comfortable. I'll tell your waiter you're here so you can get going." He leads them to a table next to a blazing fire in the fining room.

"Aren't you eating with us?" Ryan asks.

"I hadn't planned to. Thought you could use some private time."

"Sit down, Eric," Jason says. "We've got the whole trip back to ourselves."

"Okay, then. I'll just let my mother know." He takes out his phone and heads toward the bar.

"His mother's sick," Ryan tells Jason.

"I know. He told me about it."

Ryan would like to have heard how Eric talked to another guy about his mother.

When he returns from the lobby or the men's room or wherever he went, Eric points toward the terrace. "The reception will be out there under a tent."

"And if it's raining?" Ryan asks.

"There are sides to the tent that can come down, and it can be heated if necessary. They can also open that wall of French doors and add the dining room to make it one big space, but give it a warmer, cozier feel. I went to a wedding here where that happened, and it was fine."

"We decided to have the ceremony at St. Anne's, unless they've already got a wedding that day and time."

"You can still have the cocktail hour out on the terrace here."

Jason takes a warm roll from the basket the waiter has brought, breaks it in half and begins to butter it.

A platter of popcorn shrimp, mini egg rolls, chicken skewers, and stuffed mushrooms appears. Good, Ryan thinks, but nothing to write home about. Eric senses her lukewarm reaction.

"Remember, there's a long list to choose from." He hands her the manila envelope he's been carrying. "Everything's here: brochure of the place, pictures of the rooms, the catering menus. This is just a tasting, remember. It'll be a big buffet."

Too bad you can't sample a few years of marriage, the way you can wedding food: a PowerPoint of variations on how life together might turn out; a baby for a month; photos of how you could look in old age.

"These sirloin tips are outrageous!" Jason says.

Ryan isn't even aware that the waiter has brought over a small platter of them, along with one of chicken Milanese and another with herb-encrusted faro salmon that reminds her of what they serve at Golden Meadow rehab, and yet another with two large Portobello mushrooms stuffed with Asiago and mozzarella cheeses. The salmon is dry, and the chicken is drenched in too much lemon juice, but beggars can't be choosey. The small bowl of ziti with marinara sauce that he brings next isn't bad, and the deep-fried cauliflower patties drizzled with aioli are to die for, as is the beef tenderloin with a shallot and red wine reduction glaze. Jason is happy to see roasted new fingerling potatoes. All in all, it'll be okay. Her family won't lose face. What did you expect from a catering house? As long as they avoided the rubber chicken with rice pilaf and green beans, even her father might be happy.

"Something for the carnivores, something for the vegetarians, even something for the vegans. We're good," Jason says. "Do we have to worry about kosher?"

"With Faye? Are you kidding? Another type of green salad, maybe. And maybe some gluten-free bread. That should do it."

"Talk with Karen. I'm sure she'll work out whatever you'd like." It's been a long day. Eric will probably swear to anything to see them on their way.

* * *

"Maybe the cake should be all chocolate," Jason says, settling into the driver's seat and fastening his seat belt.

Lisa Anderson has agreed to make three tiers: one chocolate and one carrot to be sliced for the guests; one small one to be kept in Ryan's and Jason's freezer and eaten on their first anniversary (although all her friends have said they threw their anniversary tier out because it didn't keep). Instead of more tiers, Lisa will make two additional sheet cakes of each type to feed the guests, since the cake will be cut in the kitchen and guests won't know whether their piece came from the main cake or the sheet cake. "Saves time and money," Lisa said. When Ryan told her the florist had suggested that Lisa decorate the cake with green sugar vines, Lisa had bristled and said Annie should stick to making centerpieces.

"Sure you don't want me to drive? We can share," Ryan says.

"I'm good. Get some Zs. I'll wake you if I need to."

"We could have stayed over."

"And miss Faye's wedding?"

"No, silly. We could have left really early in the morning."

"I thought you didn't want to do that."

"I didn't. Just talking."

"I've been thinking."

"How unusual."

"I've been thinking I'd like to teach—philosophy."

"You mean on the college level—get a Ph.D.?"

"Yeah."

"Well, that's a change."

"It's what I'd have done to become a Jesuit. That was what I wanted for a discipline."

"So much more time in school, Jase."

"Yeah, but I'd work too. I don't care if it takes me longer—at least until you finish law school."

"I don't even know about that anymore. I just know I don't want to be at the Law Center next year. We're twenty-eight and we don't even know what we want to do."

"Maybe because there aren't that many jobs to choose from right now."

"Maybe because we have too much choice."

"It'll work out. Get some sleep." He mumbles something about a teaching job he's heard about at Driscoll, but she's too tired to get into a heavy discussion now.

"Do you like the idea of flowers on top of the cake?" she asks.

"Better than vines crawling down it, like she described."

"And what about having those chocolate candies for favors? I thought we weren't going to have any favors. They're always left at weddings I go to, and not everyone likes chocolate. Some people are allergic to it." She fiddles around for the lever to lower the back of her seat.

"They'll give them away," he says.

"I liked the darker chocolate one with the sliver of ginger on top."

"The Kahlua one was good too."

"But we should have one milk chocolate and one dark," she says.

"Nobody likes milk chocolate anymore."

"I do."

"Okay. The dark chocolate with the ginger on top and the milk chocolate salted caramels." He turns up the heat.

"Deal."

"The box with the lavender ribbon was nice. Matches the irises in the centerpieces," he says.

"Whatever. At least if there's any left over we can eat them ourselves. The only thing more useful and ecological than chocolate would have been toilet paper."

He laughs. "I like Eric."

"That was obvious."

"He invited me to join his fantasy baseball league next year. I just might. We may even take in a Sox game when he gets down to Boston next summer."

"Does he get to Boston much?"

"I don't know. Says he likes Fenway. Must go there enough. By the way, good call with the pedal rickshaw."

"Thanks."

"So what's left, my bride-to-be?"

"One more trip up, unfortunately, during the week to get the license and a final fitting. Fran says I have to. That's it, babe. I know this drive is a real pain."

"And the DJ?"

"You can call him. I don't want to deal with it."

"You got it."

"What about gifts for Emily and your brother?"

"I don't know. We'll come up with something. He asked me if you were going to change your name."

"Your brother?"

"No, Eric."

"What does he care?"

"He just asked."

"Ryan McDermott. It's so Irish."

"And that's a problem?"

"It's just not me. I'm not Irish. Everyone already thinks I am because of Ryan. When I was little I wanted to change my last name—it's so long and never gets spelled correctly and nobody can pronounce it. But it's me, and now I don't really want to give it up. Be like taking on a whole new identity."

"Then don't change it."

"You don't mind?"

"Hell, no. Why would I?"

"I love you."

He smiles.

"Can you believe how much we settled in one day?"

"Yeah. Kinda blew Eric's mind—with relief."

Eric, Eric, Eric.

"I don't know why it takes everyone over a year," she says through a yawn.

"Well, we did have a leg up, you've got to admit."

"Maybe two."

"Happy?"

"Very. Except for the Pre-Cana thing. I really don't want to do it."

"Okay. We'll work it out. There's one more thing—we haven't told our parents yet."

But she's fast asleep and doesn't hear him.

When they arrive at the apartment a little after midnight, they barely undress, and without so much as brushing their teeth, fall into bed.

At just about the same time, Eric Boulanger approaches his mother's house and seeing the rusty Schwinn bike leaning against the side of the garage, slumps back in his seat and phones Michael, who has been on the same mission: driving around town in search of Bicycle Girl.

"Got her," he tells his friend

"Cool."

"Hey, thanks, Mike."

"No prob. Come over for the game tomorrow. Beck and I got news."

"You're pregnant."

"Hot damn! For a single guy you got that on your radar?"

"I'm a photographer. I'm observant—especially where the body's concerned. When?"

"September. We don't know what it is yet."

"And the wedding?"

"No wedding. Beck doesn't see a need, at least for the time being. You know she thinks outside the box about most things."

"You down with that?"

"I want to marry her. She'll change her mind—eventually."

"Tell her she's bad for business. Hey, Mike—"

"Yeah?"

"I'm happy for you. I love you."

"I love you too, bro."

Chapter 19

Sunday, April 13

AYE AND HAROLD cannot wait. They're like teenagers aching to elope but finding themselves without money for carfare. They have no time to waste: As Faye said: They're melting faster than ice cubes on a summer day. They will not wait. They have no one to answer to. They will listen to no one. For that reason they pushed the wedding up a week. They also did it because Ryan couldn't get them a reservation for Easter Sunday.

Ryan is convinced the frenzy to marry is just Faye's attempt to beat her and Jason to the punch.

"Come on. She loves you to death," Jason tells her as he knots his tie.

"That doesn't make her less of a drama queen. What do you wear to your eighty-six-year-old grandmother's wedding?"

"Same thing you wear to any wedding."

"No, no, no. This is Faye, Jason. If Filene's were still open, she'd probably go to the Running of the Brides, wheelchair and all."

"The what?"

"The big designer wedding gown sale in Filene's basement. When I was thirteen, I had to go for my mother's cousin's daughter. My mother wouldn't go, of course, so Faye made my father drive me all the way up to Boston to take my mother's place. I had to sit in a corner on the floor and not move, while Faye and her sister and her sister's daughter and granddaughter grabbed gowns off racks, along with hundreds of other women, dumped them on me, then went off to hunt for more. Do you know how heavy some bridal gowns are? When they got the goods, the brides just undressed on the floor, trying on gown after gown until they found *the one*, and everybody started clapping. That's what you heard, this clapping every five minutes. My mother was smart not to go."

"So you never went again."

"Oh yes. Another cousin's wedding, before they closed the store. But that time I was a runner and not the dumpster."

"I don't understand how women can subject themselves to such abuse." He takes his new sports jacket off a long hook behind her bedroom door where's he's hung his clothes.

"It's the bargain gene all women carry, except for a few mutants. It's what we do. How's this?" She holds up a blue sheath with white polka dots. "Or this?" A short white crocheted one.

"That's nice."

"Maybe I shouldn't wear white. Then again, Faye's not. But better to be safe."

"So the blue one."

"I also have this." She pulls out a white sheath with a thick black stripe running across the top from armhole to armhole and another down the center."

"Is that a cross? Looks like a priest's vestment."

She tosses it into the pile of discards on the bed, then drops to her knees in search of a pair of black patent-leather pumps at the bottom of her closet.

"Is Tiffany coming?" He's leaning against the doorjamb, arms crossed, observing her move about as though she were in a scene from a movie.

""No. Why would she?"

"I don't know. Faye likes her."

"This is only family and a few of their friends. Besides, I think she went home for the weekend. I know I have a black evening purse somewhere."

"It's not evening."

"It's just what you call it."

"Why do you need a bag?"

"How can you go without one?"

"Easy. I have everything right here." He puts his hands under his jacket and removes his wallet, phone, and key from the pants pockets.

"Not even a comb?"

"I'll borrow yours."

"Well, where would I put my makeup—and the comb and mints that you will also borrow—and my phone and keys and wallet? Most of our clothes don't have pockets—not even our pants, and if they do, the pants are so tight even a tube of lipstick bulges and digs into your pelvic bone."

"You see? There you go again, subjecting yourself to abuse. Why do you women put up with it? Either don't wear makeup, or demand deep pockets. Look at you." He watches her trying to close a bursting evening purse. "You can't even fit what you have in that little pouch anyway. And how can you walk in those torture devices? I had a great aunt—Helen. You remember her. She wore those high heels every day of her life. At ninety-five, she couldn't even walk around the house without them because her feet and leg muscles had all shortened. She was like a living Barbie doll."

"We wear them to look good for you."

"I don't need you to wear them. Wear something comfortable."

"If it were summer, I'd wear dressy sandals, but it's still too cold out." She looks at the shoes and hesitates. She'll keep them on. She loves them; they were a great deal. She thinks how easily they've fallen back into being a couple. "Next time around I'll come back as a man."

"Me too," he says, approaching her and putting his arms around her. "A gay man," he adds bending over to kiss her.

"Don't mess up my makeup."

"Is this shirt okay?" He's wearing a collared French Blue one, open at the neck, black sports jacket, no tie.

"Oh, now *you're* worried about what you're wearing."

"Just checking."

The blue brings out the color of his eyes. She loves his eyes. "Yes. It's perfect. Are you upset about not being able to go to Mass today? It's Palm Sunday."

"I could have found an early Mass somewhere."

"Why didn't you?"

He shrugs. That's what he gets for marrying into a family that's half Jewish. Everyone has to make concessions.

* * *

The wedding takes place at the new Harbor Inn in a corner room with a view of the parking lot.

"Where's the harbor?" Joe Toscano wants to know.

"Across the street," his wife, Lauren, says.

"So why didn't they call it Across from the Harbor or The Parking Lot Inn?"

Lauren giggles. This is good, Ryan knows. After all these years, after the betrayal and the heartbreak, she is still taken with his sense of humor. Always has been. Ryan has never found her father to be that funny. In fact he's downright corny at times, but her mother thinks the man she swore she'd hunt down with the gun she didn't own, the man she said had lost his fucking mind, the man who made her cry nonstop for thirty straight days was hilarious. And the gratitude his dreamy dark eyes, shadowed by heavy lashes and brows, directs at her says he still thinks she's as beautiful and sexy and talented and desirable as she was thirty-five years ago—and, yes, blessed with such good taste in men.

They are so meant to be together. She is striking, everyone said when Ryan was growing up, with the paper-thin body of Audrey Hepburn and the face of Ava Gardner. Ryan didn't know who either of the two actresses were until she saw *Breakfast at Tiffany's* on a plane ride to Europe and *The Night of the Iguana* in a film and theater class on Tennessee Williams in college. She followed up perusing old albums her mother had relegated to the basement to discover a more youthful Lauren, and she saw it: an amalgamation of the voluptuous

Gardner and the nymph-like Hepburn. Lauren was Ava without boobs and Audrey with a seductive face. Ryan can still see it as she observes Lauren in her white-and-lime flowered shirtwaist dress, her bare arm brushing the suit-covered one of dark, solid, and muscular-to-this-day Joe, with his full head of thick black hair. He is a magnet to which she gravitates. Together they are stunning.

Lauren greets Jason as she would a New England spring: with a cautious embrace that speaks relief but at the same time mistrust—this might just be a tease. Joe is friendlier, conveying the understanding that men screw things up. The two men no longer simply share an x and a y chromosome: They have hurt women they love deeply, and they are looking for redemption.

Ryan spots her aunt Robin fussing around Faye in her wheel-chair. Beside Faye is the aide they have hired for the day at the nursing home's insistence: Faye was not ready to venture out alone, to be transported, the authorities maintained, by a family that knows nothing about handling the compromised bodies of octogenarians. Though Harold has made great strides in his recovery, he's having a hard time maneuvering his walker between the men's room and the party. They could have held the affair in the Multi-Purpose room at Laurel Manor, but Faye and Harold wouldn't hear of it, fearful that the uninvited residents would descend like vultures to participate in the festivities. Faye's childhood friends Pearl and Tilly have made it today. So have Pearl's sister Eunice and her husband, Fred, a lifetime smoker who wears tubes through which oxygen streams from a tank into his nostrils. Eunice and Fred's daughter Patty has accompanied them.

Aunt Robin and Uncle Jake are more what one would expect adults in their late fifties and early sixties to look like. Robin always says she accepted the worst features from her parents in order to leave the best for her younger sister. Robin is not homely by any means; she is just plainer—the woman you pass in the supermarket aisle or sit across from on the T day after day and of whom you take little notice. Jake has not kept in as good shape as Joe, and through no fault of his own looks much older, because he's nearly bald and insists on combing a few hideous gray strands across his scalp.

"You should come more often," Ryan tells her mother, who holds a long-stemmed glass, as slender as she, with an extended arm, taking care not to spill her margarita.

"You're right. But it's hard for me to see her like this, to see them all in that place. It's easier for you: Their timeline isn't on your radar. All I see is a sign that says *Next Stop.* I know it's cruel—and cowardly—but the last year has been hard for your father and me, and we need some time to rebuild."

Faye said getting old wasn't for sissies, Ryan thinks.

"I'm glad you're here for her, but I don't want you to burden yourself with her, Ryan. I mean that. And she doesn't want that either. She didn't do it for her own mother, and she doesn't want us to do it. And I don't want you to do it for me. Understand?"

Nice in theory, but unlikely. Furthermore, Faye's parents died before Faye had reached adulthood.

"How were they able to go for a marriage license?" Lauren asks.

"I helped them out with that."

"See what I mean?"

When Ryan had phoned her parents about Jason's return, her mother was quiet, sending anxiety through the ether while her father filled it with positive energy: Everyone deserves a second chance, he used to tell the grade-school Ryan when she quarreled with friends, and he sure as hell was relying on that to be the case for him at the moment.

"So how's it going?" Lauren sips on her drink.

"You mean with Jason?"

"No, the Easter Bunny. Of course with Jason." (Who at the moment was accompanying Harold to the men's room.)

"Great." *We're getting married,* she neglects to tell her. She and Jason had decided to wait until after today. This was Faye's show.

"Well, take your time. He's a nice boy but a little mixed up is what I always thought. Marriage is easy to get into and hard to get out of. And don't listen to my mother; she's living by World War Two standards."

"She does use that *passions were flying high; time was running out* line a lot."

"*We married in a hurry before the boys shipped out so we could sleep together.* I know my mother. Believe me. She might act like she's in the twenty-first century, but she can't shake those old taboos. She nearly went ballistic when your father and I waited ten years before we had you. Oh, she's come a long way and I admire her for trying, but it's tough to let go of those notions. Just take your time, sweetheart. Take your time."

"She said you baby boomers think you invented sex and you'll probably think you're the first to ever die. She also said there's never a right time to have children, that you just have to go for it. If you wait too long, you could find yourself out of luck."

"I knew she was filling you with that!" Lauren says, then seductively licks the salt-crusted rim of her glass. "And I suppose she told you that women should wear lots of jewelry so everyone will think their husbands are doing well."

"Something like that. You know, Mom, she's not all off base. I have friends who feel the same way—about not waiting too long, that is."

"She's not altogether wrong, but that's not a reason to rush. Your biological clock's got a lot more ticking to do. We fought hard in the women's movement. Use your freedom wisely."

I have two mothers, Ryan thinks. Two very smart mothers.

Faye and Harold are adorable: he in his light gray suit, white shirt, navy tie with salmon diamonds; she in a silk salmon pants suit she purchased off the home marketing network (along with Harold's matching tie), and the double strand of pearls and large mabe pearl earrings nestled in 14-karat gold she insisted Lauren retrieve from the safe-deposit box. The justice of the peace (Harold refused to have a rabbi, even the Reform one who agreed to officiate in a restaurant) is a middle-aged woman who terms the pair a stellar example of finding love in the twilight of one's life. Ryan wishes she had left that last line out, while Lauren, a witness alongside Robin, shoots a glance at her daughter that says *See, take your time.* The couple exchanges matching

Fimo clay rings they made in crafts class. (Faye said that real jewelry would only get stolen in the nursing home, where certain residents were prone to "shopping" in other residents' rooms.) They say, "I do," and lean in to one another to bestow a kiss. They drink champagne to Joe's toast, despite their medication restrictions.

The room is too small for waiters to walk among guests with platters of appetizers, and besides, half of the guests are too old to stand for any length of time, so they sit down to servings of calamari with *pomodoro* sauce on the side, oysters on the half shell, crab cakes with drizzled lemon butter, and scallops wrapped in bacon—to which Pearl and Tilly raise their eyebrows. For whose benefit? Faye has never followed a kosher diet, and Harold believes in the aphrodisiac powers of oysters. Fred's buttered roll gets caught in a tug of war between his teeth and trembling hands; Joe expounds on the merits of olive oil and garlic but cannot refrain from observing that the ringlets of breaded squid are a bit rubbery.

Time to choose entrees from a limited menu.

"I never know what 'seared' means," Jason whispers to Ryan

"Me neither."

"I'll stick with the lobster ravioli."

"I'll get the filet mignon. We can share."

"What's frizzy salad?" Jason asks a waiter whose nametag reads John but who introduced himself as Jawn, like any good boy from Revere, where he said he was from.

"It's *frisée*," Ryan says, correcting Jason's pronunciation.

"Yeah, but what is it?"

"Endive. It's like lettuce with hairy edges," Jawn says loud enough for everyone to hear.

Later, Faye and Harold feed each other cake with coconut-covered white icing, their unsteady forks threatening to miss their marks. Pearl chokes on a thread of coconut, but Robin, who is adept at the Heimlich maneuver, quickly dislodges it.

Lauren and Joe had spent the previous day directing a small moving company to transfer some of Faye's belongings from her home to the new apartment in the independent living building at Laurel

Manor for when she and Harold are ready to make the move. Lauren hung some of Faye's favorite artwork and even a macramé planter she had made for Faye one Mother's Day and that Faye will not relegate to the trash despite its being dated. Robin wants to put Faye's house on the market, but Lauren insists on waiting: She knows Robin will not stick around the East Coast to help prepare it for the sale.

The staff at the Golden Meadow unit at Laurel Manor has put a cot next to Faye's bed and made the bed as level with the cot as possible. They placed a long-stemmed rose on each newlywed's pillows. Tonight, they will help them into their nightclothes: a pair of striped pajamas with an open fly and a silk nightgown that will easily slide up. The couple will be cautious and inventive and their own judges of their success. Joe and Lauren will head back to New York, Robin and Jake on to a golf tournament at Hilton Head before returning to the west.

* * *

Jason's body is warm and smooth as they lie naked, face-to-face. He strokes her hair, her cheeks, fondles her nipples. They grow hard together. He is tender, smothering her mouth with his, entangling his tongue with hers.

"I love you," he murmurs over and over.

"I love you," she responds.

They loll around in bed until late morning; it's Patriot's Day. Maybe they'll go out to brunch. After the bombing last year, they are determined to be out in the streets and not hiding. Faye and Harold's wedding has instilled in Ryan a nostalgia for an era she had never experienced, a time when holidays were meant for leisure and not shopping, for a time when suspension of mail delivery meant just that. She remembers dinners at her father's parents' home in Brooklyn on Sundays and special occasions, when her grandmother started cooking early in the morning to make her tomato gravy and macaroni for a seven-course meal.

But even by then things had begun to change: Her father was always in a hurry to go back to Long Island to mow the lawn, or paint the trim on the house, or clean the garage; her aunt had to catch a big sale at the mall.

"We never did this kind of work when I was a boy," her father would say. "We sat at the table for hours and in nice weather in the driveway with coffee and pastries. Sundays and holidays were days of rest. They were for family."

"Then why do you do it now?" Ryan asked.

"Times have changed. There's so little of it."

She remembers being unable to comprehend that. Time was time. There were still twenty-four hours in a day. Today she longs to go back even farther, to Faye's youth, when women in long dresses and big sun hats sat in one end of a boat while a gentleman in a suit rowed them along the river. Well, that was an exaggeration: She didn't want to be rowed, and she didn't want to wear a long, restrictive outfit, but she did want to take a boat out and row and row until her arms ached and the city became nothing but landscape, a study in stillness bordering peaceful waters. She longed for a time when meditation class wasn't the only way to find uninterrupted solitude.

"Let's watch the marathon for awhile. I really want to support the runners this year. And then go out on the Charles if the police let us." She has barely finished saying this to Jason when her cell plays its familiar tune.

"Ryan, darling, I hate to bother you so early, but can you take Harold to the ER?"

"What's wrong?"

"He can't keep anything down."

"Harold can't eat," she tells Jason. "Faye wants us to take him to the ER."

"Can't the nursing home send him in an ambulance?"

"Apparently he won't let them."

"I'm not going anywhere," Ryan hears Harold say.

"If he doesn't want to go, he can't feel that bad, Faye. Why don't you give it until tomorrow?"

"Because tomorrow you have to work."

Maybe her mother was right about Faye. "Jason doesn't. Listen, Faye, we can't force him to go. He probably ate too much yesterday and with all the excitement—"

"All right, *bubeleh*. I'll wait. As long as Jason can take him if need be."

"If he wants to go, Jason will take him." To which Jason nods in assent. "But I'm sure he'll be better later today."

"Listen to me, darling. Do something fun today, since you're not going to the ER. That's an order."

"We plan to, Faye. We're going rowing on the Charles."

Chapter 20

WHEN ERIC SAW Danni's text the night before Ryan and Jason's visit, he didn't answer it. *Call me. We need to talk.* It had been his experience that when a woman said that, she was about to come down hard on him about his shortcomings, to pummel him with demands and ultimatums, to chastise him for his lack of sensitivity, and to stick him wherever it hurt for being a coward in the face of commitment. It didn't matter that they each viewed the relationship differently. What mattered was how *she* desired things to be, regardless of what had or had not been expressed: They were not friends, not even friends with benefits; they were a couple. His initial pursuit had been enough to sanction it and any sharing of good times to solidify it.

That the words came from Danni could not have annoyed him more. He had heard them from her over the course of their friendship, and they were the reason he held her at bay. He tried—really tried—not to lead her on after their encounter at Baby's so long ago, but Danni had just kept coming back for more. The round was over; the bell had rung. Yet there she was, justified by their having spent so much time together during the past year collaborating on the contest, coming up for the punch, demanding to go the distance—or so he imagined.

Shame on egotistical you, Eric Boulanger. You are the misogynist you pride yourself on not being, Satan in the flesh. This is what he

188

thinks of himself for ignoring the text, for waiting for Ryan and Jason in his car outside Licks and Relics so he wouldn't have to spend an extra moment with Danni, who, he must admit, in her leadership role, has matured in his eyes. She's become more self-assured, conducting the Chamber meetings with decisiveness and competence, which is no small feat in the face of members like Hank and the crotchety repairman. She looks less often to Eric for support, and when she must seek him out, the longing stares are gone.

Danni might actually be happy, and Eric has had nothing to do with it. She's over him, like previous girlfriends. Everyone is over him. Everyone except him. That Danni has come close to being annoyed at Eric is not surprising: The entire Chamber is fed up with his excuses about *the* couple and their lack of enthusiasm, with their downright absence, for that matter. So much time has been spent by the Chamber, so much effort expended, so many hopes are hinging on this ungrateful couple's big day.

"It's not as though Brackton is going to implode if this plan doesn't live up to your expectations," Michael has told him. "Go easy on yourself, man. You tried."

Yeah, he'd tried. But at the moment, he's tired of trying—to be a good son, a good photographer, a good friend, a good citizen, a man women find attractive. He's tired of driving around in search of Bicycle Girl when she doesn't go home nights. Tired of being beholden to so many. Tired of being alone. Tired of listening to the whining of his fucking mind. Tired.

When he called her from Licks & Relics on learning of her accident, Danni hadn't been the least bit angry with him for not having responded to her text, as though for the first time she understood why he might not have wanted to. In the deliberate speech of one pumped up on drugs yet still in discomfort, she explained that she hadn't broken her leg (it didn't take long for news to get distorted in Brackton), nor had she undergone surgery yet. She had shattered her kneecap— slipped while standing perfectly still at the bottom of the run when she turned to see if her friend was behind her, her knee coming down hard on a large chunk of ice hidden beneath a thin layer of powder.

There'd been a hard smack, then the sickening feeling that washed over her as she heard the nasty crunching sound when she tried to move, saw the concavity and felt the bony lump where there had been the protective cap.

"You need anything? I'll come and visit," he said. He would make it up to her for not calling sooner. He's a Monday morning quarterback, always backpedaling, working overtime to right the wrongs.

"Don't bother. I'm fine, Eric. My sister, Linda, is here, and a friend. I just want to get this surgery over with Monday morning. They have to wait for the swelling to subside. The doctor said it could have been much worse and won't need too many screws and wire to put the knee back together. He said I'm young enough to heal quicker than a lot of people it happens to. Isn't that good?"

But *I'm* your friend, is all he wanted to say.

"I'll be home in a few days, have to stay with my parents for awhile. I feel so bad about not being there for Ryan and Jason. I'm really sorry for leaving you to deal with today by yourself."

"No worries. We'll be fine. You hurting much?"

"Enough. Morphine helps."

He could see her wincing, waiting for nurses to come with that legal high, and afterward thanking them and laughing her Danni laugh.

"Just get better." As though she would choose to do otherwise. "Is there anything I can do at your house? Feed the cats?"

"Thanks, Eric. My dad has it covered. Say hello to Ryan for me."

She had asked him to pass along the greeting, but he hadn't. Damn him. He never did that. Why not? He didn't know. Maybe he saw it as a formality, something people just said but didn't expect you to carry out because it usually took away from the situation at hand and obliged him to reveal when and where he had seen the person who extended the greeting and under what circumstances. He'll do it from now on, he swears. Michael does it: *Becca says hi.* So does his mother when she tells him Maisie Billings or Lisa Anderson sends regards. He's certain Jason McDermott does it; he's that kind of guy who wouldn't let anyone down, and after all, isn't someone entrusting you to pass something on? Isn't it your responsibility to follow through?

Ryan is lucky to have a guy like Jason and was stupid to risk losing him by being indiscreet with Eric. But wasn't it he who had come on to her first? He can't remember the sequencing. Still, it had been up to him to take responsibility.

He thinks she handled it well yesterday during the visit. He thinks he did too. And despite finding her a bit of an enigma, he still finds her hot. *Jason* is lucky.

He'll phone Danni this afternoon to find out how the surgery went this morning. Then he'll go over to Heavenly Baked Goods and Plantasia: He wants to have flowers and something yummy waiting for her at her parents' house when she goes home.

Chapter 21

Tuesday, April 15th

J ASON HAS BEEN inside a church. Ryan can tell this by his smell. It's how she used to know that her uncle Vincent, the dentist, had just come from his office: Uncle Vincent smelled of tiny particles of amalgam mixed with eugenol that flew out of mouths when he excavated old fillings. When her carpenter grandfather Toscano returned from work, he smelled of sawdust. Artists like her mother smell of oils and turpentine, landscapers of manure and cut grass, mechanics of grease and gasoline. Lawyers and accountants like her father have no occupational odor other than their own heavy daily dose of aftershave and the occasional breath that reeks of Scotch from a long business lunch. With priests it's the spicy scent of frankincense and myrrh, the clouds of smoke that get shaken out of a little golden canister so often that they never disappear. Not only has Jason been in a church, but been there a long time—probably at Mass—because the scent is so strong she can almost hear the bells beckoning the faithful to bow their heads and pound their breasts—once, twice, three times—out of respect for the consecrated host being raised for all to see.

She cannot help but feel she's been betrayed. When he embraces her, it's like inhaling the perfume of another woman. But it's not another woman. They live in a free country with freedom of worship. Still she asks: "What did you do today?"

And so he tells her, as she chops parsley and garlic on a cutting board, and sets a large pot of water to boil, and sautés garlic until it's crispy in the olive oil she's poured into a small frying pan. She's chosen to make *aglio e olio* because it's easy and needs few ingredients, because she has the desire, or *voglia,* for it, as her father would say, because the intensity of its aroma will fill up the kitchen and living room of the small apartment and obliterate any trace of religious adoration.

He unscrews the twist cap of a bottle of California Chianti (watching his purse strings has already taken precedence over impressing her) and pours them both a glass. She dumps a handful of salt into the turbulent rolling water. He sets the table with large shallow bowls her family has trained him to use for pasta and asks if Tiffany will be joining them. She doesn't know. She hasn't seen her in several days.

"Should I text her?" he says, taking out his phone.

"You have her number?" She's surprised.

"I'm in that thread you sent about donating to your mailman's retirement."

"Right."

His phone signals a text, but not Ryan's, which sits on the counter. Tiffany has made the effort to respond only to Jason, which really disturbs her.

"She's not sure when she'll be back. Says to start without her."

But she's coming. He puts out a third place setting. He uses paper napkins and puts the fork on top of the plate instead of to the left, something that irritates Ryan, but she says nothing because she knows it'll irritate Tiffany even more. She puts a pinch of red pepper into the sizzling garlic, followed by the parsley, lets it sauté for a very short time, adds a little water, and turns off the gas. He produces a loaf of crusty bread—a *bastone*—he picked up in Davis Square from an Italian deli and searches among Tiffany's set of expensive knives for the long serrated one. He begins to slice.

"Not too many," she says. "Trying to cut down on carbs."

He removes a butter dish from inside the door of the fridge. She grimaces: Her father's family never used butter at the dinner table; it was reserved for breakfast. Even her mother had gotten on board with that one. He used to know this, and yet it was as though his year and a half in the novitiate had cleansed his memory of such things and he was starting all over again.

He nods and stops sawing.

"What were you doing in Somerville?" she asks, eyeing the address on the empty white paper bag the bread came in that now sits on the counter in a mess of crumbs. Oftentimes, as now, her speech is guided by her emotions and she forgets to preface her statements the way the shrink she saw when Jason left her advised her to do. She is like her mother in that respect and envies women—and men—who have the restraint to count to ten before they open their mouths. She pours the oil mixture into a shallow pasta bowl, gives the spaghetti she has dumped into a colander a few shakes to dislodge any water, and adds the spaghetti to the bowl. She mixes it quickly with two forks so as not to let it get cold, and sprinkles it with parmesan cheese. They sit down to eat.

"It's kind of a long story." He butters a slice of bread. "I went over to Driscoll to see Larry Wolfson at the outreach program. To check out volunteering, maybe with refugees. When we were in school, I tutored kids from Somalia. He told me about this St. Gerard's parish and high school in Medford that's was looking for a sub in computer science for the rest of the term. The teacher's out on early maternity leave. It's about a fifteen-minute walk from the train station at Davis Square, so I stopped in at this great Italian food shop on my way home. You should have seen it: hanging dried salamis and sausages that you like, little pizzas, oils, pastries, just like in the North End. You'd love it. Had no idea Davis Square has gotten so trendy—lots of cafés and shops. Unfortunately, the downside to that is the neighborhood is full of young singles. The parish had to close the elementary school. Not enough families there anymore."

"You're digressing, Jase."

"Sorry, but it was so lucky. A paying job until June twentieth."

"You can teach computer science?"

"At this level I can handle it. Three classes. Two preps. Fifty-eight students."

"When would you start?"

"Monday." He dips a chunk of the buttered bread into the oil that's collected at the bottom of his plate. Watching him mix the butter with the olive oil would normally disgust her, but his words have trumped his actions.

"Whoa!" She holds a forkful of spaghetti bound for her mouth in mid air.

"I love kids that age. Won't be a problem. The pastor, Father Coluccio, is from Rome. They've got a priest from Colombia." He is full of enthusiasm. "So I went over to the school—did I tell you it's junior high and high school? Great faculty. Small but dedicated. This order is only about thirty years old, founded in Rome, a really small order but they're all around the world. After I met with the director of the school—a guy named Todd Neisman—"

"Also a priest?"

"No. After I talked with Neisman, Father Coluccio let me into the church, which is next door. Beautiful modern stone church. You'd like it."

Does it matter whether or not she likes any of what he's describing?

"I couldn't stay for Mass because it was too late, six thirty, or even the Adoration of the Eucharist at five thirty, so he said I could just sit there for awhile. I needed some self-reflection."

"You can't do your soul-searching in a park or an empty apartment?"

"You never know when Tiffany's going to show up here—besides, it's not the same. I guess I'm used to the ambiance of a church. I won't lie. It settles me. We can't go rowing on the Charles every day. You said it yourself: We have to find our places of solitude."

"Yup. And I guess a church is yours."

"Come on, Ryan. Don't be that way. I'm not sitting in some dark watering hole in the middle of the day. The religious community will always be a part of my life, but just not the way I was thinking. More wine?"

He is so pleased with himself, as if he's just discovered the passwords to all his online accounts he thought he'd lost, as if he can eat all the chocolate desserts in the world and never gain an ounce.

"It's hard to raise kids, be active in their lives, work two jobs, keep your relationship on track, besides being tied to a group of priests," she says as he refills her glass.

"Less demanding than being a Jesuit." He smiles.

"What are these priests called?"

"Missionary Fraternity of St. Charles Barromeo. They're Italian. I thought you'd like that."

She rolls her eyes.

"Listen, Ryan. I'm not going to be one of them. There are quite a few lay instructors at the school. I told you I think I might like to teach."

"Philosophy."

"Maybe not. Maybe I'll teach high school. Or maybe I'll finish up law school and teach law."

"Maybe I'll enter a convent."

He laughs. "I'm just trying to find my way back into the work world and see where I fit."

"You're right. It is a paying job. Good for you. You just should have told me sooner."

"I was going to tell you during dinner—"

They hear the key in the door, and it marks the end of their discussion. Tiffany is glowing—rosy from a number of downward dogs and a long shoulder stand at yoga class, high that she's in a new relationship, about which she refuses to divulge information. In fact, she's been in a good mood ever since Jason showed up—an alluring mood. She may be a lesbian, but she's a rich, spoiled, hot lipstick one who plays the femme fatale or hard-nosed feminist whenever either suits her. Ryan has known quite a few lesbians-turned-heterosexual. She can't think of one gay male who has reversed his course. Tiffany thinks nothing of prancing around in front of Jason in panties and see-through T-shirts when she's there, which, thank God, isn't too often lately. But what's happened while Ryan's been at work and the other two are alone? Tiffany's had trouble with boundaries with roommates in the past, but convinced Ryan that she was the victim in such disputes. The two before Ryan had been a lesbian couple.

Ryan has never lived alone, which is something she regrets: She has her selfish side to consider, one that doesn't like to share, that wants to keep things—and people—to herself. She can't imagine ever writing a cookbook (beyond the fact that she isn't a good cook), can't imagine how chefs give out secret recipes despite being paid handsomely for them. If anyone asks her how she made something, she always leaves out an ingredient or says she'll give it but never does. She even hides things from herself, jotting down thoughts in her notebook with such intentional carelessness that even she cannot decipher her scribble afterward.

* * *

When Jason is fast asleep, Ryan gets out of bed, takes her laptop to the couch in the living room, and goes on Facebook to check out Tiffany's most recent posts, to look for photos of Jason in her albums or timeline, to see if she's changed her relationship status in any way. Absurd. Yet she searches. The only image she finds of him is a selfie of the three of them on the back porch eating breakfast several days ago. Is she searching for excuses as to why he cannot change sufficiently for her? But he cannot be the only one to change: There must be compromise in a relationship; there must be acceptance, a melding of philosophies, a commitment to forgiveness, and trust. Her mother taught her to be selfish, but she was learning that her mother was too selfish for her liking. Ryan knows she can get Jason to the altar, but she needs to know he wants to be there.

Tomorrow is Easter Sunday, and she'll suggest they go to Mass together. She can do this. She can sit there and maybe be lucky enough to garner some little piece of wisdom from one of these cool priests who just might surprise her, or else she'll simply bathe in the comfort of community. And if she can't, she'll compose their grocery list in her mind or think up a plot for a new short story. If it gets really bad, she'll resort to the times tables. That's what might be missing in her life—the glue, the moral fiber to guide her. She's no longer a rebellious coed; she's an adult playing in the major leagues. She can baptize her children. She can send them to religious instruction because that's where this will lead. But she can also reinforce that the Bible is a storybook of parables, that doctrine, like government, is man-made, an invention devised by humans to get through this life.

She can make Jason comfortable and happy, and in turn ease him back into the life of the laity. Maybe their children will be more grounded than she is, maybe they'll know how to find a love interest like themselves because they'll have more of an identity, the identity Ryan's grandparents used to tell her parents Ryan would never have. And when they're old enough, their children can choose to stay the path or go along another; it will be up to them—no strings or guilt attached. She can do all this because she knows her and Jason's relationship won't succeed without a change in attitude and behavior from both of them. What she can't do is second-guess his every conversation, every smile with other women, every minute spent with priests. There can be no others in this relationship.

Chapter 22

Sunday, April 20

J ASON IS DELIGHTED when Ryan offers to attend Easter Sunday Mass at St. Gerard's. She insists they drive to Medford, telling him that if he took her car to work and not the T every day, it would cut his commute in half. He complies for this day only, reminding her how committed she is to public transportation and reducing her carbon footprint.

She likes the heavy oak doors with their brightly colored Tiffany-glass panels. And she's never seen a ceiling carved out of wood. Aside from that, everything about the church is modest: pink plaster walls, white rectangular columns, more Tiffany windows with simple outlines of saints that resemble pen and ink drawings, a modern altar.

The priest saying Mass in his white-and-gold chasuble is middle-aged and reminds Ryan of photos of her father when he was younger, with a black beard and long curly hair that crept down his neck and covered his ears and wide sideburns.

"That's Father Coluccio," Jason whispers.

In the pew in front of them, a couple not much older than Ryan and Jason sit with their two children. The little boy, in a suit with short pants and a crooked bow tie, plays peekaboo with Ryan, his brown eyes open wide, his skin plump and dewy, while his younger sister, in a frilly dress with matching bonnet, sits comfortably in the father's arms sucking on a pacifier. Ryan studies the mother. She did this, she thinks; she produced these two little adorable beings. She can envision two munchkins squirming between her and Jason, eagerly waiting to drop their pennies into the basket when it's passed. She can see how this community might be supportive, how ritual can instill security and discipline. Choice is so distracting and at times unnerving. Eliminating some of it can make for a simpler world less fraught with decisions.

When a lanky teenager steps up to the pulpit, Ryan is unprepared for his eloquent reading of the gospel. Father Coluccio's homily does not start out as pertinent to modern world issues, focusing instead on the mother of Jesus and the ultimate anguish she experienced and the joy Christ's resurrection now brings her—brings all of us. Maybe he does this because Mother's Day is around the corner. Women are valuable, essential, hardworking gifts from God, who sacrifice for their children, he says. The Blessed Mother is the epitome, the representative of all to whom we owe thanks and, to those who have been made to suffer, an apology. He is welcoming and almost as charismatic as the new Pope. He does not mention that women, for whom he urges great respect, can never be ordained, cannot be joined together in a same-sex marriage, cannot be supported in their right to choose. He cannot change dogma, this disciple of the new and popular Pope does not admit.

That's what Ryan hears the Irish attorney in her office remark on every news article involving the new Pope, with whom the woman has a love-hate fascination. "Even the Episcopalians have been ordaining women priests for almost forty years; the Jews have women rabbis; but no, not the Catholics," she says. "Jury's still out with the Orthodox," Josh Levy, another attorney, reminds her. Ryan never gets involved in the discussions; she hasn't really cared about women's roles in the Church, or whether it recognizes gays and divorced members, or condemns abortion. She hasn't cared about what the Church professes because she hasn't cared about the Church. But if today signals a change in her participation, she will have to take a stand.

For now she chooses to tune out and say the Our Father, the Lord's Prayer, before the moment for the congregation to recite it. She repeats it over and over again in her head, making her own adjustments: "Our

Father—*and Mother*—who art in heaven ..." She has always liked the
prayer and for some reason uses it as a mantra for distraction in times
of distress. She doesn't want to analyze the words too deeply; it's one
of the only prayers she learned as a child. She likes its cadence, and
actually doesn't mind the sentiment, except for the part her father
says wasn't said when he was a boy, the part about the power and the
glory and the kingdom, which sounds like something from a Harry
Potter novel.

It's time for Communion; kneelers are lifted. People rise and head
to the center aisle. Jason looks at Ryan uneasily, but she smiles. "This
is the best part," she says as she stands, the part where you get to actually do something, the part she knows gets to Jason because she
has never received her First Holy Communion. He lays his hand on
her shoulder to hold her back, but she shrugs it off. "Jesus wouldn't
want me not to partake, would he? If you're invited to dinner, you eat,
don't you?" She's daring him, leaving him no recourse but to let her
join the line leading up to Father Coluccio and his golden chalice of
consecrated wafers.

When Communion is over, the faithful resume their singing.
Father Coluccio marches down the aisle, led by an altar girl who holds
up a large heavy-looking gold cross. That wasn't so bad, Ryan thinks.
She has reflected deeply on a relevant topic; thought about how to
end her short story and, in doing so, passed the hour quite pleasantly.

After Mass, a beaming Jason introduces Ryan to Father Coluccio,
who stands outside greeting other parishioners. With others lined up
behind them, they don't engage in lengthy conversation, but he's genuinely warm as he takes her hand in his: "I cannot tell you how happy
I am you both are here." She wishes the comfort of his familiar accent
could compensate for the failings of his homily, but it doesn't. Can she
really do this week after week? After mourning Jason for over a year
and getting a second chance with him, she has to.

They walk to Davis Square for lunch, but when they get there,
Jason suggests they take the T down to Back Bay and eat there instead.

"Why would we do that?" she asks.

"Because you love Newbury Street."

"We can explore here."

"I want to take you to Newbury Street."

She relents. "So let's drive."

"Why walk all the way back to the car and then have to drive around for a parking place or spend a fortune in a garage?"

He takes her hand and pulls her down the station stairs to the inbound Red Line. She fails to see any logic in his thinking, since now they will have to come all the way back for the car. But he is on a high, and she will ride it with him.

On the train, Ryan asks: "Do you believe in the Trinity?" Her question was prompted by the recitation of the Apostles' Creed at Mass. The inquiry surprises him.

"Of course," he says.

"I have to admit I don't get it. I mean, how can they say, *And he sits at the right hand of the Father*? How can Jesus sit next to God the Father when He and the Holy Spirit and God are one and the same? Makes no sense."

"I know you didn't go to religious instruction, but didn't you learn that in theology class at Driscoll? At least one was required."

"I got out of it by taking the Metaphysical Poets in the English department."

"We never talked about this before."

"Religion didn't seem so important before I started dating an ex-priest."

"Well." He furrows his brow and considers, as if the answer were posted in the advertisements above the windows across the aisle. "Each of the three persons in the godhead has the same divine nature; so they are the one true God in essence or nature, not three distinct gods. The Father begets the Son, but that occurs within the inner life of God. So they're two persons distinctly related, while remaining one in being. The Holy Spirit proceeds from the Father and the Son, but in a different sense: It's spirit—love—that the Father and Son—God, if you will—releases unto us."

He relaxes, pleased with his answer, but she looks at him as though he has just produced a rabbit via sleight of hand.

"Okay," Jason tries to explain. "St. Augustine says: I am a knowing and willing being, and I know that I am and that I will, and I will to be and to know. One life, one mind, one essence—man. But above man—or woman—" he smiles—"is that immutable being which is and knows and wills immutably."

"Still gibberish, Jason," she says as the train screeches into the Park Street station.

"No. Listen." He is intent on making himself understood, as they switch to the Green Line train already in the station. Yet she has to work hard at getting him to divulge most other thoughts and feelings. "God is the being one; the son, Jesus, is the knowing one, the word who proceeds from the Father; and the Holy Spirit is the willing one, the bond of love between the Father and the Son. Three distinct realities in one being. Look, a mother, father, and child can be three distinct persons and yet have the same nature. The Father, Son, and Holy Spirit are like the family—three distinct persons with the same nature. Combine the two analogies and you have three relationally distinct realities within one being anthropologically, and three relationally distinct persons sharing the same nature in the analogy of the family."

He smiles with satisfaction. She returns the smile, eager to drop a subject she regrets having brought up. Relieved when they ascend into the airiness and sunlight of this warm April day, she leads him toward her favorite hat shop, hoping to discover a killer sale.

Some café owners have already set out their patio furniture. Ryan and Jason agree on one of their old favorite haunts and sit outside, where her new wide-brimmed straw hat trimmed with black grosgrain ribbon—bought at full price—fails to shade her face. The Bloody Marys are numbing, the sun blinding. They'll telephone their parents tonight and reveal the wedding plans; they compile a makeshift guest list on a napkin. Should they search for their own place in JP or move back to Brighton or maybe Brookline? Jason thinks Medford or adjacent Somerville might suit them and their budget better.

* * *

Jason wants to tell Ryan's parents first; he'll confirm what his mother already knows in their weekly email exchange. Ryan calls Lauren and Joe on their landline so the couple can both talk at the same time: her mother in the bedroom, her father in the kitchen. Despite the fact that there are two of them, the air on the other end goes dead when she informs them about the upcoming Brackton affair.

"Well, *that's* news," her father says, breaking the silence, partly shocked, partly proud of his daughter's resourcefulness, and thankful for Jason's commitment. "We'll get things rolling."

Ryan has her parents on speakerphone, and Jason grins at Joe's compulsive nature to take on—and over—a project. Still, Lauren has not responded.

"You don't understand, Dad. There's nothing for you to do. It's all taken care of: the place, the music, the food, the dress, the tux, photographer, invitations, even the rings and the maid of honor's dress."

"I'm able to give my only daughter a wedding, you know. You're not a charity case. Then again, that leaves more for a gift, a house, your honeymoon—or are they picking up the tab for that too?"

"No," Ryan says. "And I appreciate your generosity." Jason points to himself to be included. "*We* appreciate your generosity."

"It's a bit of a trip for my family to take, but I guess these destination weddings are the rage now."

"It's Vermont, Dad, not Turks and Caicos."

"Well, okay then. Congratulations to you both. Send us our invitation. Great news, isn't it, Lauren?"

"I didn't ask your permission, Joe, since I've already done that once," Jason explains. "And we did get carried away in the excitement of this whole unorthodox affair."

"You don't need my permission, Jason. We're not old-fashioned. Ryan can make up her mind. But I appreciate your consideration."

Lauren breaks her silence. "A marriage is a lifetime. Or at least it's supposed to be."

"We know that, Mom."

"Do you? Your generation is so caught up with the *wedding and its perfection*, the size and style of the diamond, the execution of the proposal, the makeup and hairdo, down to the personal meaning in the favors, as though you were shooting a scene in a movie. A wedding is a lot of hoopla about one day—actually more like five or six hours. Then you wake up the next morning without your professional face paint, with your matted 1930s upsweep, your two-thousand-dollar gown a crumpled heap of lace and silk on the floor, and your rose-colored glasses askew, and there you are naked, and hungover, like any other couple, facing each other for years on end—"

"Oh boy," Joe says, hoping to quiet his wife.

"Wow," is all Ryan can muster. Why can't her mother be as negligent about analyzing the ins and outs of Ryan's life as she is about cleaning the house or cooking dinner?

"Just because your generation wasn't into big weddings didn't mean they had a better success rate," Ryan says. "Do you always have to critique everyone's happiness? Do you always have to make it a generational or societal issue? Can't you just let things *be* sometimes? Take care of your own problems? Can't you be happy for us? I've saved you the bourgeois task of going gown shopping with me. I thought you'd be relieved."

"Ryan—" Jason attempts to divert her.

"As my mother used to say, *Si vedono loro*," Joe states.

"I don't even know what that means, Dad."

"They only see themselves, you people are only concerned with yourselves."

"That's what she used to say about *you*, Dad, right?"

"Yeah," he says, wistfully. "That's what she used to say about me."

Lauren says: "If you're happy, I'm happy for you. But a free wedding is no reason to rush into marriage. I just want you to be sure."

"How sure can anyone ever be, Mom?"

"She's right," Joe tells Lauren.

"She's channeling Faye. And, Ryan, you're not going to sign up for one of those registries, are you?"

"Why? We haven't given enough wedding gifts to our friends' and family's kids," Joe says.

"Let them decide what to give you. Don't tell your guests what to get. Money for travel and a house is useful. A registry is so—"

"So what? Conventional?" Ryan says.

"Maybe they'd like more than the dripping homemade candles people gave us when we got married," Joe says. "We would have been better off telling them what we needed, Lauren."

"We didn't have a big wedding, Joe."

"You have an answer for everything."

"While you're going the old-fashioned route, you can wear my opal earrings that always discolor the piercing in my earlobes: something old, borrowed, and blue all in one."

"Thanks loads, but that parakeet I got tattooed on my left hip will cover the color requirement. Besides, opals are bad luck if you're not a Libra."

"Okay, ladies. Easy does it," Joe says.

Ryan recognizes that they have ruined her parents' evening, which will now be spent arguing about how badly Lauren handled the phone call. Followed by several hours of her mother not speaking to her father, who continues to cave in to his daughter's every desire, according to Lauren. Followed by a lengthy discussion at the Chinese restaurant as to whether or not Lauren and Joe should have gotten back together, let alone Ryan and Jason. Followed by Joe's concession to Lauren because he is still treading in very deep water. Followed by (Ryan hates to think of it) lovemaking and a commitment from both of them to start anew from that lousy point they always get stuck on.

Chapter 23

Friday, May 9

THERE ISN'T MUCH prep work to be done for the computer classes; curriculums already exist, in addition to quite a few lesson plans left by the teacher. Still, Jason sits up each night at the kitchen table with his laptop and prepares. He does not want to fail—at anything in this experimental period of his life that has quickly become a done deal. He cannot help but warn his new students not to spend too much time with this technology that takes them away from time that should be spent cultivating new relationships, from learning and doing new things, from communicating in person with friends. There is no substitute, he tells them, for direct human contact, which means looking someone in the eye.

"Yes there is. There's Skype," a student says.

"Ah, but you can't really look someone in the eye on Skype. It's even worse than a phone call, because it's forced—like you're performing, like you're onstage."

He knows they've tuned him out and, despite his beseeching, will carry on in their beloved cyberspace. This includes the girls who find the young rookie teacher irresistible and will later purposely pass by his classroom to catch a glimpse of him through the glass panel of the closed door and titter as they make their way down the hall. Today he'd like to stick around after school to chat with some of the teens who live within walking distance and don't have to catch buses or run to an athletic practice or a music lesson, which he's done since he began several weeks ago. Instead he heads over to Faye and Harold's new apartment at Laurel Manor.

When he knocks at number 31 he's welcomed by a young Cape Verdean home health aide who's been there since early morning, and who, at 6 p.m., will be relieved by a middle-aged woman from Minsk, the city Faye's mother emigrated from so many years ago. Faye prefers the slender soft-spoken Cape Verdean to the bossy Belarusian who'll spend the night dozing on and off on the sofa bed, waking up to Faye's calls into a baby monitor and accompanying her to the bathroom. Faye has graduated to a walker and Harold has shed his completely, relying solely on a cane, and only for extra security.

Harold's inability to keep food down after his wedding went away, just as Ryan assured Faye it would. Its source, however, was not indigestion, or food poisoning, or a result of too much excitement, but an aborted attempt at something else. While he resumed his normal eating habits for a short time at the new dining hall in the independent living unit, a week ago he began to refuse to accompany Faye there, and when he did, he pushed the food he'd ordered around with his fork, leaving it scattered but untouched. His behavior was not lost on Faye, who asked Ryan to take him to the doctor. Once again Harold refused to be taken anywhere, returning to his recliner, where he remained until it was time for bed.

He offered no excuses for his actions—no stomach aches, no constipation, no sore throat or tooth pain—except that he was not hungry. Four days ago, he began turning down liquids too. Three times a day a tray was brought to the apartment for Faye, who couldn't bear the questions of fellow residents who sat at their table and inquired about Harold's condition, for which she had no answer. Ryan and Jason brought him fish from Harbor View, and Boston cream doughnuts—his favorite. The Belarusian aide baked him an apple strudel. The Cape Verdean brought him *canja,* a thick chicken and rice soup.

Within days Harold grew gaunt looking. His fair complexion became chalky and sallow. They tried to persuade his doctor of twenty years, who denied knowing of any secret illness on Harold's part, to make an exception and do a house call, but he had come down with the flu and suggested the ER. Laurel Manor sent in their social worker; Harold would not speak with him.

So today Jason stops at Friendly's and picks up a chocolate fribble, hoping Harold will feel nostalgic and at least sip some of the milkshake. Jason has given up on the healthy smoothies laced with supplements he purchases from a juice bar in Davis Square at which Harold repeatedly turns up his nose.

Jason unwraps a straw, places it in the hole of the cover, and positions the tall plastic cup at Harold's lips. It has been seven days since his last intake of solids, three days since his last sip of liquid. Harold shakes his head; Faye wrings her hands.

"Please, Harold, for my sake, darling," Faye says, begging. "Drink. Just a sip."

"For your sake, darling, no. Only a little water with my blood pressure medicine." He doesn't want to have another stroke.

"Ach!" Faye cries. "*What*? What's wrong? Tell us, goddamn you! What is wrong?"

"Nothing." Harold waves his hand in the air and smiles.

"Call a psychiatrist! I've married a psycho. My daughters were right. I should have waited. They were all right. I married a *meshugganah*. Call a psychiatrist! Jason, do you know one?"

"Enough, Faye, darling." Harold is calm as he speaks. "All right already. I'll tell you what's up."

"Thank God!"

"Faye, dear, with you and Jason and—" He looks up at the aide, who utters her name—"and Jocelina, I say that I have never been happier in my life. To be here with you, such a beautiful and intelligent and loving woman, as my wife is a dream I never thought I'd see come to fruition in all my years on this earth. I am floating in the clouds, delirious, yes, but with love, with peace, with contentment."

They hang on his every word, awaiting further clues to his madness.

"I'm eighty-nine years old. Thanks to some recent expert medical care, apart from a little balance problem and high blood pressure, I'm a healthy son of a bitch. I even have most of my hair. I could never be happier than I was the day I met you, Faye, except for the day you married me. And this is how I want to die—a happy, healthy son of a bitch, and not a broken-down, up-shit's-creek burden to you, or worse, a man twice divorced. Be happy for me, Faye. I'm a lucky man."

They stare at him in disbelief. They are speechless.

* * *

A little after 5 p.m., Ryan approaches the T station at Downtown Crossing, where she passes a man holding a sign that reads *Homeless with a family*. He stands in the spot where her mother has told her that, when she was a young woman, Hare Krishnas, with their shaved heads and flowing garments, used to play music and dance and chant for hours on end to reduce their karmic debt.

"Please, Miss, for my children," he murmurs.

She ignores him and is about to enter the station when, out of the corner of her eye, she realized he is not an angry drug addict or lazy shiftless individual who prefers begging to working but a man whose pained expression has gone from hope to despair with her passing. Whatever his reason for being there, she decides it is genuine, and she fishes in her bag for a five-dollar bill, turns around, and hands it to him, saying she's sorry, but she hadn't heard him. What's five dollars to her, even though she and Jason are watching their spending? She'll go without her morning cappuccino tomorrow and the next day. She should have given him a twenty; Jason would have.

She arrives at Faye's at the same time as the Belarusian aide, Anastasya, to find Faye sitting at the kitchen table, head in her hands, an untouched dinner tray in front of her. In the bedroom, Jocelina folds laundry from a white plastic basket. In the living room, Harold is where she left him the day before. Jason sits in front of him on a footstool, his awkward wiry body bent like a paper clip, as he leans in toward the recliner and talks to Harold, eyes closed, who shakes his head from time to time. Jason acknowledges Ryan with a slight smile;

he barely notices as Anastasya and Jocelina exchange shifts. He concentrates on Harold, murmuring something Ryan can't hear clearly. He takes Harold's hand, returning to long moments of silence, and then, as though having dug into a bag of spiritual tricks of persuasion, begins again.

Ryan has almost forgotten to say hello to Faye. She kisses her grandmother and pulls a chair up to her.

"Oh, Ryan, *bubeleh*, it's worse than we ever thought. He wants to die."

"What?" She looks to Jason for confirmation. He nods.

"He wants to leave me. He's starving himself. Some honeymoon, eh?"

"Shouldn't we call his children?"

"I don't even know who the ingrates are," Faye says with disgust.

"How does a good man produce two bad seeds?" Anastasya chimes—her accent thick—as she moves about the apartment, tidying up magazines and pillows that Jocelina has left out of place.

"It takes more than good genes to raise a child," Faye tells her, stirring sugar into the cup of tea Anastasya has poured her. "You should know. I thought you said you had children back in Belarus. It takes more than one person. You know, they say it takes a village. Well, it takes more than that. People are born with their own personalities."

There's a knock at the door and a young girl with a chestnut-brown ponytail and a nametag that reads Amanda timidly pokes her head in. She knows about Harold. Everyone knows about the new residents, the man and his wife who haven't shown up at the dining room for several days, about the man who refuses to eat.

"Can I take your tray?" she asks Faye.

"Yes, darling. Thank you."

"Are those earrings *inside* your ear?" Anastasya does not hold back, referring to the three-quarter-inch in diameter white disks nestled in Amanda's lobes.

"Yeah. They are," Amanda says.

"What in world you pierce your ear with?" Anastasya says.

"They were just pierced like normal," the girl says, laughing. "Then I stretched out the hole. It took a long time."

Anastasya shakes her head as though to ask why she would ever have done that. Amanda steals a peek at Harold in the recliner as she quickly picks up the tray and tiptoes out.

"Such a sweet girl," Faye says.

"What a shame such sweet girl does that to herself."

"Have you eaten?" Faye asks Ryan and Jason. She is indifferent to Amanda's ears.

"We'll go out later," Ryan says.

"I'll ask them to bring you something. It's on me. Here's the menu. It might be too late for anything more than grilled cheese or a hamburger."

"Grilled cheese sounds good. How about you, Jase?"

"Hamburger, please. Thanks."

"Good. That's settled," Faye says, who has finally accomplished something she hasn't been able to do for the past week: she's fed someone.

Harold has confessed that he got the idea on the day of the wedding. What if this were the end? How happy he would have been to die that way. But he didn't follow through then. He waited a month to be sure, and then put his plan into action. He didn't say anything because he didn't want to be dissuaded. He wanted to be far enough along to be sure of his decision. This is not the first time he has entertained the notion of killing himself: he had been a member of the former Hemlock Society, collecting information on methods for making a dignified exit.

It was for people who are suffering, who are in pain, whose days are numbered, Faye said she had told him. And that's what he had always thought, but even with Faye in his life—because of Faye—getting older seemed unbearable. He'd had a taste of what it was like not to be able to care for himself after the stroke. He didn't want to wait until his lungs failed him and, like Fred, had to go around hooked up to oxygen, or until another stroke permanently left him in a wheelchair or impaired his vision so badly he couldn't recognize Faye.

"No," he responds loudly to something Jason has whispered. "I do not want to sit across the table from that woman, deaf, dumb, and blind. I will not deteriorate before her."

"But we've already deteriorated!" Faye tells him, as though giving him the good news that the worst is over.

"I do not want you to see me in diapers or with a tube inserted in my penis."

Ryan thinks she and Jason should leave. They are intruders on this intimacy. She motions to Jason, but his look tells her that it's right for them to be there, that it's weak for them to leave.

"I don't want to go back *there*." He points in the direction of the nursing home. "When I was a little boy, I helped an old man struggling to open the door to my father's candy store. 'Don't ever grow old, sonny,' he said to me as though I had a choice. I thought he was crazy. 'Don't ever grow old.' When you're young you can't understand that getting old means losing your energy, your friends, your autonomy. I've had a full life. I'm the happiest now I've been since I can't remember when. If all I have to look forward to is giving up things and people, I want to take control of my life before it takes control of me. That's what that old man meant: make a choice before it's too late. It's taken me a lifetime to understand it."

Jason can only do this if he continues to try to convince Harold to live. Like a senator engaged in a filibuster he talks. But the more he talks, the more he appears to convince Harold that what he is doing is right.

"Just pray. Your prayers help," Harold tells him.

"I'll call a rabbi."

"No. Just you. I like the way you pray. I like your voice. I don't care what you're saying."

"It's not fair to put this on Jason," Ryan whispers to Faye.

"Let him do it for me, Ryan. Please."

Jason offers Harold a sip of water. He refuses. "No more," he says, putting up his hand. "Not even water."

* * *

"It's his choice," Ryan tells Jason as they sit up in bed well after midnight. "Assisted suicide is legal in some states. We even had a ballot question here a few years ago."

"It was for physician-assisted suicide for the terminally ill, if I remember correctly. And it got voted down. Ryan, the man's not sick."

"But he *is* suffering. He's tormented by what he sees for his future."

"So we're all going to commit suicide? That's fucking insane."

"It's dying with dignity. It's making a choice."

"It's still suicide. The Church is very clear on that. Listen." He pulls up something on his phone and reads: "*From the Vatican Congregation for the Doctrine of Faith: Nothing and no one can in any way permit the killing of an innocent human being, whether a fetus or an embryo, an infant or an adult, or an old person, or one suffering from an incurable disease, or a person who is dying. Moreover, we have no right to ask for this act of killing for ourselves or for those entrusted to our care, nor can any authority legitimately recommend or permit such an action … a violation of person, crime against life, and an attack on humanity.* That's from the Declaration on Euthanasia."

"How old is that?"

"It's from 1980."

Ryan throws up her hands. "First of all, it's outdated. Secondly, Harold isn't even Catholic, so it doesn't apply to him. And most importantly, you know I believe in a woman's right to choose. That stuff drives me nuts."

"I know that. Let's not get into that now. Let's stick with euthanasia. And Harold may not be Catholic, but he's asking me to be his accomplice."

"So what if it is suicide? So what?" She tugs at the sheet to cover her bare breasts while she fishes under the pillow for her oversized T-shirt. She's cold.

"I don't know if I can be a part of this. We're talking about, and I quote: *a violation of a person, a crime against life, and an attack on humanity—*"

"Enough! He's doing it with or without you. You have a chance to comfort him." *And end this torture between us.* She pulls the shirt down over her head.

"I wish I hadn't taken this job. I'd be able to spend the day with him tomorrow."

"It's already tomorrow. It's a quarter to one."

"I almost had him there today. I know I did. I almost had him change his mind."

"And then he might have changed it again. You would just be prolonging his suffering, playing with his body that's already pretty fucked up. Then how would you feel?"

"Life is a God-given gift. To be taken by the giver."

"Not everyone believes that."

"Do you?"

"I do believe it's a gift. I also believe that once you give a gift, you relinquish your possession of it, your power over it, or else it wasn't a gift a all."

"I'll be back in five. Want anything from the kitchen?"

"Tiffany hasn't come home yet," she says, reminding him that he's naked. He gets out of bed and slips into a pair of jeans he picks up from the floor. She knows he's going to pray for guidance, for Harold's soul, and that he can't do it with her beside him. He cannot help obsessing about everyone's problems, from absorbing everyone's angst. Being in bed with him is like sleeping with the entire city of Boston.

"You didn't ask what I would do if it was *you* doing this to *me*," she calls after him.

"I guess I can't see us that far down the road."

"What do you mean?"

"Being old like that. Like Harold said: It's hard to envision."

"Maybe it's because you'd never consider the idea. Suicide, that is."

"Maybe."

"TGIF."

"Can't hear you," he shouts from the kitchen.

"Thank God it's Friday," she yells back. "You can spend the whole fucking weekend with him." Of course she'll be there too—with Faye. Where else would she be?

* * *

Eric is not in the mood to meet a new woman tonight. He's tired. Are thirty-two-year-olds supposed to get tired? He doesn't dare express his fatigue in front of the older generations, who'll come back with something like *What have you got to be tired about?* Or *Wait until you get to be my age.* Or the one he really hates: *When I was young, I never slept.* He spends enough time thinking about what he should be doing when he's not driving his mother to chemotherapy or grocery shopping or worrying about the contest. He spends enough time thinking about how sometimes *all* he'd like to do is sleep.

Worry, he has found, takes the greatest toll on one's body—even a young body. But Becca is hot on him meeting a woman from her yoga class who's just joined a veterinary practice in Rutland. And so he showers and puts on a clean pair of jeans and the light-gray long-sleeved polo shirt he's never worn that his mother ordered from L.L. Bean last Christmas. He makes a minimal effort to make himself presentable; he doesn't want to look too good. Not that that isn't hard to achieve. It's just that he feels too weighed down right now to take on a relationship.

* * *

When he arrives at Michael and Becca's, bottle of wine in hand, he finds Bicycle Girl straddling her Schwinn and peering through the kitchen window, as he too has been guilty of doing. Michael tells Eric she's been there for an hour.

"She only shows up when you're here," Michael says as they stand in the open doorway. "It's as though she knew you were coming. Like she was waiting for you."

"That's possible," Eric tells him, unmoved. "She could have overheard me tell my mother. She's at the house most days for one meal or another."

"Let's invite her in."

Eric looks at Michael perplexed. His friend knows the deal. "No."

"Just for a few minutes."

"No!"

"Why not? What makes you so sure you're handling her the right way? Maybe ignoring her isn't the answer. Maybe she's craving to be included."

"You want to ride around all night again when she takes off? Come on, Mike. Cut it out."

"There's a lot of new research being done on autism and antisocial disorders, nonthreatening ways to communicate with them and have them reciprocate. We have kids at school on the spectrum who—"

"I said no. You don't know what's been done for her all these years by her parents, my mother. You don't know what sets her off. You don't even know what's wrong with her. You don't know *everything*, Mike."

The restraint Michael is exercising is palpable: Eric recognizes it's impossible for Michael not to act on his impulses when he believes they're based on sound reasoning.

"Let me try," Michael insists, taking a step in Bicycle Girl's direction, then freezing when his friend grabs his arm. Eric releases his grip but the damage has been done, the tone for the evening set.

A car pulls up and a petite brunette with long wavy hair gets out. Bicycle Girl rides away. Eric isn't worried, knowing she's gone off of her own accord and that, barring any unwanted advances, she'll eventually wind up at her father's house or Eric's tonight. He also knows that he and Michael will get past their little altercation soon enough—maybe with a beer and pithy apologies or just a slap on the back—but for the next three hours, they are tolerant of each other, making an effort to put the pretty and pleasant veterinarian at ease. Over Becca's paella and several glasses of Pinot Grigio, Eric inquires about the doctor's life; she asks him about his, both knowing that neither will take the initiative to arrange a second date anytime soon.

Chapter 24

Saturday, May 10

SOMETHING HAS HAPPENED. Something has changed. A calm presides over the stifling apartment by Saturday morning. Ryan and Jason find Faye in the armchair next to the bed, wearing a pink cashmere sweater and glasses, reading the *Globe* aloud to Harold. Jocelina has brought a box of doughnut holes and turned on the coffee maker in anticipation of the couple's visit, as though it is nothing more than a casual social call.

"How is he?" Jason is disappointed to see that Harold has declined since the night before. He was counting on trying new tactics.

"Anastasya put him to bed last night after you left. He hasn't gotten up except to go to the bathroom. Jocelina brought this." She points to a portable commode next to the bed. "She's very good that way. I don't know where it's coming from, but it keeps on coming," she says referring to Harold's incessant need to urinate.

"Not so loud. I have my hearing aids in." The voice from the bed is fainter but his speech is fluid. Eyes wide open, he smiles with lips that are drier than they were the night before, cracking at the corners of his mouth. "Sorry if I have bad breath."

"Would you like to brush your teeth?" Jason asks.

"Nope."

"It might make you feel better."

"Nice try."

"This is your show, Harold. You make the calls."

"So you've come over to my side, young fella?"

"I've always been on your side."

"Faye's come on board. What a woman. I'm such a lucky man." He smiles at her and she returns the admiration with an added shrug of her shoulders, as if to say: Do I have a choice?

If she's such a wonderful woman, why do you want to leave her? Jason thinks, but the tide has shifted and he will no longer swim against the current; rather he'll let it take him wherever it carries Harold.

"Is Ryan here?"

"Running some errands. She'll be here soon. Would you like to listen to some music?" Jason asks.

"There's a box with some CDs in it we haven't unpacked yet. It's under that thing that looks like an old radio. It *is* a radio, but there's a CD player in it too. Pretty nifty, eh? Got it on sale at Caldor before it closed."

Jason fishes through the box beneath the side table in the living room, puts a CD in the retro radio, and *Moonlight Serenade* turns the place into a ballroom.

"Care to dance?" Harold asks Faye.

"If only we could. I'll fix Jason a cup of coffee." Jocelina appears at her side, helping her to maneuver the walker.

"Maybe the music makes you sad?" Jason asks Harold.

"Hell no! The fact that we can't dance only confirms my position. You know, when I was a young man in Brooklyn ... Did I tell you I grew up in Brooklyn?"

"No. I didn't know that."

"My older brother and his friends had a block party and paid next to nothing for Glenn Miller and Louis Armstrong to come. Can you imagine?"

"That's pretty amazing."

"Of course, they were just starting up then. But they were popular just the same."

"How'd you end up in Boston?"

"After the war. I went in right after high school, just in time for the Big One. The war was pretty much over after that, and my buddy told me to come and start a furniture business with him. I figured what the hell. Something new. So I went."

"And your buddy?"

"He had no luck. Survives the Battle of the Bulge and gets taken out by pancreatic cancer at thirty-eight."

"That must have been tough on you."

"On me? Tough on his family. Tough on him. Life is tough."

"So is dying."

"Can't give up, can you?"

"I didn't mean it that way."

"Let me tell you something. When you're ready, it's easy. It's just that easy."

"I admire you, Harold."

"No you don't. You think what I'm doing is wrong. A sin against God."

"It doesn't matter what I believe."

"For the record, there are no sins against God. Just against people. That's where I stand."

Ryan walks in with a box of breakfast sandwiches from a café and package of swabs.

"You're a genius," Jason says, giving her a peck on the cheek. "Harold, can I moisten your lips? Ryan brought these for you."

"Okay." He finally agrees to something.

"How about we eat these on the patio? Is that all right, Faye?"

"The patio. That's a good idea, Ryan. It's cruel to eat in front of him. Come, Jocelina. Bring the doughnut holes and coffee. Have some breakfast."

Jason picks up two chairs from the kitchen table and follows Ryan and Faye out the sliding doors into the narrow sitting area with its bistro set. They fit snugly around the table, like rolled-up anchovies in their compact can, on this beautiful morning.

"Faye, shouldn't we call hospice? A rabbi? Shouldn't we call *someone*?" Ryan speaks just above a whisper, as though tiptoeing on sacred ground, even though Harold can't possible hear her.

"Jason is here. He feels comforted by Jason." She shrugs her shoulders. "Maybe he's a *goy* deep down."

Jason knows that's a funny line, but he can't seem to laugh or even smile.

"There might still be time. Let me try," he says.

"No. Someday you'll understand." Faye becomes serious. "You move slowly, Everything takes so long. You nap a lot. It's hard to read, to hear. And the worst part is, people treat you differently. Life gets just a little too small."

"But Harold isn't doing badly at all," Ryan tells her.

"This takes courage. Don't let him fool you. I've been to a ninety-year-old's birthday party where the guest of honor is doing great. Then you see her a few years later and it's a different story."

"Promise me you won't ever do this, Faye," Ryan says.

"No promises, *bubeleh*."

Faye's phone rings, and Ryan runs in to answer it. It's Lauren; she usually calls on Saturday mornings. When she finds out what's going on, she's furious. "Why am I not surprised? What did we know about him? Harold is committing suicide, and the kids are helping," she tells Joe.

"What the fuck!" Joe can be heard saying as he gets on the extension phone in the bedroom. "What the hell's going on? This is not right. You two kids should not be dealing with this."

"I warned you, Ryan," Lauren says.

"I'm driving up to Boston!" Joe says.

"No, Dad. It's under control. We can handle it."

"What do you know about dying, about making arrangements?"

"Harold has it pretty well covered. Really. He even wrote his own obituary—one handwritten sheet of paper in the top dresser drawer, with the number of the funeral home and all. Says Faye can do what she likes with the ashes. It's okay, Dad. We've got it."

"Give me that undertaker's name and number. Just give me his name. Let me take care of this."

"I already called him, Dad. He said to call when it's time."

"I don't like this. Is there someone helping you?"

"Jason."

"Other than Jason."

"She can do it, Joe," Lauren says. "She wants to—and obviously Faye wants her to."

"We'll come up for the funeral," Joe says. "We'll come for Faye."

"No funeral. He wants to be cremated."

"A memorial?"

"No. Nothing. He doesn't want anything,"

"That's wise," Lauren says.

"That's pitiful," Joe says.

"Ryan, find out who his doctor is and have him send someone from hospice."

"Mom—"

"It's for his sake, Ryan. Call the doctor."

"Would you like to talk to Faye?" Ryan asks her parents.

"Yes. Put my mother on."

"Don't yell at her, Mom," Ryan whispers into the mobile as she carries it out to Faye.

"What do you think I am? An insensitive moron?"

"And Mom, in case I forget tomorrow, with all this, Happy Mother's Day."

"I'm sorry, Mom," they can all hear Lauren tell Faye. She has not called her mother "Mom" in years.

When she was in college, Lauren decided to call her mother and father by their first names. Her father found it amusing; if Faye was upset, she didn't let on: it was the Age of Aquarius, and they were all equal in Lauren's eyes—men, women, parents, grandparents, and children. When she had Ryan, she taught the baby to call them all by their first names as well. But as time went on, Lauren began to envy her friends whose children addressed them as Mommy and Daddy; she began to tire of the odd stares and occasional questions as to the true relationship between her and Ryan, and so she told Ryan to call her Mommy. But it was too late—too hard for the little girl to make the switch.

Then, one Mother's Day, when Ryan was in high school and she asked her mother if she would like anything special (a question to which Lauren had always answered no), Lauren admitted that she would very much like for Ryan to call her Mom. Ryan found the request surprising and a little problematic, because she liked calling her parents by their first names: It made her unique among her friends. Nevertheless, she made the effort, and when the next Mother's Day arrived, she was no longer even tempted to cross out the *Mother* in her card and write *Lauren*, as she had done in the past. The same went for Joe, who had always preferred being called Dad.

Ryan's parents became like all her other friends' parents: They were Mom and Dad. Joe's parents had never allowed Ryan to call them by their first names, considering it disrespectful. In their family, everyone even had a title that accompanied their names, like aunt, cousin, uncle, or *comare*. When Ryan asked Faye and Sid if they would also like her to make the changeover, both said she could call them anything she cared to call them. Such nonsense over nothing, her grandfather said. Call me grandpa, *zayde*, Sid, *schlemiel*. And so they remained Faye and Sid to Ryan—and to Lauren.

Chapter 25

EARLY IN THE morning Jason phones Father Curran for the second time since he's taken his leave. It's not against the rules: He's already told his mentor he's not returning to the novitiate. This time he's asking for advice as a member of the Catholic Church—not the Jesuit community. The priest is not surprised either time; nothing rattles him.

While Jason is talking to Father Curran, a fully dressed Tiffany comes into the kitchen and Jason steps out onto the fire escape. She plops a backpack on the floor, pours herself a glass of OJ, and fills a bowl with granola and milk. Slicing a banana, she asks Ryan what all the secrecy is about. She knows what's going on with Harold; Ryan had to tell someone, and Tiffany can, on occasion, have a good take on extraordinary circumstances.

"He's talking to his advisor."

"In the seminary?"

Ryan nods. "Where you headed?" she asks Tiffany.

"Hiking in Vermont."

"Alone?"

"With a friend. I'll be gone a few days."

"Talk about secrecy. You never bring anyone here anymore, Tiff. We'd like to meet your friend."

"It's gotten kind of crowded here," Tiffany says, fishing through some fruit in a wooden bowl on the table and selecting a green apple.

"Do you resent Jason being here? It's just for a short while. You've certainly had friends here for long stretches."

"We don't have time for each other anymore," she says, examining the apple.

"You're jealous of Jason? You're never around. At least not when I'm here. And when I am—"

"What?" She looks at Ryan.

"Forget it."

"No. What were you going to say?"

"Sometimes you have no concept of privacy. You run around half naked."

"Sorry if I've invaded your space." She decisively drops the apple into her backpack.

"You don't get it," Ryan tells her.

"No. *You* don't get it. *I'm* not your problem," Tiffany says, shaking her finger at Ryan.

"What's that supposed to mean?"

"*You* figure it out."

Ryan doesn't understand Tiffany's obsession with their relationship. It's not as though they've known one another forever. The girl wasn't even able to tell her she had a booger in her nose at lunch with Eric and Danni at Baby's Grill in Brackton. When she confronted Tiffany about it later as they shared the queen-sized bed at the Daffodil House, Tiffany said she hadn't wanted to embarrass Ryan.

What kind of friend lets her girlfriend sit there with snot in her nose? Ryan asked her. Tiffany told Ryan that she had already made an ass of herself lying about Jason and what he did for a living. Ryan accused her of an over-the-top performance with the vendors, to which Tiffany had no defense except that she had just gotten into it because she found it so exciting. And with that, Tiffany asked something she'd never asked her: Did she ever consider being with a woman? It was a natural question. If Ryan had, for some matter of convenience, found herself in bed with a male friend of hers, he most likely would have asked if they could, for just that night, be friends with benefits, and he wouldn't have been the first guy to ask the question. But she wasn't even sure if that's what Tiffany was suggesting for the two of them since Ryan hadn't given her the opportunity to elaborate. She had simply said, no.

"Look, Tiff," Ryan says, trying to make peace with her roommate. "I can't help it that Jason's back in my life now."

"He never left."

"Let's have lunch when everything with Harold is over. Maybe go to a movie."

"Sure," she says, slinging the backpack over one shoulder.

"Are you dating a guy?" Ryan asks.

"I'm not dating. I'm having a good time."

"Any decisions on school?" Ryan admits she hasn't shown much interest in Tiff's life lately.

"I'm getting closer."

"How's your Italian class going?"

"*Finito.* Over. Guess you'll be at Faye's again today?"

"Where else?"

"Good luck. I mean it." Tiffany puts her glass, spoon, and bowl in the sink and washes them. "You were more fun when you were just pretending to be getting married," she says on her way out.

Ryan is growing tired of Tiffany's evasiveness, her phobias about clutter and foul-smelling dishwashers, and her know-it-all manner of doling out advice when everything else in her own life is anything but fastidiously tended to.

"Where'd Tiff go?" Jason asks when he comes back into the kitchen.

"Hiking," she says.

"Why you so pissed off?"

"Sometimes she just gets under my skin."

He is too preoccupied with Harold's situation to press for more information. In fact, he cannot seem to talk to her about much of anything else.

"Father Curran," he tells her, "said that while he can't condone Harold's decision or recommend it, he says lots of old people reach a point where they're tired of living, especially in a lesser physical state—which as we know isn't entirely Harold's case, or at least it wasn't until he started this thing—and give up. Basically, he described everything Harold has already said. He said Harold has the right to refuse his medications. That it's not my role to preach or teach here, but to help Harold make some meaning out of the life he's lived, to help him find that peaceful place at the right time. He said I should stay open to him, walk on his journey with him, hold him up as best I can. If I'm a comfort to Harold's soul, I should comfort him into this next life, and accept that we have no control over his life and death. 'It is not your sin. It's not his, either. Just pray for him and let God take care of the rest. And I, my son, will pray for you.' That's pretty much what he said."

"I think I like Father Curran."

"Let's go to bed," he says.

"Now?"

"Yeah."

Afterward, he rolls over on his back, moist eyes closed, and sighs. She knows he's disappointed in himself, not only for thinking of his own needs at the moment, but for having failed to save Harold. She wipes his tears from her shoulder, then wipes her own.

* * *

Overnight, Harold has grown weaker and his speech and breathing become more labored. He refuses his blood pressure medicine. Discomfort is apparent, though they have no idea how much he may be suffering, and Ryan is glad she took Lauren's advice and phoned Harold's doctor to ask him to have a hospice volunteer come and evaluate the situation.

"You have to help me die," Harold tells Colleen that afternoon. She is a woman around Lauren's age. Everyone of consequence seems to be around her parents' ages. She is a former nurse with a clean, scrubbed face and short, light brown hair that hugs her scalp like a bathing cap.

"At this point, we can make a diagnosis to warrant our participation," she tells Jason and Ryan, and Ryan is relieved to have professional help and to be told that this drain on their own bodies—on their lives—will soon be over.

Colleen smiles at Harold and sits down on the bed, telling him she can offer morphine for pain and shortness of breath, and something for anxiety. She tells him that it is okay to do this, to speed things along. He thanks her. She says she'll return tomorrow. She takes Jason into the living room and gives him the Comfort Care Kit: liquid morphine that is to be administered by a dropper under the tongue (he will not need much, she assures Jason, and less and less each time), lorazepam for anxiety to be taken with the tiniest sip of water, and more cotton swabs for his dry mouth.

"Morphine is very constipating," Colleen says. "Each day without nutrition the system breaks down, but the body still makes stool. The drug, however, slows down the motility in the GI system. That can be uncomfortable."

For the first time, Harold asks for a glass of water.

"It's better if you don't drink it at this point," she reminds him.

"Oh yeah. No," he says.

On Monday afternoon, when Jason arrives after work, Harold has stopped talking and his breathing has become more labored. Jason gives him another dose of the pain medication. On Tuesday, he is semiconscious: Jason gives him an even smaller dose of morphine and slips a diaper on him; he helps Faye onto the bed, where she lies next to him and holds his hand. By Wednesday, Harold has passed into a coma. When Jason and Ryan arrive on Friday, Faye is lying alongside Harold and Jocelina is sitting in the armchair next to the bed. At 3:14 a.m. on Saturday, Harold lets out a few mild gasps and stops breathing. It is as Colleen said it would be—relatively peaceful. Ryan phones Colleen: There will be no need for her to come today. She phones the funeral home. They will pick up the body in about three hours.

"Not that soon," Faye says.

"Please, Faye," an exhausted Ryan entreats.

"All right. Tell them to come at seven. Seven will be fine."

Chapter 26

RYAN IS ANGRY with Faye for having brought all this about, although she knows this is bigger than Faye and Harold, that her anger is about Jason's intimacy with faith, which leaves very little room for their own intimacy. Yet he takes her again that day as they try to recoup lost sleep. There is no caressing, no foreplay. He climbs on top of her and, burying his head in her shoulder, he enters her, but not before asking permission: To use her as a confessional; a holy prostitute; a source of absolution for his sin and a release of nearly two weeks of internal struggle?

"Is it all right?" he murmurs, leaving no time to negotiate because he's pumping once, twice, three times, as though beating his breast while crying *Mea culpa, mea culpa: through my fault, through my fault, through my most grievous fault, bless me, Father, for I have sinned.*

* * *

He grows pensive in the days following Harold's death, which is reminiscent of the time before he left her.

"You're in your head too much, Jason," Ryan tells him one evening as he prepares his lesson plans. "You think something, and next thing you think you've said it but you never did. Even philosophers have soapboxes."

"No reason to go ballistic on me."

She throws her hands up into the air. "Ballistic? You think *this* is ballistic?" She *is* shouting now out of sheer frustration. "You men push and push us to our limits, and then when we explode, you call us psycho."

"I never said you were psycho."

"You intimated it. All I have to do is raise my voice and you think I'm yelling at you—I'm 'ballistic.'"

"You're exaggerating."

"And you're making a good offense the best defense."

They have makeup sex that night and tell each other it's all right now. But it's not all right. There is not much right about them. And yet they go on like this for two more weeks, until one morning they don't speak. Later that day, she texts him at work and suggests they meet in Cambridge at a restaurant they've never been to before.

Chapter 27

S HE'S THERE BEFORE he is, sipping a glass of Merlot. He enters smiling, telling himself he has no idea what's about to take place, only that he knows she's all business by the way she nervously fondles the glass of wine so dark it resembles blood. She's had a bad day, one that's about to get worse.

"Sorry I'm late. Todd Neisman called a last-minute meeting." He does not dare cross that electric fence and kiss her. He takes his seat across from her.

"No problem. I just got here."

"Did you order for me?"

"Why would I do that?"

"To save time. You must be hungry."

He's trying to keep afloat and her buoyed with him, and so he dances around her heaviness in the hope that any minute she'll return to her usual levity and lose the strained look in her eyes, but there's nothing but thin ice to step on here.

"You too," she says, still somber.

The waiter in a floor-length white apron asks if he can bring Jason a drink. Jason inquires what they have on tap and listens to a recitation that he wishes were longer to take up more time, stretch the minutes like an elastic band between now and when Ryan starts talking again. He selects a beer, barely conscious of what he's asked for. It arrives promptly, and he gulps most of it before she's done ordering her entrée, waiting for it to numb some part of him, any part of him. When it's his turn, he requests the first thing he sees on the menu—and another beer.

"How'd you sleep last night?" she asks.

"Okay. Why?"

"You were all over the place."

"Sorry. Guess you didn't sleep well yourself then."

"It's okay. I wasn't tired." But her words are void of emotion, spoken with effort by someone who is fatigued.

He knows she's gone through his school bag and found his copy of *The Confessions of Saint Augustine*, a white paperback with a light green border, dog-eared in many places, especially to a page where the book practically opens up on its own, the page where he saw a fresh tea stain this morning when he found the book not in its usual place and the half-drunk cup of tea left on the coffee table in the living room. She has never been able to be secretive: She's too messy and thoughtless about cleaning up after herself. The folded corner of the page leads to one of his favorite passages, highlighted in yellow, an excerpt from "The Examined Life."

> *Too late have I loved you, O Beauty, ancient yet ever new. Too late have I loved you! And behold, you were within, but I was outside, searching for you there—plunging, deformed amid those fair forms that you had made. You were with me, but I was not with you. Things held me far from you, which, unless, they were in you, did not exist at all. You called and shouted, and burst my deafness. You gleamed and shone upon me, and chased away my blindness. You breathed fragrant odors on me, and I held back my breath, but now I pant for you. I tasted, and now I hunger and thirst for you. You touched me, and now I yearn for your peace.*

He is not angry that she saw and read it; he is relieved to know that she knows what he contemplates, struggles with, confronts, and, as she often claims, does alone within the confines of his mind. Still, he fights her when she says it's over. She cannot compete with God, she tells him, and she shouldn't. She tells him she sees his strength, his faith, and his power to help. It's all blended together and cannot be separated or spread over a spiritual world and a lay world, like individual wheat or gluten-free canapés on the same platter. It's all connected; it's all one.

He knows it. She knows it. How did she think they could do this? she asks. How did he? He cannot deny feeling hunted down by God at times, wishing God would just leave him alone. But his own persever-ance is also relentless: How can he sleep without her by his side? How can he come home to anything—anyone but her? He's tried so hard not to be afraid, not to care what others think. How can she throw away what they have been working on these past months? How can they fail again? Their only failure, she says, has been trying too hard to make right something so very wrong.

"Don't you love me?" he asks, aware of using the turquoise eyes she loves to penetrate hers like a laser beam that will produce the desired response.

"I do. I love you for all you are, for your intensity in all you be-lieve. But that's the problem, isn't it? I can't share it. I wish I could. We can spend our lives getting over one hump after another, trying to fit together. But the only getting over is the fact that we don't make each other happy. I can't just be in love with love."

"You're just running scared, Ryan. You do that. You act like you want something, but then you can't follow through. You can't even find an end to your stories."

"Fuck you! I'm not the one who left." She does not lower her voice.

The waiter heading their way with a cloth-wrapped water pitcher executes an about-face. Jason is embarrassed.

"You're not going to lecture me on following through," she says. "And for your information, I've hardly been able to get a word down because I've been spending all my time with you!"

He hadn't meant what he said. He just needed to punch back. He was coming undone. "I just don't understand why this is so sudden. You keep everything in."

"Me? You're the one who needs a mind reader, unless you're explaining church dogma."

"What are we doing, Ryan? Come on! We're good together. We make each other happy." He tries to be playful—to *lighten up* as Father Curran urged when Jason was deciding whether or not to leave the seminary.

"But we can never sustain it," she says having regained her calm. "And that makes me sad."

"We'll go to counseling." He forces a smile.

"It's bigger than that. I've seen you succeed, Jase—with Harold, kids at school, people in your outreach programs. I've seen what you're best at—I guess what you're called to do. But you need to understand that while I admire you for it—love you for it, just like everybody else—I don't share enough in it. It's always me looking at you, admiring you, getting frustrated by you. But it's never me in the picture. It's damn tiring trying to fit in where you don't belong."

He plays his last card. "There's talk of Pope Francis being in favor of priests marrying."

"It's about time," she mumbles sarcastically. "No—really, Jason. That's awesome. But it won't matter for us. You need to be an integral part of the Church in a way that has no room for me, and frankly, I have no room for it or any other religious institution."

He looks down at the table. He's quiet for a long while.

"You have no room for *me*, is what you mean." He can no longer feign levity.

"You're intent on making me the bad guy, aren't you?"

"That's it, then," he concedes reluctantly.

"Jason, I hated you for leaving me, and I love you so much for trying again. It's made me feel guilty and shitty and lonely. What it doesn't always make me feel is good, and it can't make you feel good either. We're in each other's way. And you know it as well as I do."

"So we failed—again."

"No, Jase. We learned."

He has underestimated her, taken her for granted at times, and feels the pain of losing her now more than ever. But in his heart he knows what he's always known is demanded of him, what he's read over and over in another highlighted passage:

Truly you command that I be continent from the lust of the flesh, the lust of the eyes, and the pride of life. You have commanded self-restraint from fornication, and as for wedlock itself, you have counseled something better than what you have permitted ...

"Is it okay with you if I say goodbye to Faye?"

"Of course! How can you even think you need to ask my permission?"

"Will you come with me?"

She takes a deep breath. He knows it's so hard for both of them to deny one another, to deny themselves. But this is the beginning of the end.

"No," she replies.

"You want me to tell Eric?"

"I've got that. I got us into it; I'll get us out. The lying is over."

"I'll leave tonight." He cannot envision spending a night under the same roof after breaking up.

"You don't have to."

"Yeah, I do. I'll go back with you and get my stuff. I'm sure I can stay at the rectory at St. Gerard's until school is over. Just three and a half weeks left."

"I'll drive you over there after you get your things."

"Better if I take the T."

"It'll be late," she says.

"Okay. I'll take an Uber."

"Will you go back to the novitiate?"

"Where else would I go?" Her question surprises him.

"I thought you might want to pursue the Brotherhood. You like them."

And for once he sees things clearly: It's not this or that or the other possibility. He knows where he belongs; because if this thing he has always felt about God is real, he needs to share it with others—bring it to others.

"I'll always be here for you," he tells her.

"I know. Me too."

Can one feel relief and pain at the same time? In any kind of death, do they bear equal weight?

Their meals arrive and they dig in with gusto; they are hungry to get on with their lives. But they draw out the end, taking small spoonfuls of the shared crème brûlée then sipping slowly on their brandies. When they finally leave the restaurant, it's with arms around each other, supporting each other like an old couple who have just fallen in love.

Chapter 28

Monday, June 2

THE DOCTOR SAYS Danni has made remarkable strides since her accident. Today she shed her immobilizing brace for a flexible one that allows her to bend the knee and, with the support of crutches, put a bit of weight on her injured leg. Just in time for the emergency Chamber meeting Eric called as acting chair in her absence.

He has visited her at the hospital and numerous times after she came home, bringing her and her parents takeout from Chez Alexandre's and Baby's Grill, along with his mother's two-year-old canned peaches and jam. One night he made her tofu curry and rice, one of his mother's favorite recipes. Thank God she is back to chair tonight's meeting. It's enough that *he* has to drop the bomb. At least Ryan had the decency to call him and not leave a text or an email. When he listened to *her* message saying they needed to talk, he phoned back immediately.

"Shoulda figured as much," the grumpy appliance repairman, known as Electric Ed, barks when Eric announces the wedding is off. "This harebrained scheme of yours, Boulanger, was bound to be a bust."

"Why would you say that, Ed?" Mother Twinkle asks. She sits up straight and closer to the table, her soft voice now within the old man's limited earshot. "These things happen between young couples."

"Cut the horseshit," Electric Ed grumbles.

"It's just so unfortunate for Brackton," Maisie says.

"Oh, you think so?" Hank the mechanic bellows. "You think being the laughingstock of the county—of the state—is a bit of an inconvenience? You're damn right it is."

"I don't know why you're so bent out of shape, Hank. Didn't affect you in any way. I didn't see your name on the list of vendors," DJ Rich Rinaldi says.

"What was I supposed to contribute? A lube job?"

"If someone needed it," Rich tells him.

"I can try to sell the dresses," Fran Costantino says, trying to hide her disappointment. "It'll be hard—the sizes are small and there's no room for more alterations. I can put them on eBay or Craigslist."

"I haven't baked the cakes yet, but I did give up two other wedding requests from other towns," Lisa Anderson laments.

"Well, that only shows how much the contest was working," Mother Twinkle pipes in. "All that advertising has brought new business to Brackton."

"All that advertising we paid good money for, Little Miss Sunshine."

"Hank, I'm going to ask you to speak respectfully, at least while you're in these meetings," Danni admonishes.

Some agree with Hank, while others can't deny that the contest has created a certain amount of notoriety in northern Vermont.

"It's brought many of us who were lagging behind into the twenty-first century. I know I've learned a lot about the Internet and using it to my benefit," jeweler Raphael O'Leary says.

"I agree," Danni says.

"I just mailed the invitations to Ryan two days ago," Annie Chalis says. "And the printer did me the favor of a rush job."

"He'll never know they weren't used," Danni tells her.

"What about you, Mark, and you too, Terry?" Maisie Billings asks the owners of the Daffodil House and the Brackton Inn. "You two had the most to lose—a whole other affair you could have held that weekend. And the food! Can you cancel the orders?"

"Too late for that. Look, as we say on Wall Street, that's business," Mark says. "We'll donate it somewhere. It was a good idea,

Eric. Maybe we just selected the wrong couple. Maybe it's *all* our faults."

"*I* didn't want them," Hank says, picking his greasy fingernails.

"Only when you thought they were gay," Rich Rinaldi reminds him.

"Can we get another couple at this late date?" Maisie asks.

Eric has remained silent, eyes closed, slouched against the back of the slatted oak chair, his head dangling onto his chest, looking as though it might fall off. "We can try," he says dully, as he comes to life like a collapsible doll whose strings have been tightened.

"How do you figure?"

"There might be a couple who didn't get married because they couldn't afford it. Or maybe they got married in a city hall and would love to follow up with a big party, even do the ceremony over. Worst case scenario, not as many people as they might have liked can make it."

"I'll contact the runners-up tonight," Danni says, shuffling through her papers, searching for her list.

"Don't make us look hard up," Hank tells her.

"Do what you have to do," Eric advises.

"You better hope she's a size six," Maisie tells Fran.

Fran laughs, already energized with a bit of hope. "I've got some dresses from last season I'm dying to get rid of."

"Before I ask for someone to make a motion to adjourn, I have an announcement to make.," Danni says. "I'm resigning from the Chamber."

"Starting when?" Fran asks, as surprised as the others.

"Right now."

"Are you kidding me?" Hank says with a cold stare.

"Young people don't know nothing 'bout commitment," Electric Ed whines.

"Because of your accident? It's completely understandable," Maisie says.

"In part," Danni explains. "I'm far from ninety percent, and everything takes a lot more time and effort. And there's the Fourth of July parade and picnic, and then the Fall Festival bazaar, the Children's

Halloween Rag Shag and Pumpkin Party, and the leaf peepers' events to get ready for. I'm just a bit overwhelmed and limited at the moment."

"Stands to reason, sweetie. Don't know how you even made it here tonight," Mother Twinkle says.

"I guess that keeps *you* acting chair, Mr. VP," Hank says to Eric.

"You know, I feel I've got a bit of conflict of interest here at the moment. Annie, you're treasurer, think you can be chair until someone else comes forward and we take a formal vote. Just to get us through this quarter?"

"Oh, Eric, summer is really my busy time, in addition to Valentine's Day and Mother's Day."

"How about you, Lisa?"

"I'm swamped this time of year too."

"I'll do it. Tax season is over." Accountant Rob Burns is itching to take command.

"Just for this quarter, Rob." Eric knows full well that once Rob gets hold of the reins, he won't let go.

"I'll fill you in on the particulars after the meeting, Rob, if you can stay. Otherwise we'll make a date," Danni tells him.

Rob smiles. He doesn't think for a second he needs to be brought up to speed.

"Wait! What about the runners-up, Danni?" Fran asks. They all nod as though they haven't lost track of this minor detail.

"I don't mind getting in touch with them later. Technically my term won't end until midnight."

"Take your time," Hank says with newfound empathy.

"You take your time, young lady," Rob Burns echoes louder.

"Today, tomorrow, I don't think anyone minds," Hank says. "You've worked hard on this. You should be the one to follow up with these folks and take it to the finish line."

Hank is glad Eric has recused himself. He's always wanted him out of the picture. And that's just fine with Eric.

They all assent, not wanting to pass up Hank's unusually considerate posturing. Danni calls for a motion to elect Rob acting president and for her to continue as liaison to the new couple; Eric makes the motion; Terry Stewart seconds; there's a resounding aye. No further business. Meeting adjourned.

* * *

"Why didn't you tell me you were stepping down?" Eric asks after everyone has left.

He picks up her large black tote bag filled with papers, a loose-leaf binder with all the agendas and minutes from the past two years, and the Chamber's bylaws she is never without at meetings, while she adjusts her crutches under her armpits.

"Honestly, I wasn't considering it until today. I hate to admit it, but it's too much now, Eric, I won't be able to do justice to it all—and to everyone. I would have liked you to take over, but I understand why you don't want to. By the way, thank you for the meals and the roses and the cupcakes you brought over."

"I was going for the sunflowers but Annie said you like roses."

"Annie always pushes roses."

"Recovery's made you snarky."

"I don't mean because they're expensive. Annie just likes roses."

"It's okay to be snarky. Basic bitch suits you just fine."

"Oh, Eric," she says, blushing, the old Danni apparent. "The color of the roses you sent over last week was so unusual—my favorite shade of pink."

"You think we'll really be able to get another couple?"

"We can try."

He's taken the Subaru because it's easier for her to get into and out of. He settles her in the passenger seat and throws her crutches into the back, for once grateful for the Pollyanna personality that manages to lift his spirits an inch and make him optimistic that she might have something up her little puffed sleeve.

Chapter 29

Saturday, June 27

THE NEW COUPLE has followed the plans set in place for Ryan and Jason, from the gowns that Danni mailed to the bride down to the favors, with the exception of the ceremony that will be held at the Congregational church instead of St. Anne's. The rings were resized as were the tuxes, and delivered to the Daffodil House. No need for a rehearsal dinner; the small bridal party will be briefed the morning of the wedding. The responses from the late-date e-vites sent out by the pair reduced the guest list to seventy-six, which thanks to Danni's promptings includes her family and close friends along with members of the Chamber who were encouraged to attend for appearances sake and in support of the vendors who had contributed. Danni especially wanted Michael and Becca to come: Becca had been so kind as to make house calls and give her massages during her recovery, and Michael, she assured Eric, would ease Eric's anxiety.

At their final Chamber meeting before the wedding, Danni told the members that everything had been handled via long distance since there hadn't been time for a visit. "The new couple is thrilled," she assured them.

"Aren't you even going to tell us their names?" Lisa Anderson had asked.

"After the commotion that caused last time, let's not even go there."

She was getting so smart, Eric thought. Everyone had laughed at the comment. She had learned how to put them all at ease.

"It suffices to say they're on board and very pleased and grateful and looking forward to their dream wedding."

"That's good enough for me," Hank assured her.

"Get this damn thing over with," Electric Ed roared.

* * *

Eric lays his charcoal gray suit—his only suit—white shirt and red and navy striped tie on his bed; there is nothing more for him to do for the wedding scheduled to take place at 4 p.m. but show up.

His mother and Bicycle Girl eat breakfast on the screened in porch: waffles that he prepared with wild blueberries grown in their yard. Facing the morning sun in a T-shirt and jeans, he is barefoot, feet free from being cooped up for too many months in thick thermal sox and laced up boots, every pore of his body happy to breathe. At last he understands his mother's enthusiasm for spring cleaning, for opening every window, vacuuming spider webs beneath the chairs and sofas, for sweeping away sticky silky threads hanging from the ceiling, that have suddenly become apparent in the new stream of sunlight. Wash the curtains that smell and feel like dust. Scrub the pine floors where dirt not confined to the mudroom has been tracked in all winter and ground into the grain. Let the house breathe too.

That's what he's been doing for her for weeks—under her supervision and probably not enough to her satisfaction, but willingly nevertheless. That's how he intends to pass the day. But for now, he succumbs to freeing the cobwebs of his mind. He takes in his mother's smile and enthusiasm for her backyard: the pink and white peonies she transplanted from her mother's garden years ago—their heavy blooms like freakish heads too big for their necks—and the purple cone shaped lupine whose name he hates hearing his mother utter because it sounds like another disease. The border of lily of the valley and buttercups around the porch needs to be weeded before the clover overtakes them. She's been enjoying a good stretch, with more energy than she's shown in recent months, more appetite, more of the signs that, he'd been told, often signal an imminent decline.

He takes it all in this morning: her laugh, her eyes and teeth yellowed from drugs, her enthusiasm, her delight in watching Bicycle Girl slowly and methodically eat her breakfast, like a robot with dying batteries, eyes fixed on the edge of her plate or whatever it is she sees. And he wonders if he's loved his mother more than he loved his father, or if his feelings for her are the result of a longer time spent together and a greater dependency on each other. Both demanded of him more than they ever would have wanted, and he has come to appreciate that. But what is a life without demands placed on you by others? A life without love?

He picks up his camera.

"Oh, Eric, not now. Look at me. I'm not even dressed!" Marie Boulanger cries, trying to wave him off as he snaps away, zooming in on the fragile complexion and the once blond head now topped off with the turban that makes her look as though she's luxuriating at a spa; zooming out to capture the red plaid pajama bottoms peeking out of her white terrycloth robe that has fallen open at the waist. He clicks away as she brings a forkful of waffle to her mouth, her other bony hand cupped under her chin to catch the dripping syrup. He wants to capture her while she still cares about her appearance— about everything.

"You be careful," she tells Bicycle Girl as the young woman abruptly gets up from the table and sets off for her day on wheels. No smile returned. No words of thank you. No hint at when she will return. But she always does. Sometimes for breakfast, sometimes for dinner. Even on the nights when his mother sends him out to search for her, he knows a reconnaissance isn't necessary, that Bicycle Girl will show up sooner or later, either at their house or her father's, up on the ridge.

Marie had intended to go to the wedding; after all, it's her baby's project. However, when 3:30 rolls around and Eric checks to see if she needs help getting ready, he finds her lying on her bed. She was too ambitious today and overdid it—puttering around in the garden planting herbs, cleaning out the fridge, and feeling so damned good doing it. He'll look in on her from time to time, he says. No need, she tells him. He sets her up with a pitcher of ice water, her pills, and some buttered rye toast she's been craving which he cuts up in bite-sized squares as though for a toddler, so she doesn't fill up too fast and get sick. When he pops in later despite her protests, he'll heat up a slice of leftover quiche he bought yesterday.

He showers and shaves, parts the hair he has been growing out, dresses, sprays himself with cologne, and heads over in his pickup to the Congregational Church at the Brackton-Peterbury town line. He had asked Danni if she wanted him to pick her up, but she said she was going with her parents. The new couple has gotten a beautiful day for their wedding; one thing to check off the list of what could go wrong, or, if he were more like Danni, what has gone right.

* * *

There's a decent crowd pouring into the church. There being no ushers or groomsmen to direct foot traffic, Eric hesitates in the vestibule, contemplating where to sit. He realizes that it doesn't matter which side of the aisle he chooses, since he doesn't know the bride *or* the groom. The seating appears lopsided with the majority of guests on the left, and so he turns right, taking a seat in the last row, where he'll be able to scan the church for all those in attendance.

He sees Maisie and a date, and Fran and her mother diagonally across the aisle from him. Mother Twinkle is behind them, her long white hair flowing over a glittery gold shawl. Like Eric, rivals Lisa Anderson and Annie Chalis, who have just entered the church together, take pity on whoever is represented by the right and sit in front of Eric. Cary Clarkson is there, undoubtedly hoping to sell the newly married couple, or one of their guests, a country home.

With two cameras hanging around her neck, Sarah Bentley photographs the alter flanked with giant pots of wildflowers. She faces the congregation and clicks away. Good move on her part to capture all the guests in one take, a shot most photographers overlook because they're concentrating too much on the couple.

Eric thought Mark Goldman would show, but then again, he and his wife must be busy overseeing preparations for the reception, and

Richard Rinaldi will be setting up his DJ equipment. He hasn't spotted Danni yet either: He should have offered to pick her parents up along with her, and he worries that she's fallen or that her father's had another heart attack. He identifies the back of Chair Rob Burns—his wife to his left and a younger woman to his right—smack up there in the second row front (no surprise) of the crowded left side. And lo and behold, even cantankerous Hank has shown up. Michael and Becca slide in beside Eric just in time to hear the organist give the notes for all to rise.

The traditional wedding march does not follow, but a slowed-down version of what Eric swears is Stevie Wonder's *You Are the Sunshine of My Life*. With no maid of honor or bridesmaid, the procession is headed by a beautiful woman with raven upswept hair and delicate features in a pinkish wedding gown and carrying a bouquet of pink and white roses. Her arms are linked to those of an older couple—he in a tux, she in a long beige dress—who beam with unmistakable parental pride. Eric feels a nagging familiarity about this bride and wonders if Danni has picked a local out of that puffed sleeve of hers. The eyes of the congregation follow her, heads turning toward the altar where the smiling minister, Margaret Jeffreys, stands with an open notebook in her palms but where there is still no groom or best man. Not really that strange: Eric has attended several weddings where the groom and his parents also walked down the aisle, or the groom strolled down solo, but usually they process in before the bride.

It's at this moment that Eric gets a full-face view of the broadly grinning woman with the unmistakable wild copper hair concealed in a bun who is standing alongside Rob Burns. As she anticipates the bride's approach, he makes the connection. Beneath all the makeup and changed hair color, the bride, now being kissed on each cheek by her parents, whom Reverend Jeffreys directs to stand to the right, is Tiffany, the formerly green-haired roommate of Ryan Toscano. As he leans over to enlighten Michael, the crowd takes the minister's lead and returns its gaze to the back of the church, where, to the amazement of some, in hobbles Danni, sheathed in full-length shimmering champagne, supported by crutches and on either side by Molly and George Pritchard.

Lisa and Annie question Eric with raised eyebrows.

"Who knew?" he says with a shrug.

"My oh my." Michael seals his surprise with a grin.

"Looks like we've come full circle," Lisa whispers.

The vows are short, the homily brief. He is the first in the receiving line to congratulate the couple in the vestibule of the church.

"I just wanted to protect you. That's why I didn't say anything," Danni whispers in his ear when he kisses her.

"You didn't think I'd have a problem with it, did you?"

"Not about Tiffany and me, but I was worried you would think I was taking advantage of the contest. That's why I had to quit the Chamber. Not one of the other contestants was remotely interested. I couldn't see all our work go down the tubes. As far as everyone else is concerned, you never knew."

"I didn't."

"You're not mad at me?"

"I'm happy for you."

"So we're good?"

"Yeah, we're good." He laughs. She has no idea how good they are. Better than they've ever been. It's like finding the missing piece to a jigsaw puzzle that never existed. "I'm happy for you both," he says to Tiffany.

He has a decision to make: wait outside the church for Ryan, who will be among the last to exit, and deal with the surprised reaction of the Brackton crowd now, or beat it to the reception. He decides he needs a Moscow Mule—heavy on the vodka—under his belt before he confronts any of them.

* * *

It doesn't take long for the Chamber's board of directors attending the wedding to approach an amply fortified Eric and form a little group in the lobby of the Daffodil.

"Isn't it wonderful?" Mother Twinkle purrs. "I get so overcome at weddings." Her shiver sends her gold shawl fluttering.

"And just one day after the Supreme Court declared same-sex marriage legal in *every* state. Way to go, Eric!" Maisie congratulates him.

"Yeah. Just dandy," Rob Burns says, despite his wife's tugging at his sleeve in an effort to restrain him. "Bad enough the winners had to come from home, but from the Chamber itself? Can't wait to see how this flies."

"Nice move, Boulanger. You could have given us a heads-up," Hank says. He appears amused.

"Surprise to me too," Eric informs them one after the other, then finally stops since they're not buying it. He says he and Danni thought it would be better that way.

He's been keeping an eye out for Ryan but doesn't see her until the cocktail hour is over and the guests are told that dinner—a buffet with no arranged seating—will be served in the tent. She enters from the direction of the ladies' room, and he excuses himself, telling Michael and Becca to grab a table and save him a place.

"Been hiding?" he asks.

"Not really. I had some calls to make and—except for a few who are ignoring me, the vendors have been very sweet—sympathetic. You know—the jilted bride. Fran wanted to know if it was hard to see Tiff in my wedding gown."

"Is that what you are? Jilted?" he asks.

"No."

"Did you tell them that?"

"What?"

"That you were jilted?"

"No. I assumed you did."

"I just said the wedding was off. Period. That's what you told me."

"I told you more than that."

"Not much. Besides, it's none of their business—or mine. It took a lot of courage for you to come, Ryan. I admire you."

"Thanks. I'm sorry. I really am. For creating such a mess."

"Hey, looks like it all worked out for the best." He gives a nod in the direction of Danni and Tiffany who have just entered the Daffodil, hand in hand.

"I know you turned yourself inside out to accommodate me and Jason through our craziness."

"I just wanted things to go well all the way around." He knows his hand is warming his drink, but he keeps it firmly wrapped around the glass nevertheless in an effort to steady it.

"I appreciated it. Still do."

"Listen. It didn't go sour because of what happened in the dark-room, did it?" He feels compelled to ask.

She shakes her head. "Jason and I weren't even back together then. Hadn't been for well over a year."

Her statement takes him aback and he squeezes the glass.

"Let me get this straight. You entered the contest when you weren't engaged? Not even going together?"

She nods.

"Wow."

"I know. I just kept hoping Jason would have a change of heart. And he did."

"Wow." He is so angry now that this is all he can muster. That and swallowing the remainder of his drink. "And you didn't even confess when you called off the wedding."

"Kind of after the fact. I swear I didn't know about Tiffany and Danni. I didn't think I'd ever see you again."

"Sorry for the inconvenience." Jaw tightly clenched, he inhales deeply.

"Why'd you even come here today? You should have quit while you were ahead."

"I wasn't going to. But I wanted to for Tiffany. I haven't been the best roommate lately. And I'm trying to be more honest with every-one—including myself. It's not like I go around doing this kind of thing all the time. I wanted to formally apologize. The contest just got me at a vulnerable time, and I grabbed onto it."

"Today's about Danni—and Tiffany. Not you."

"Yes."

"So you played us like it was all some joke. Just a bunch of little ol' country folk. No biggie." He can feel the heat rising within him. He really needs another drink.

"I wanted so badly for something to work. It was selfish. But I didn't think of you all in a bad way—I liked you. You were so nice it made me want it to work out even more. I didn't know how to get out. And then Jason showed up. I regret it, and I'm sorry. I guess I lost myself inside of someone else. But hey, Tiffany and Danni met."

"You think this contest is the only thing going on in these people's lives here? The only thing they have to deal with? You don't know the half of it."

"I don't know what else to say, Eric. I made a mistake. Haven't you ever made a mistake?"

"Yeah. Falling for you, for one."

"When you thought I was engaged."

"Right. Big mistake. I guess you're here with friends of Tiffany's?" The eyes are squinting but he's not smiling.

"No. I came alone. I don't really know Tiff's friends well, or her family. I don't plan on being here long. I wasn't even going to stay for the reception, but I wanted to talk to you. Apologize in person."

"Can I get you a drink?" He might as well offer while he gets his own.

"A dirty martini would be great," she says as she walks with him to the bar. "Jason's a priest, you know. I mean, he's been in the seminary. Gone back to it."

"Have to say I'm not that surprised." Good people, complicated circumstances. Soon gone for good. He can see through the French doors leading into the tent that the tables are full. "My friends saved a table. I think you'll recognize them."

Michael has kept an eye on Eric and reserved two seats.

Ryan sits between Becca and Eric, spending most of her time chatting with Becca, who makes an effort to put the only other female at ease. Three young men from Tiffany's family occupy the remaining seats at the table, and Michael makes attempts to engage them in conversation—about sports, school—but the teenagers from New York City are not very interested in socializing.

They go up to the buffet when signaled. They sip their champagne and clink glasses when the toasts are made. They eat. They do not talk. They clap when the cake is cut. Michael and Eric bring back two plates of carrot cake, two plates of chocolate cake, and four cups of coffee from the dessert table. Michael doesn't suggest they take some out to Bicycle Girl, who stares in at nothing in particular from outside the tent. The dishes are cleared and Rich Rinaldi announces the first dance. They watch Tiffany and Danni float around the portable plywood surface and kiss. Ryan gets up to leave: she's staying with friends in New Hampshire and wants to get on the road before dark.

"Don't forget your favor," Becca says, handing her the small silver-foil box of chocolates tied with a lavender ribbon. Inserted beneath the ribbon is a smooth rose heart-shaped stone with a tag attached stating what it symbolizes: *Romance, Passion, Positive relationships with others.* Compliments of Mother Twinkle.

Becca stands and, despite her substantial belly, gives Ryan a warm embrace.

"Nice meeting you," Michael says, taking her hand in both of his.

"Bye," she says to Eric.

"Drive safely," he tells her.

Chapter 30

Wednesday, July 2

I T WASN'T THE same-sex marriage that made the Brackton Is for Brides Contest a disaster. That, as Eric had initially envisioned, turned out to be the good part: Taking place on the heels of the Supreme Court decision, the media was all over it. While Tiffany's prominent Big Apple parents placed the announcement in the Sunday *New York Times*, the newspaper bumped it up to the Style section with full-blown half-page "Vows" coverage of the courtship. In a phone interview, the pair was discreet enough to say that they had met on the ski slopes, not wanting to expose Ryan and Jason as the couple who had broken their engagement. The paper ate up the suspense and irony of the local gal and organizer of the contest secretly saving the day for the town in time to celebrate a landmark decision: *A great twist to the perfect ending; the couple could not have timed it better.*

That the crutches she sported were the result of the very activity that had brought the women together only added another layer of icing to the cake of irony. There was an expansive pastoral backdrop shot of the two women, not unlike those featured in *Vermont's Book for All Brides*, compliments of wedding photographer Sarah Bentley. The day after the piece ran, the phones at the Daffodil House and the Brackton Inn rang off the hook with requests for reservations, in addition to an unprecedented number of hits on their websites.

But it is not only about the money in small towns that breathe and bleed along with their inhabitants. In communities like these, everything is personal. News of the *New York Times* Sunday spread followed local reports, of course, from the *Rutland Herald* down to the *Brattleboro Reformer,* that went as far as to say that the couple prevented what would have been a crushing financial and emotional blow to the town: not a lie by any means, but a painful insult all the same, one that Rob Burns had called on the day of the wedding. With deeper investigation, the *Burlington Free Press* touted the fact that the winner had not only been a member of the Chamber's board of directors but its longtime president and a close friend of Eric Boulanger, originator of the contest. *How clever of that hamlet,* they intimated; *how desperate and dishonest,* the town of Brackton's residents interpreted.

The deepest injury came from the *Rutland Herald* and local television shows that followed another lead they couldn't ignore. Every family has its rotten apples, and Tiffany's was no exception. The wait staff at both inns shared stories about guests and their condescending comments: The Daffodil House was cute, rustic, a wannabe for the Vanderbilt mansion, and the recently renovated Brackton Inn simply tacky, with décor no better than that of a 1950s Sag Harbor cottage. Mark Goldman, it was rumored, had offered (in his best New York accent) to drive one of the rude women back to the Upper West Side early, assuring her that he knew the way, upon hearing her complain that she couldn't get hold of any Uber drivers because there were none here in the sticks.

Most guests were more gracious, labeling everything *so charming,* their repetition of the word damning. Tiffany's great-uncle, whether due to dementia or kleptomania, was caught taking bottles of wine from tables and burying them under thick white towels—an upscale Scandinavian hotel's logo embroidered on their corners—in the trunk of his BMW. Thanks to him, such amenities as mouthwash, pain relievers, tampons, safety pins, breath mints, and other sundries arranged in white wicker baskets disappeared early in the evening, along with rolls of toilet paper from the restrooms at the Daffodil.

It was the cousins, however, the Park Avenue bad boys, the trio of two high school seniors and one college freshman who had sat at Eric's table, who delivered the greatest insult to Brackton, the coup de grâce that would put an end to any future Brackton Is for Brides contests. Seeking to extend the party beyond the neighborhood's noise code deadline, the boys, already infused with alcohol they had illegally stashed away in their hotel room, strolled into town shouting their intention to find some action in "this shithole."

All they found open was Baby's Bar and Grill, where they engaged in a game of pool. When Jimmy Goulet refused to serve the plastered teenagers with their fake IDs, the youngest boy and member of his high school wrestling team jumped the bar, secured him in a headlock with his left arm, and began pummeling his face with his right fist. The attempt to pull him off by the only other two men in the bar drew the remaining cousins into the fray. By the time the patrol car came by, the scene resembled one in a bad western. Jimmy was taken to Rutland Regional for stitches and the boys were thrown into lockup, only to be rescued soon after by their lawyer uncle, who was no less angry with the police than with his nephews. Hefty payments to Jimmy managed to get the assault charges dropped, but they could not prevent immediate coverage of the altercation by the local press and television news. *The boys were in town to attend the wedding of their cousin to former member of the Brackton Chamber of Commerce and winner of the Brackton Is for Brides Contest,* Vermont newspapers and local anchors stated.

* * *

"An outrage." "A damned shame." "A fool's folly." "A good attempt."

Opinions at the Chamber meeting following the wedding fly around the room like bullets.

Eric sits passively, waiting for the fallout to end before he apologizes. He's glad Danni isn't there to take any flak. "It's like after losing the College World Series. You tried your best. Now you leave it all on the field and hold your head high. And when you can't hold it up anymore, hold it higher," Michael told him.

"I'm sorry." Eric says.

What else can he say: *It seemed like a good idea at the time*? To some of them, it was never a good idea.

"There's no need for that." Mother Twinkle waves away his apology. "We were all in this together."

"The hell we were," Hank bellows.

"I'm booked for next season," Mark Goldman says about the Daffodil House, as he sits back in his chair, satisfied.

"Same here," Terry Stewart says about the Brackton Inn.

"No complaints with me either." Rich Rinaldi gives a thumbs-up.

"You got *your* wish there," Hank tells him.

"If you'll remember correctly, Hank, I was originally opposed to the couple being same-sex for fear it would put them up for ridicule. But I was wrong. It's out now. All of it. And we were a part of it. It was the right thing."

"We all got justice," says Jimmy Goulet, who had suffered the most but was proud of his battle scars. "We should feel good. We went the distance. There were gains and there were losses. As Mark would say: That's business."

Mark nods.

"And my shop got mentioned in the *New York Times*!" Fran Costantino exclaims.

Yet despite the acknowledgment that business will increase some, and in light of their differences of opinion as to whether or not the reputation of the Chamber has been damaged, on one fact they sadly concur: Whether or not the town of Brackton is respected or disrespected—now or in the future—is out of their control. And so they vote unanimously not to hold another contest—it simply took too much out of them—and move on to the next order of the day: the Fourth of July fireworks.

2015

Chapter 31

Wednesday, April 1

FAYE HAS NEVER completely reverted to her old self. While she no longer requires constant care, she uses a cane (though a walker would serve her better): She doesn't want to grow dependent even on a gilded one, however, and doesn't want other residents to see her with it. Since Harold left his entire estate to her, she is more than financially set to stay in Apartment 31 with an Assisted Living package that provides help in keeping her medications straight and performing tasks she finds a bit too difficult to manage. Lauren and Robin insisted on the package rather than have their mother attempt anything foolish again that would land her back in the nursing care facility for good.

Of course, Faye still attempts foolish things—she is, after all, Faye, who prefers to climb up on stepstools to change light bulbs and shower on her own. A black eye on one occasion; a goose egg on her forehead on another. She's been lucky so far. She insisted that Ryan attach her call-for-help pendant to a string of bling. The Home Shopping Network still provides entertainment, and weekly poker games with Pearl and Tilly (to which Faye takes a cab or the Senior Transport Bus) keep her in the sagging loop. Sixteen months since her biking accident. A year since Harold's death. Not much time to take her down, yet she's been diminished.

"I'm not aging well," she tells Ryan, sitting at a card table covered with jigsaw puzzle pieces. She uses an emery board to file down the

259

edges of a dark brown piece so she can complete the portal of a castle in Scotland.

"Are you kidding, Faye? You've aged incredibly well. And what you're doing with that puzzle piece is cheating."

But despite Faye's babbling about the inconvenience of getting old, Ryan understands that Faye hasn't really seen herself as old until now: Aging is something new to her, to be tackled from now on.

"You look ten years younger than you are, Faye."

"I feel ten years older. Don't go away. I have to piddle." Faye heads for the bathroom. "Turn on the TV please, *bubeleh*? The makeup lady is on today."

Ryan hopes this is just a phase her grandmother has been going through. Tomorrow she'll settle into her new situation and fully assume her old Faye persona until the next decline. It's all Harold's fault: his choosing to die, his giving her love and then pulling the rug out from under her for no reason. Faye was fine before he turned up. Ryan still can't understand why Faye isn't bitter. It will take years for Ryan to comprehend this, Lauren tells her daughter. Years for both mother and daughter—with any luck. "We were made to grieve and move on," Lauren says. "Don't forget that."

"You like it here, don't you, Faye?"

Faye smiles.

"This is my life now, darling. I like it enough."

Ryan doesn't hear from Tiffany much since she moved to Brackton, where she's finally found her niche running Licks and Relics with Danni. They invited Ryan up for Thanksgiving, but it was too soon after the contest for her to make another appearance. Besides, she wanted to spend it with Faye. Lauren and Joe drove to Boston, and for the first time they all had Thanksgiving dinner out—at Durgin Park, one of Faye's favorite old haunts still in business. Seated beside complete strangers at a long table covered with a red checkered cloth, they washed down their butternut squash soup, roast turkey, baked ham, prime rib, baked beans, and mashed potatoes with mugs of spiked mulled cider, finishing off the feast with pumpkin pie and apple pandowdy.

Next week is Easter, and Faye has agreed to make the trip to Long Island with Ryan for Joe's traditional feast. She hasn't even put a qualifier on the journey, like *Depends how I wake up,* or *If I'm still here,* or her grandmother Toscano's favorite, *God willing,* which irritated the hell out of Faye, who found it utterly morbid. Faye is set on going, and Ryan is convinced she's about to turn that corner Ryan's been waiting for her to encounter.

Ryan's new roommate, Mehool, a grad student from New Delhi who is getting his PhD in chemical engineering at Northeastern, will also be joining them. He's never been to New York before, and Ryan plans on going a day early and taking the Long Island Railroad with him into the city to the parade. He's most keen on seeing the Brooklyn Bridge, been obsessed with it ever since he was five and an Italian tourist gave him a pack of gum with a picture of the red iconic structure spanning the wrapper.

Mehool is quiet and considerate, cooks great Indian food, minds his own business, and doesn't care to socialize much either in school or out, which suits Ryan just fine, because she's been working overtime to tie up loose ends at the law center before she starts her MFA program this summer at Emerson College. She made up her mind during therapy sessions with a woman adept at helping her clients tap into what truly makes them joyous. Just as Jason always knew, creative writing uplifts her; legal writing does not. One of the writing samples she submitted was the story she finally finished about the naïve young mother whose decision to rent a room to a disturbed vagrant causes her seemingly perfect marriage to unravel. The second was a new story about a young woman who appears from nowhere in a small Vermont town—a woman without voice or identification who rides around all day and night on a rusty two-wheeler, a person everyone calls Bicycle Girl.

She and Jason keep in close touch: They are finally what they were destined to be—best of friends. In several months, he'll take his vows of chastity, poverty, and obedience. He is ready for that, and for the next three years of academic work at Fordham or Loyola or St. Louis, working as a scholastic or a brother to prepare him to teach in a school and live in a Jesuit community in yet another two years of Regency at a Jesuit institution.

If he still wants to pursue the priesthood and be eligible to administer the sacraments after that, he'll enter the Theology stage of study that might bring him back to Driscoll and Boston for three years. Then ordination. And after fifteen years as a Jesuit, he'll embark on his Tertianship, his final months of reaffirmation and spiritual renewal, studying early and recent documents of the Society and its mission. Unlike his first vows, in which he will have offered his life, the final vows will be a confirmation by the Society itself of his Jesuit life, an endorsement of the man and a lasting commitment to him as one who has walked in the deepest waters of the Society of Jesus and surrendered to that Society of God.

He tells her this in his emails and occasional phone conversations, and says that he prays daily for her, for the country, for the world, and for himself. It used to make her feel uncomfortable to hear her name mentioned in his litany of spiritual requests, as if she were dying or falling prey to some lethal addiction, but now she accepts it, even likes it: *I've got your back,* it says. Never hurts to cover all your bases.

And by the way, he emails her, *I'm going to see the Pope when he comes in September. I mean really see him. A group of us have tickets to his Mass at Madison Square Garden.*

That's great, she emails back. It *is* great for him, greater than attending any basketball game or rock concert there could ever be. *I'll look for you on TV. Let's see what he has to say.*

She hasn't dated much—no time. Well, not true. More like little interest. But just as she's optimistic for Faye, she senses that she too may be turning a corner. Faye has a simpler explanation for it: spring fever. Ryan checks Eric Boulanger's Facebook page from time to time to see if he's put up a photo in place of his anonymous thumbnail, one that would give some indication of how his life is going: The cover photo changes—always a breathtaking New England landscape in different seasons; no exotic location to suggest travel; no woman who might be a girlfriend; no thumbnail photo. *Eric only shares information with his friends. If you know Eric, send him a message.* She does not. She hesitates to ask Tiffany anything about him. Tiffany never mentions him.

Ryan's relieved not to be pushing upstream in a measured but ineffective breaststroke. There are limits to control—and selfishness. She luxuriates in the return of Daylight Saving and the fact she can hop on the Green Line at Park Street after work on Thursdays, when the museums are open until 9 p.m., and pay a visit to Isabella. Ryan finds her on the third floor in the Gothic gallery of sacred art, her shapely figure draped in full-length black with a strand of pearls (and a few rubies). She's waiting for Ryan, arms and cleavage bared, head strategically placed against the print of a Renaissance fabric that forms a halo around her brunette head and that presents her as a pagan deity among the images of the holiest of holies in the room.

Ryan is filled with admiration and gratitude for this life-sized vision of Sargent's in a gilt frame—for the generosity of this woman of means and foresight who knew what brought her pleasure in life and cared enough to preserve and share it. She wonders why she and her mother have never come to this museum together, why she has never brought anyone else here. Because it's a private retreat that she intends to keep as her own? How contrary to Isabella's intent. Her mother would love this museum.

Bring her, Isabella beckons. *Time passes only too quickly in a world of uncertainty. You know that now.*

She'll take it from me.

She gave it to you.

I'm afraid I'll lose it.

What good is it to possess something you love if not to share it with others?

I have trouble sharing.

Does a good writer keep her thoughts to herself?

I wish you were my mother.

You choose death over life?

You aren't selfish.

Ha! Oh, but I am. Look at what I amassed for my own pleasure.

But you've left it for us.
Could I take it with me?
Come on. You always intended to share.
Yes.
It is our common ground.
Then open your heart. Open your eyes. Find your common ground.

Chapter 32

Saturday, June 6

MARIE BOULANGER HUNG on longer than expected, through the hottest summer on record into an unprecedentedly mild and colorful fall, refusing to participate in ending the suffering that included short but frequent hospitalizations, and only reluctantly acquiescing to hospice care when her defiant body was just about to quit on her, or she on it. Nothing about Eric's ordinary mother was ordinary.

He couldn't work after Marie died. The precious time he had wished for during the months of her illness now lay stretched ahead of him. How could he have felt so bereft, after having had so much notice, so much time to prepare? After days and nights of reading the Book of Psalms to her at her request because it calmed her, how could the solace he had at first taken in knowing she no longer suffered have turned into such emptiness? But it had.

He was empty and lonely and sad, floating through his days without direction or purpose. The evil foreman of sickness, who had provided structure to his days and nights, told him when to punch in and out for three years, had closed up shop and moved on to another unfortunate house to dictate to new employees the structure of each minute and hour. He woke up the morning after his mother's funeral paralyzed—a little boy lost—his eyes timidly scanning the perimeters of the room, his ears straining for a familiar call for help, and he asked himself: *What do I do now?* He had returned to Brackton for her, but now she was gone. And he was free. Yet death seemed to have shrunk all other needs.

* * *

This spring morning he sits alone in an Adirondack chair on the deck in a pair of shorts, feet bare, his laptop on the glass of the wrought-iron table. He is reminded of the morning of Danni's wedding, of the Contest, and he smiles. He longs to talk to his mother. Just touch her again. She's there, he knows: in every blade of grass the wind bends, in the scent of the hyacinths and tulips she planted, in the new young owner of the house next door who, in denim capris and a red bandana, stands high on a ladder stripping gray paint off her old Victorian.

Bicycle Girl too is gone. When Marie took a turn for the worse, her father placed her in a group home in Burlington. It was something her doctor had been urging Bicycle Girl's father to do for a long time: It was safer for her; it was best; her father wouldn't be around forever. But her dad knew that if he had moved her sooner, the girl would have become even more lost without Marie. And neither he nor Eric wanted to deprive Marie of Bicycle Girl.

He scrolls through his contacts in an effort to create a mailing group to which he'll send a notice about his new one-man show of mirror-image photos he has lined up at the Brattleboro Museum in July. He's added quite a few new pictures to the collection that he's been working on since Marie died, in between his paying jobs. They may be—he thinks—his best ones, for he has begun to see more clearly, is able to envision the possibilities in advance, without rushing to achieve an end purpose, delighting in the serendipity of the results.

He hesitates when he comes to the name Ryan Toscano. With a decisive click followed by a fleeting pang of regret, he deletes her information and obliterates her from his world of cyber relationships—from his life. He puts on his running shoes and heads over to Michael's house. The two will take turns pushing the jogging stroller he gave Becca and Michael when Jack was born up and down hills, around the pond, trying to beat their best time. Jack was a good name, and while Michael and Becca refuse to admit that they named their son after Jackie Robinson (probably from fear of putting any weight of expectation on him), Eric is sure of it.

And what about Eric? Baseball practice began a month ago. Has he tied himself to Brackton—to these boys—indefinitely? That is what his mind asks when he goes to bed each night and when 2:20 in the afternoon rolls around and he heads to the field. But then they gather: arrogant, timid, frustrated powder kegs of testosterone, eager to prove themselves, frightened to fail. They need him to succeed. Without him there is no hope for a winning season, no release from lives fraught with the heartache of unrequited love, overbearing parental expectations, domestic dysfunction, and shame.

He feels the weight of that power but he is not burdened. His fantasy team may be in place, but it is this team that has his heart. For how long? He pushes away questions that serve only to disarm him. Perhaps this will be his legacy to Brackton. He laughs out loud at the absurdity of his tenacity. *Play ball,* the breeze tells him. *For God's sake, Eric, will you get out of that damned head of yours and just play ball?*

When he returns from his morning run with Michael, he finds a white legal-sized envelope with no return address in his mailbox among the medical bills he's still receiving and junk mail he thumbs through. He takes the stack of mail into the kitchen and drops it on the table, takes a quart of dark green vegetable health drink from the fridge and gulps from the bottle. He showers, grabs his camera, and heads down to Woodstock to see what happens when he turns the Taftsville covered bridge upside down. He'll drive home by way of Burlington and get a few bikers on the Island Line Trail to ride toward him, then reverse direction and ride away. He'll shoot trees so that they will look as if their canopies were rooted in Lake Champlain.

He won't open his mail until late that evening, when he fixes himself some spaghetti and mixes it with leftover slices of sirloin from Buy

One Get One Free Night at Baby's, and finds in the hand-addressed white envelope a ticket to a 3 p.m. game at Fenway Park on June 14th. Red Sox vs. Yankees. A box seat behind home plate.

Sweet! What good fortune! It's not even his birthday, he'll exclaim to himself. Someone really wanted to make it worth his while to take a trip to Boston. Someone, he'll imagine, who will be sitting that Sunday in the seat next to him.

Acknowledgments

I AM FOREMOST grateful to the indefatigable and brilliant Michael Mirolla and everyone at Guernica Editions. To my patient and stellar editor, Chris Jerome, for making me look much better than I am. And to my niece, Amanda Medori Hallauer, who first planted the seed for this story in my brain.

All manuscripts need fresh eyes before they are even handed over to an editor. I would like to thank the following readers for their time and insights: Michael Wohl, Joann Kobin, Betsy Hartmann, Roger King, Mordicai Gerstein, Susan Harris, and Zane Kotker.

And many thanks to those who graciously provided time and details, and to those who may be surprised to find a page or line from their own lives: Ellen Augarten, Pauline Bassett, Lawrence Biondi S.J., Neil Broome, the late Enzo Finardi, Barry Feingold, Margi Gregory, Craig Kirouac, the late Pat McDonagh, Lorraine Mangione, the late William Neenan, S.J., Jeanne Ransome, Jeff Ross, Ariana Wohl, Carina Wohl, and Marcie Yoss.

Special thanks to Elysa Piccirilli, Ellen Augarten, and Brionna Burke for help with the cover.

And, as always, to my husband, Martin Wohl, who has made all the difference.

About the Author

Marisa Labozzetta is the author of *Thieves Never Steal in the Rain* and *Sometimes it Snows in America*, both Eric Hoffer Award finalists; *At the Copa*, a Binghamton University John Gardner Fiction Award finalist and Pushcart Prize nomination; and *Stay With Me, Lella*. Her short stories have received the Watchung Arts Festival and the Rio Grande Writers' first prize, and honorable mention for Playboy's Victoria Chen-Haider Memorial Award. Her work has appeared in *The American Voice*, *Beliefnet.com*, *The Florida Review*, *VIA*, *Italian Americana*, *The Penguin Book of Italian American Writing*, *Show Me a Hero: Great Contemporary Stories about Sports*, *Celebrating Writers of the Pioneer Valley*, *KnitLit*, and the bestselling *When I Am an Old Woman I Shall Wear Purple*, among other publications. She lives in Northampton, Massachusetts.

For a Reading Group Guide to *A Day in June*,
and to contact Marisa Labozzetta for a speaking engagement visit:
www.marisalabozzetta.com.

Printed in February 2019
by Gauvin Press,
Gatineau, Québec